AN IMPERFECT TRUTH

Priscilla Masters

**SEVERN
HOUSE**

First world edition published in Great Britain and the USA in 2023
by Severn House, an imprint of Canongate Books Ltd,
14 High Street, Edinburgh EH1 1TE.

severnhouse.com

British Library Cataloguing-in-Publication Data
A CIP catalogue record for this title is available from the British Library.

ISBN-13: 978-1-4483-1189-7 (cased)
ISBN-13: 978-1-4483-1190-3 (e-book)

This is a work of fiction. Names, characters, places and incidents are either the
product of the author's imagination or are used fictitiously. Except where actual
historical events and characters are being described for the storyline of this novel,
all situations in this publication are fictitious and any resemblance to actual persons,
living or dead, business establishments, events or locales is purely coincidental.

All Severn House titles are printed on acid-free paper.

Typeset by Palimpsest Book Production Ltd.,
Falkirk, Stirlingshire, Scotland.
Printed and bound in Great Britain by
TJ Books, Padstow, Cornwall.

Praise for Priscilla Masters

"Gripping . . . *Silence of the Lambs* fans will want to
check this out"
Publishers Weekly on *A Game of Minds*

"A page-turner that keeps you reading, with well-drawn
characters who make it a pleasure"
Kirkus Reviews on *A Game of Minds*

"With its unresolved personal story and chilling conclusion,
the novel suggests that Masters has another successful,
character-driven series ahead"
Booklist on *Dangerous Minds*

"A tense cat-and-mouse game . . . A twist ending"
Publishers Weekly on *Dangerous Minds*

"A captivating tale"
Kirkus Reviews on *Undue Influence*

"Appealing . . . the increasingly tense plot builds to a
surprise ending"
Publishers Weekly on *Undue Influence*

About the author

Priscilla Masters is the author of the popular DI Joanna Piercy series, as well as the successful Martha Gunn novels, the Florence Shaw mysteries and a series of forensic psychiatrist mysteries featuring Dr Claire Roget. She lives near the Shropshire/Staffordshire border. A retired respiratory nurse, Priscilla has two grown-up sons and two grandsons.

www.priscillamasters.co.uk

ONE

The day started as usual, sitting in the kitchen in her dressing gown, the radio playing softly in the background, tuned into a local station, her fingers simultaneously scrolling down her iPad, her mind already racing through the day ahead.

Which, judging by the local news on both radio and iPad, would begin with a traffic jam.

As she waited for the kettle to boil, her attention was focused on the details of her route to work, so she was paying scant notice to the radio announcing the local headlines. All she heard was a name: Patricia. It held no particular significance to her. The kettle reached a noisy boiling point and the rest of the story didn't register at all because all her attention now was focused on brewing the first, much needed, very strong coffee of the day. While she was drinking it, still sitting at the breakfast bar, she scrolled down her tablet, hoping for more detail on the current traffic situation, which had recently been dire, wondering whether she needed to plan an alternative route. In the background the sparse facts of a story trickled out from the radio and into her consciousness.

Found dead in her own home by two of her children when they returned after a night out.

Police investigating.

Post-mortem later today.

Almost automatically she stitched the sentences together and jumped to a superficial judgement. A deranged partner. Which meant it wouldn't take long for an arrest to be made. She drained her second mug of coffee and poured out a bowl of cereal.

It was only then, as she crunched through her breakfast, that she picked up her iPad again, tapped on the local headlines, and found herself scrolling down to read the details of this crime against an unknown woman.

The headlines were lurid.

Forty-two-year-old woman butchered to death in frenzied attack.

She tried to dismiss it as tabloid talk. The use of the word *butchered* instantly commanded revulsion and the attacks were always *frenzied*, weren't they?

She read on. The paragraph below was couched in similarly dramatic lines.

Pools of blood, *multiple* wounds and a fact which would make many uncomfortable – the assault had taken place in the victim's *own home while she had sat alone, watching television.*

The victim's own home. The one place she would have felt safe, relaxed enough to switch on the television, blank out the world and chill. Claire looked around at her newly fitted kitchen – dark blue units, walls and floor pale grey. And over it, with far too much imagination, she superimposed an intruder, terror, the assault, arcs of blood still pumping, screams and finally silence, followed by two teenagers coming home to find their mother *butchered*.

She blinked the images away and turned the radio up. It too was covering the night's gruesome events. She gleaned more detail.

The victim, Patricia someone or other – Claire missed the surname – was described as a mother of three who'd worked as a teaching assistant at a local school and was divorced. *Vox populi*, in this case the usual friends and neighbours, who'd popped their heads up for their moment of fame to pay tribute to someone they'd possibly hardly known, described her – equally predictably – as a *lovely woman* who had *worked tirelessly for her family* and had had *no support* from her *ex-partner*.

Again, Claire reflected, the reporting was following well-worn tram lines. She could have written this herself with her eyes closed. The script was designed to maximize drama and horror by using selected phrases a robot could have spat out. Her suspicion was still a deranged partner. But she'd picked out something else that edged towards the personal. The address where the murder had taken place, she noted, was one of the nicer areas of Wolstanton, close to the centre of Newcastle-under-Lyme. Claire actually knew the street, set behind the main road, the A527, which ran through its centre. The road consisted of a leafy suburb with a triangular central area of parkland lined with substantial Victorian semis which had short front drives, generous bay windows and solid front doors. She'd looked at one herself when house hunting and had been impressed with the accommodation and outlook before she'd finally settled for a larger place in Burslem with Grant Steadman, currently her on/off boyfriend. So perhaps it was her familiarity with the area – indeed the very street –which set a bell ringing softly into her consciousness as she reflected that it was just possible that she'd even viewed the actual house where this woman had been sitting, quietly watching television, believing herself to be safe. Perhaps it was that which persuaded her to scroll down even further. She felt a creeping empathy with the unknown woman and her unsupported family, while still acknowledging that this hastily gathered set of clichéd quotes were probably missing most, if not all, the salient details. She yawned; her coffee had yet to take full effect. Most likely, she thought, hand cupping her chin, the ex-partner who had given *no support* had rejected his wife's appeals for financial help and decided to put an end to her bleatings once and for all. That was the way the police thought. She poured herself a third cup of coffee. *Put your hand on the collar of the next of kin and you have a forty per cent chance of being right*, an officer had told her once with a wink and a smirk, while all she could think was that meant you had a sixty per cent chance of being wrong and accusing someone, newly bereaved, of murder. She consoled herself with this comfortable assertion: stranger crime is, mercifully, rare. She returned to the road updates. Nothing to do with her.

TWO

8.32 a.m.

While in the shower she turned her mind to a more immediate and personal problem.

In little over a month, she had a wedding to attend. Adam, her half-brother, was getting married to Adele, and she had nothing to wear. Or at least nothing suitable. What does one wear to attend one's half-brother's wedding while running the gauntlet of your mother and stepfather's wrath? The wedding of someone you had once hated so much that as a child you had considered stuffing a pillow over his face, until he had looked at you with trusting eyes and you had thought, with a child's desperation for approval, maybe he won't hate me too. Revisiting that moment and seeing it through an adult's eyes, with the insight studying psychiatry had given her, her mouth twisted and was suddenly dry. Part pain, part grief, part guilt, part stubbornness which she should fight. She *would* go to the wedding, chin held high, in her something-or-other outfit and play her part. Not that her mother and stepfather would pay much – any? – attention to her. All *their* attention would be on their beloved boy, Adam-the-perfect and his beautiful, clever bride, Adele. Her presence as well as her outfit as the 'French Frog', the derogatory sobriquet they'd attached to her, would hardly register on the Richter scale of attention. She could turn up in funereal black or bridal white, scarlet sequins or a zombie outfit. They wouldn't bat an eyelid. Because they wouldn't even notice.

But Adam and Adele would, and for them, whom she had learned to love, she would make the effort. She tilted her face up to the jets of water and faced another hurdle to leap over, which could add to the difficulties of the day. Reluctant to attend on her own, she had, in a moment of weakness, replied that she would be bringing a 'plus one'. In this case Grant Steadman, whom, she sensed, would highjack the wedding and grab the opportunity to renew his marriage proposal, an invitation he aired so often it felt threadbare, and which had a whole host of complications in its wake.

Like his needy mother, for one.

Like his desire for a quiver full of children, for two.

And like his resentment of her job with its unpredictable hours, for three.

In *his* mind, every hour she spent working over the forty-hours-a-week limit (according to him) made him sulky and petulant, which was yet another reason why she knew she never would marry him. She couldn't bear the thought of having to explain and justify the long hours she spent working, the off-duty time she spent studying articles in journals and breakthroughs in forensic psychiatry and the study courses which could, at times, take her all over the world. At some point she was going to have to be honest with him and finish it properly. Not this ragged half on/half off relationship which was unsatisfactory for them both. But so far she'd shied away from severing the connection completely. It felt too final. Besides, she told herself, he would be hurt, and she didn't want to hurt him because, for all his faults and deficiencies, Grant Steadman was a decent person. He was also a wonderful lover. But every moment spent avoiding the truth and trying her best to deceive herself, the conviction grew. It wasn't working and it never would. And she was being a coward.

She came out of the shower, a towel around her hair and a bath sheet knotted around her body. She patted herself dry, sprayed deodorant and moisturized her face, sticking her tongue out childishly at the image which scowled at her from the steamy mirror. Somehow or other thinking about Grant almost always made her smile initially – but sometimes that smile melted when she peered into the future. If she continued avoiding the truth she would, one day, drown in the place she was digging for herself with her milky self-deception. Because even though *she* knew it would be a disaster, *Grant* could be very persuasive both mentally and physically. Momentarily she felt warm as she recalled his touch. Hands gently roaming. 'It won't work,' she said as she pulled on a pair of camel-coloured, loose-fitting trousers and a pink sweater. 'It won't work,' she repeated to the woman in the mirror, but she read scepticism in the normally calm visage and clear grey eyes. *Really?*

Why do we do this? she wondered. Why proceed with a relationship which we know will ultimately destroy us?

There was a knock on the bedroom door. 'You decent?'

'Yes.'

The question was followed by a head popping round. 'I wondered if you wanted a lift in?'

Simon Bracknell, sandy-haired, tall, skinny, bespectacled. Her Aussie registrar and, for the last six months, her lodger, who rented the top floor of the Victorian semi she'd originally bought with Grant, then bought him out when his objections to her workload had made the relationship uncomfortable. She'd needed distance.

'Yeah. Thanks. Just hope we're ready to leave at the same time. And, judging by the reports on the local radio, I think we might have problems with some roadworks.'

'OK. I'll keep an eye on the traffic situation with my phone.' He followed that up with, 'Five minutes do you?'

'Great. I'm more or less ready now.'

She spent the five minutes cleaning her teeth and applying light make-up – foundation, mascara, lipstick– but she recognized in the face that grimaced back at her that it was the face of a coward, ducking away from an unpalatable truth.

Simon was already in the car and threw the door open as she

was locking the front door behind her since she'd felt compelled, with a shiver, to double lock it with the deadlock. Even after she'd turned the key twice, she still checked that the door was, indeed, locked and secure, pulling and pushing it to check.

Simon was watching her curiously with the heightened perception through which a psychiatrist notes an unusual action. He'd given her lifts plenty of times before but had never witnessed such belt-and-braces behaviour.

But he made no comment, limiting his curiosity to a raising of one ginger eyebrow. A movement which she picked up and tried to shrug off. 'Oh, just a story in this morning's news.'

He still did not ask, so she volunteered.

'Some woman murdered in her own home.' She followed this with her own version of a solution. 'Probably the ex-husband.' She wondered whether the police had made an arrest yet. Had she been in her own car she would have explored this via Radio Stoke.

Simon gave her a sharply perceptive look before focussing on reversing out of the drive.

On the way in their talk was mainly centred on their current inpatient load. And in particular, one patient who was causing concern – Dana Cheung, who had severe puerperal psychosis. This psychosis had affected Dana from late in her pregnancy when she had tried, on two occasions, to cut the foetus out of her. Luckily the wounds had been superficial, but they had been enough to put her on the at-risk register, her pregnancy supervised by the Greatbach Secure Psychiatric Unit and, when she had reached full term, to have an elective caesarean section at the maternity wing of the Royal Stoke University Hospital. That had been a month ago. Since then she had remained an inpatient.

Still believing her baby was the devil incarnate – the resurrection of one of the many evil witches rife in Chinese legend – Dana was convinced her month-old baby was plotting to have her killed. When, supervised, she was encouraged to be in the same room as Lily Rose, Dana would back into the corner, forming her forearms into a protective cross. She screamed out the two deities she was convinced her child was possessed by: E Gui, the hungry ghost, whose small mouth stopped her from eating, and Baigujing, the White Bone demon, who would murder any young mother and crunch her bones to dust. Her terror was horrifyingly real and had required hefty doses of sedation. Added to that her nutritional state was causing real concern as she had pulled out nasogastric tubing on more than one occasion and they dare not risk inserting a tube directly into her stomach – percutaneous endoscopic gastrostomy, known as PEG feeding – because she would likely pull that out too, convinced they were poisoning her. Having so recently given birth, she was weakened and anaemic, and her management was proving a real challenge. Her poor suffering partner, Graham Cheung, who had to be kept away for the moment as he too was a focus of her paranoia, was trying to cope with his job in Qatar as well as a new baby. Obviously an impossibility, so he had moved his mother into their home. Fangsu Cheung was a Chinese national with a very traditional outlook. Between them they were trying to give Lily Rose the start in life that her mother could not. Because from the very moment of birth Dana could *never* be alone with her daughter. Lily Rose had been cared for initially by the team at the maternity hospital before being moved to the loving and safe hands of the nursing team in the paediatric wing of Greatbach Secure Psychiatric Unit. Now she was home with her grandmother and father. But the longer this separation continued and bonding was delayed, the wider the chasm between mother and daughter would become. And there was another angle. Graham Cheung had confided in Claire that his mother had never really liked his foreign wife and regarded her with deep suspicion, particularly now when, in her eyes, her daughter-in-law was possessed by a devil. Claire had seen the way Graham's mother looked at Dana, with fear and suspicion.

In the beginning, trying to manage Dana through the illness, Simon and Claire had used major tranquilizers as well as anti-psychotic drugs but, so far, they were having little effect. Dana didn't even acknowledge Lily Rose as her daughter but insisted she was a changeling planted by one of the two evil spirits. Graham was a civil engineer, and soon he would be recalled to Qatar, where he was overseeing the building of a residential complex. Fangsu was desperate to take the baby home to China but both Claire and Simon knew that if this happened Lily Rose would never be united with her mother. The bonding process had to be introduced, and soon. At some point her puerperal psychosis would be resolved, but the timing was all important. Introduce mother to baby too soon and the baby would be imperilled. But leave it too late and bonding rarely happens. Which had led Claire to wonder, in a rare moment when she attempted to confront her own personal history, what had happened to the absent bond with her own mother when her French father had disappeared, leaving her mother to manage alone until Mr Perfect in the shape of Mr David Spencer had rescued her, and they had produced Little Baby Perfect in the shape of Adam. The boy Claire had at first hated but later learned to love. He was a soft-hearted, kind and loving person and his soon-to-be-wife, Adele, was equally sweet-natured.

Her mind returned to her patient.

In the now-stationary traffic, Simon's fingers were tapping on the steering wheel. 'I can't see there being a hurry to reunite mother and baby. Graham's mother is doing a good job looking after little Lily Rose.'

'Yes, but she's hostile.'

'She's doing all right. Surely?'

Claire turned to look at him. 'You know as well as I do, Simon, that the sooner we can reunite them – safely – the more chance there is of good mother and baby bonding.'

'In which case . . .' He couldn't resist a smirk. 'Mother-in-law will get kicked out.'

'Ye-es. Well, maybe that's best, if Dana can reach a point where she's capable of nurturing her child.'

'If,' he repeated. Then added, 'So, what's the next step?'

She looked across at him and privately smiled. When he had applied, from Sydney, for the post of registrar, she had pictured an Aussie beach bum, rippling with muscle, a deep tan and sun-bleached hair. The reality couldn't have been more different. He was slim to the point of thin, freckled, pale-skinned, wore thick glasses and looked as if he would struggle to pick up a surfboard let alone run down the beach and into the waves with it.

Cliché, he was not.

'We wait for the anti-psychotics to kick in.' She smiled. 'They will, eventually. We make sure her mental state is stable.'

She changed the subject, sharing her misgivings about the family wedding looming, without going into detail about her reservations about Grant. 'And I have yet to find a suitable outfit,' she finished, anticipating his response correctly.

'Can't help you there, Claire. Sorry.'

She was smiling, almost laughing. 'I sort of thought you might say that. Don't worry. I have a couple of girlfriends who'll probably step up to the mark.'

Julia Seddon and Gina Aldi, she was thinking. The doctor and the artist. Perfect.

And now they'd arrived at Greatbach Secure Psychiatric Unit.

THREE

8.49 a.m.

They walked in together under the Victorian arch and stepped across the quadrangle, rounding the grassy knoll and the beech tree which was showing the early, welcome signs of spring. 'I have a short clinic this morning,' she said. 'Only a few patients booked in. Maybe you could go up and spend some time with Dana? See how she is today, check her weight and look out for ketones in her urine. I'll join you later as we have a case conference at eleven and then a multi-disciplinary meeting about some of the patients on the top floor. A couple of them are ready to be discharged. I think at lunchtime we have a talk on new therapies for bipolar disorder?'

'And there,' he said, teasing her just before they parted ways, Simon heading straight for the wards while she veered to the right, 'is your day and mine mapped out. And Claire,' he called back, 'I suggest you make a firm date with your lady friends for the shopping trip.' He was grinning, cheerful, his mood light-hearted. 'After all, the right outfit will inspire you with confidence. And you are what you wear, as they say.'

Now he'd reached the door and passed through it before she could think of a suitable riposte.

Her clinic was in the basement with windows facing into the quadrangle where staff were walking to their shifts. Others, who had covered the night shift, were yawning as they headed out through the arches towards the car park, while a few patients wandered in the spring sunshine. The paths skirted around a couple of ancient trees, the beech and two oaks, and beneath them grassy mounds were bright with daffodils and purple crocuses as well as a seated paved area. It looked peaceful and far away from the forbidding aspect which overlooked it, which tuned into the public's image of a Victorian psychiatric hospital. This central area had been designed to calm disturbed patients and elevate the mood of those suffering from anxiety and depression. And, to some extent, it worked.

Once in the clinic Claire closed the door and scanned the list of patients she would be seeing this morning, flagging up a couple of questions she needed to check with some of them and mentally allocating appropriate times for the consultations within the limitations of the given time slots.

She picked up the first set of notes.

Professor Cornelius Rotherham, sixty-one years old, a man crippled by obsessive compulsive disorder.

She had been seeing him for four years on and off now, ever since his job had been terminated because of inappropriate behaviour – in this case asking all his students to place each sheet of their dissertations in plastic folders so he could spray them with disinfectant before reading them. He'd also insisted they all disinfected their hands before entering the lecture theatre and spray their shoes with bleach, which had caused many designer trainer wearers to refuse and complain. That unexpected dismissal by his employers had spiralled him into OCD of truly tortured proportions, washing his hands until they bled, scrubbing the tiny flat he hardly ever left to the point of sterility until his neighbours complained of noxious fumes, probably caused by mixing bleach with vinegar, releasing toxic chlorine gas. He'd been lucky not to be evicted.

His explanation? 'Bleach doesn't always make things cleaner. Not really.'

The Covid-19 epidemic had proved torture to him and he had presented at the hospital with breathing problems when his ex-wife had called the police because he had not been answering his phone. He had been found collapsed and dehydrated, his weight down to seven stone. When the Royal Stoke had stabilized him, he had been discharged into the care of Greatbach and she had been seeing him as an outpatient ever since, realizing his condition would never be 'cured' but might be managed. The community psychiatric nurses visited him at home and things had reached – and remained – at an even keel.

He walked in, wearing, as usual, disposable gloves; he would not actually touch anything inside the clinic rooms. Claire knew better than to try and shake hands with him.

He sat gingerly on the chair opposite, having first carefully placed a sheet of newspaper down, and then he gave her a tentative smile. Claire actually liked Cornelius. He was a timid man, pathologically frightened of contact and germs, but incredibly gentle and polite. He had read almost every book she'd even heard of so had a depth of knowledge which he'd retained behind a pair of very tired blue eyes and sparse white hair. Life, for him, was a struggle.

She glanced at the weight the nurse had filled in. He'd actually gained a couple of pounds. He was waiting for her to comment first and she picked up a hope that she would praise this minor achievement.

'How are you?'

He didn't respond straight away but swallowed and considered his answer. Then he gave her a bright smile. 'I'm not bad, thank you,' he said in his soft, polite voice. 'Not bad at all.'

'Give me some detail,' she said, knowing she would have to push for the truth.

He began a halting catalogue of various behavioural patterns he felt he'd been able to reduce and she listened carefully, knowing the evidence was hidden underneath those gloves, and so she asked him to take them off, and when he did she realized he was little better. Any improvement was minimal. His hands were red and raw and he knew it as he stretched them towards her, meeting her eyes with a mute apology while still trying to reassure her. 'I do *feel* better, Doctor,' he insisted. 'More settled.' His voice was as hollow and desperate as a doomed Edgar Allan Poe character. She felt desperately sorry for him. But her job was not to pretend she believed a fable.

'Are you taking the medication we prescribed?'

He hesitated and she sensed the answer.

'Cornelius,' she said. 'It is the only way to improve your condition, to make your life a little more normal.'

'Normal,' he echoed. 'Normal?' He held his hands out towards her almost in supplication. '*This* is my normal, Doctor Roget. *These* are my normal.'

She shook her head, knowing she had to persuade him. 'Isn't there something you'd like to be able to do?'

She'd had this conversation with him before. Two tears rolled down his cheeks. She had seen these before too – if not the exact ones, their grandparents. 'I would like to hold and kiss my little girl,' he said. 'But I can't expose her to this.' Again, he held out his hands.

His little girl who was now in her early thirties. Once she could have held this carrot out to him, reminding him how he would feel when he hugged her. But in the four years he had been her patient this golden chalice had lost its potency. He no longer believed she could work miracles. He was intelligent enough to know the best he could hope for was management, that he would get no worse.

That he would survive.

She let him go, reminding him to make a follow-up appointment in two months' time.

Then she picked up the notes for her next appointment. And, as she read the name along the top, she felt a shock pass through her as though she'd picked up an electric eel.

She'd forgotten that her name was Patricia. Or that she lived in one of the Victorian semis which overlooked Wolstanton's central triangle of parkland. Or maybe, she thought, as she held the notes, she'd chosen to forget it. But the fact remained. Patricia, or 'Poppy' Kelloway, as she knew her, would not be attending the clinic today.

FOUR

12.15 p.m.

Claire had worked her way through the rest of her clinic in a daze.

Perhaps her subconscious had registered it when she'd heard the name on the radio. Maybe that knowledge she'd tried to tuck away was behind the feeling of gnawing unease when she'd locked the door then double-checked it and the slight nausea that had haunted her all morning – the feeling that something, far back in her mind, wasn't right. And now she had a quandary and a duty. This would be a murder investigation. Poppy was – had been – her patient. As she fingered the set of notes, she wondered whether Poppy's psychiatric history had anything to do with her murder. Sure, Poppy Kelloway had a circle of enemies which was wider than just an ex-husband. She had plenty of enemies because she told lies. Most of the time they'd been little more than repeated and embellished tittle-tattle, but at other times they had been invented 'facts', carving out deeper wounds and causing real harm to people. Like pebbles tossed into a pond, some of those lies had spread, leaching into others' lives, other families, other relationships, costing her friends who gave her a wide berth once they understood. And on at least one occasion, those 'little stories' or 'mistakes', as she'd described them, had resulted in a death.

Harry Bloxham had been a thirty-four-year-old gas fitter who'd had the misfortune to attend Poppy's house to mend the boiler. He had been a good-looking guy with thick dark hair, according to the photographs Claire had seen. Whatever really happened – and Claire was convinced that nothing *had* happened – Poppy had accused him of sexual harassment, stopping short of rape. Poor Harry had had no weapons with which to defend himself. He was not very bright and Poppy had been all too believable, helped by a petite feminine appearance. And it was easy to see the woman as victim. Particularly one as credible and practised as Poppy Kelloway. Harry had lost his job and six months later had hanged himself.

Poppy had already been a patient of Claire's – referred by her GP because of a 'personality disorder'. So Claire had looked into the case and challenged Poppy.

The worst thing? When she had questioned her, Poppy had puffed herself up, looking pleased with herself as if she'd achieved something. She'd turned up that day in a navy dress, high-heeled shoes, and had taken extra care with her appearance. Eyes wide open, hands on her lap, knees pressed primly together as she'd insisted, 'Something did happen.'

'Go on,' Claire had prompted her, ready for her response.

Out had come the details, of inappropriate touching, his hand on her bottom when she had been standing at the sink. Claire had watched as Poppy had simpered and told her tale . . . and known the whole thing was a pack of lies. Harry Bloxham had done nothing. The papers had kept neutral when reporting his suicide, saying that there had been allegations of inappropriate behaviour in a customer's house. One customer, mind you. Not named.

Six months later Claire had received letters from Harry's sister, Lisa Graham. And now, as Claire contemplated Poppy's end, one or two phrases stuck out in her mind.

I understand that the customer who made the allegation against my brother and which directly resulted in his suicide is a patient

*of yours, Dr Roget. You should have spoken up, said at my brother's
inquest that Ms Kelloway was prone to making false allegations.
In other words, lying.*

Addressing her by her title had made Claire feel complicit. She
had waited for days before responding. And then it had been couched
in carefully bland, professional terms, quoting her patient's right to
confidentiality and asserting that she had not been asked to appear
as a witness at the inquest and it had not been her place to intervene
because she hadn't been aware of the true version of events. But
that hadn't been true. She'd been hiding behind her title. When
Poppy had attended her clinic in that demure navy dress and told
her simple story, Claire had known she was lying, and the feeling
that she and Poppy had been on the same side had stayed with her
ever since, an unpleasant taste at the back of her throat.

And now she was dead.

Today, as the headlines were published, there would be a small queue
of people who would be relieved that Poppy had told her last lie.

Claire was still for a moment, the set of notes in her hand.

And the phrases which, this morning, she had dismissed as cheap
tabloid talk but now applied to someone she had known, were graphic.
Sadistic, possibly sexually motivated assault. Butchered. Frenzied.

As her hand still held the set of notes which contained her patient's
story, she recalled Poppy's redeeming quality with a smile. In one
aspect the newspaper was right and its language appropriate. She
was a devoted mother who had worked hard and, miraculously,
provided a stable home. She *did* love her three children, two of them
teenagers now. Her mind lingered on the fact that those two teenagers
were the ones who had returned from a night out to find what must
have been a horrendous sight. They must have been terrified that the
killer was still there, in the house, waiting for them. Claire pictured
two boys running from their home, screaming into mobile phones.

She sat up straight. Poppy had three children. So where had the
third child been? Upstairs, in her bedroom? Cowering? A witness
to the terror below?

And what would happen to them now? Would their father fill the
gap?

Claire shook her head, recalling Poppy's stories about her
marriage that had spilled out of her mouth during consultations,
stories of cheating and abuse, physical and mental anguish. True or
not? Did they belong with the tales of friends who had cheated her

of money, terrible wrongs which had been done to her, jobs she had been passed over for? And those made uneasy bedfellows with her other particular brand of stories, of lottery winnings and incredible coincidence, meeting people halfway up Swiss ski slopes or mountains, of exams she had passed at unbelievably young ages, of places offered at major universities, of chances she had rejected for one reason or another.

And it had all ended like this. Someone had erupted and taken a terrible revenge. She tried to derive some consolation from the officer's words: *Put your hand on the collar of the next of kin and you have a forty per cent chance of being right.*

But riding on the back of that came her own, less welcome thoughts. You had a sixty per cent chance of being wrong.

She put the set of notes to one side. They would soon be consigned to the basement with the word DECEASED written across the front.

FIVE

8 p.m.

S he'd spent the day in a haze, listening to her patients talk, attending the lunchtime meeting on a new drug for bipolar disorder, seeing more patients. At some point in the day Edward Reakin, one of Greatbach's clinical psychologists, had approached her. 'I heard about Poppy Kelloway,' he said in his quiet, polite voice. 'Terrible. Simply terrible. For that to happen to one of our patients – someone we knew.'

'Yes.'

He hesitated. 'Will you be asked to cooperate in any way with the police investigation?'

'I don't know. Not if they already have someone in their sights. I suppose it depends on how far they get.'

'And if they ask you?' He'd looked around, making sure no one was listening.

'If they ask me and I feel I can be of help . . .' Her voice trailed away. She didn't want to picture the scene too vividly. She tried to shake the images away.

'When did you last see her?'

'Middle of last month.'

'Best you read my notes. They're on file.'

The result of this quiet conversation was that all afternoon she'd felt distracted and Poppy's notes, including Edward's most recent assessment, remained on her desk. She wondered if the police would call, but there was nothing so far. And she had nothing helpful to offer. Maybe, she hoped, they had already arrested someone and wouldn't need any input from her. The secrets and harm connected with Poppy's psychiatric history could be preserved in aspic.

And now she was home, trying to think about something – anything – else. She'd showered and changed from her work clothes into a comfortable T-shirt dress and left her feet bare. She'd tried the television but there was nothing she wanted to watch. She felt too distracted to concentrate, and so she was sitting quietly, one lamp dimly lighting the corner.

Her mobile phone rang with a vigour that demanded to be responded to.

'Claire.'

It was a deep, male voice with a sound of authority behind it, but she struggled to put a name to it. Always guarded, she responded cautiously. 'Yes?'

'Claire,' he said again. 'It's Zed.'

Then she knew and remembered. Detective Sergeant Zed Willard with whom she'd been involved in a case a year or so ago.

Though she already knew this was not a social call, she began with the conventional, 'Zed, how are—'

He cut her off mid-sentence. 'Can I have a word with you?'

'Isn't that what we're doing?'

'Hmmm.' He huffed out his impatience. 'In person.'

And she already knew what it was about. 'I'm in the clinic—' She'd been about to say *in the morning*.

But again he cut her off. 'Where are you now?'

'At home.'

'Is it OK if I come round?' His tone was still abrupt, tense. Neither was it a question. This was no romantic overture gesture. This was connected to the topic she'd been trying not to think about all day.

'Yes.'

'I'll explain it all when I see you. Should be about twenty minutes.'

He hesitated before rapping out in the same abrupt tone, 'I take it you still live in the same place?'

'Yes.'

She turned on the side light, plumped up the cushions, opened a bottle of Merlot. Then she sat and waited.

The knock came on the door twenty-two minutes later, just as she was wondering how much longer he'd be.

DS Zed Willard was standing on her doorstep, looking drained. He was a stocky guy with bright blue eyes and thick dark hair. He made an effort and grinned at her, but even that grin seemed almost too much and his face quickly sagged. He was pale and looked as though he hadn't slept for days. His jeans were rumpled and his grey hoodie had what looked like a coffee stain down the front. Perhaps he'd picked up on her negative scrutiny as he made an attempt to straighten his clothes, bunching up the hoodie and adjusting his jeans. While his further attempt at a smile held a note of appeal, asking her not judge him, his head tilted to one side in a question. He was holding a canvas rucksack by its handle.

They stood awkwardly on the doorstep, studying each other for a moment without moving, neither quite sure how to greet the other, whether to hug, kiss, shake hands – or what? After a pause Claire smiled back at him and relied on a formal, 'Nice to see you again, Zed.'

He groaned and his shoulders collapsed. 'You won't think that in a minute.'

The warning stopped her short but then she relaxed. 'Come on in.'

She led the way into her sitting room. Lights turned low. Grey carpet, red cushions on cream sofa and armchairs. She sat down and indicated he too should sit. Opposite rather than adjacent. She wanted to watch his face because she had the idea this was not going to be pleasant. His apprehension only reinforced her instinct.

He eyed the bottle of wine and shook his head. 'I daren't,' he said. 'I'm knackered. I haven't slept since . . .' He managed an achingly exhausted, shallow grin which stopped short of his eyes. 'One snifter of that and I'd crash out here and now.' He accompanied the warning with an attempt at a wider grin which reminded her of the mischievous, cheeky side to him which seemed to have been erased. Temporarily, she hoped.

She offered him tea or coffee and he accepted a black coffee, no sugar, waiting until she returned and handed him a mug. But as she'd re-entered the room she'd seen him, the epitome of despair, head in hands, only looking up when she'd placed the coaster and the mug on the coffee table in front of him.

'Sorry,' he said, without specifying why.

She waved the apology away and poured herself a very small glass of wine. She was going to need her wits about her. She waited, expectantly.

Zed Willard lifted the rucksack from the floor and pulled out a small polythene evidence bag. It contained something familiar: a small, square, white appointment card which had been torn into bits but now was pieced together with tape so she could read the words, though she didn't need to: *Greatbach Psychiatric Unit*. Disturbingly the date was today's, the time eleven a.m. and the consultant's name her own.

She faced him without comment, trying not to show how much this disturbed her. But the fact was the sight had set her nerves jangling, as loud and ominous and frightening as an air-raid siren. She drew in a deep breath and when she looked up she read questions in his gaze. And something else – a form of pity for her which was unexpected.

The question that sprung into her mind was what significance did he and the police investigation attach to this?

He was looking more alert now, the coffee beginning to revive him. 'So?'

She blinked and was cautious. 'Maybe *you* should start, Zed.'

'OK.' He was in no hurry. 'I take it you've heard about your patient?'

There was no point skirting round this one indisputable fact. He had the appointment card in his hand. She nodded. 'It's been on the radio. Some of the details, anyway.'

She knew the police's attitude to patients who had mental health issues. She knew the workload that some of her patients cost them. But she hoped Zed would not let this influence the investigation.

He shifted forward, displaying both anxiety and eagerness. 'What was she being treated for, Claire?'

She hesitated briefly, then realized that if she didn't volunteer the information now, Zed would be back again with a warrant to review Poppy's records. She sighed. 'Poppy had narcissistic personality disorder.'

'You call her Poppy?'

That brought a smile to her face accompanied by a memory. It had been almost five years ago that she had first met Patricia Kelloway. And addressed her as Patricia.

'*Please, please, don't call me that horrible, ordinary, silly name. Patricia.*' She'd spat the name out. '*I hate the bloody name. So plebeian.*'

That had warned her that this patient would make no compliant subject. And as a psychiatrist, Claire knew that to swim alongside a patient brought far better results than confronting them, so she'd smiled and acquiesced.

'So what *shall* I call you?'

'*Poppy.*' Said brightly staccato, singing the name out as though it was an aria and with it a lift of her small features. '*That sounds much more like me.*' Giggle, giggle.

So Poppy she had been from then on.

Zed was looking at her quizzically. She had to remind herself that he had probably never met Poppy Kelloway. Not alive anyway. He had never known her powerful, magnetic personality or the element of fun which accompanied her the moment she entered a room. Poppy might have been a liar but she'd had an undeniable charisma. Likewise, he had never witnessed her detachment from the fallout of her lies when Claire had questioned her about her marital break-up, or from stories about husbands making advances or a job loss when she had complained about treatment from an employer. Only one of her complaints had resulted in a suicide, but for Poppy they had been entertainment because, however dramatic the story, she could always sound convincing. She drew you into her false narrative, an accomplished actress playing a part, and she had never *sounded* like a liar, however far-fetched her stories. But there was a catch. When she realized she'd taken you in, she would laugh.

Claire found herself dropping back into Poppy's tales.

'*So I said to the judge, you find me guilty of this stupid shoplifting thing which is a clear result of that so-called store detective trying it on with me and I'll knee you in the bollocks. And you know what, Claire? He let me off. Ha ha ha. They had CCTV of me stuffing the jumper into my bag and he still let me off.*' She'd ended the commentary with another roar of laughter before she must have sensed this narrative wasn't, perhaps, dramatic enough, so she'd added, '*And they fined the shop for false arrest.*'

'Really?' Even with years of psychiatric experience, Claire had found it hard to inject enough scepticism into her response because the image of a judge receiving such a threat was actually quite funny.

Funny as well as far-fetched. And she'd suddenly felt wearied by Poppy's stories. What was the point of them? It was as though she was peering into a crystal ball clouded by soot. It was dark and grey and impenetrable.

And as for a diagnosis? That was the easy bit. The obvious one was a narcissistic personality disorder with an intense attention-seeking feature. But that label didn't go anything like far enough.

Zed Willard was watching her with careful scrutiny. 'What's the significance of the appointment card being torn up?' His voice was soft and quiet as though he feared the answer.

She hedged her response. 'It depends who tore it up.'

'As there were only Poppy's fingerprints on it . . .' He waited before giving her a fact. 'He wore gloves.'

'He?'

'She'd fought like the devil. We're working on the assumption that it was a man.'

'But she hadn't been—'

'No. She wasn't raped.'

'So . . .?' She knew he was returning to the subject of the card.

'It could have been frustration with Greatbach.'

'Yeah. A feeling that for all our input we had achieved nothing. But . . .' She was thinking out loud now, hardly aware of the words forming. 'We can't always cure psychiatric patients, Zed. We can sometimes control, sometimes modify behaviour patterns.'

She knew she owed it to DS Zed Willard to be more open with him. 'She was a chronically pathological liar.' In a quieter voice, she added, 'We saw her regularly in the hope of preventing harm resulting from her fantasies.' She deliberately didn't mention Harry Bloxham. He would already know, or soon find out.

SIX

Zed let her words sink in before prompting her. 'Go on.'

'Come on, Zed,' she said gently. 'It doesn't take a psychiatrist to take a guess at it. She wasn't going to be attending that appointment. It's a poke in the eye to us.'

'Torn up.' He mused. 'You think it indicates mockery or

resentment for failing to cure her?' He searched for the words. 'Or modify her behaviour?' He pressed on. 'Was there any significance in the fact that she had been murdered the night before she would have been seeing you? Was there anything special planned for today's appointment?'

'No. It would have been just another routine appointment.' But she recalled Edward Reakin's insistence that she read through his notes. What had he picked up on during her last contact with Greatbach?

Her openness with him led Zed to share a confidence with her. 'One of the theories we have is that your patient's killer is another of your patients, Claire. And as the appointment was with you, it could even be directed towards you personally.'

'So that's why you had to come round so urgently?'

'Claire. She was sitting in her own home, watching television, believing she was safe.'

Claire sensed the ugly undercurrent here. It was as though she had been hit in the chest. And was about to be hit again – even harder. To try and divert herself, she asked, 'Do you have anyone in your sights?'

'Not yet. But if this is another of your patients . . .' He left the phrase to hang in the air before adding, 'We need a list.'

'Of what?' She tried to moisten her mouth with a sip of wine. It didn't help much.

His response was blunt. 'Any patients of yours who had contact with Poppy and are capable of murder.'

'You want me to trawl through my patients and find likely candidates?' To the best of her knowledge, the only time Poppy had ever bumped into other patients in the clinic was when waiting for her appointments. She wondered if Zed had picked up on her slightly resentful tone. Yes, all of her patients were at the clinic for a reason, but that didn't make them all potential suspects.

She must have looked sceptical, as DS Willard pressed on. 'And if your patient's killer is someone known to you?'

She tried to stop him there. 'I can't just go through a list and tick names.'

He shrugged. 'I need your help, Claire.'

She knew what he meant. She had a duty to work with the police. But releasing the names of patients to be included in their list of suspects was not only conjecture, it was a step too far.

'You know your patients better than anyone.'

He was right. It was true. She did.

Then he spoke slowly and quietly, without drama, at the same time avoiding her eyes. 'I wasn't anxious to share graphic details with you, but maybe it's the right thing to do.'

She sat very still, not sure she wanted to hear this.

'The facts are these,' he said and drew in closer, moving to the edge of his chair, frowning at the floor as though wondering where to start. 'Her three kids.'

'Two teenage boys and a daughter.'

'They were out, at least the boys were. Clubbing in Hanley.'

'Together?' She was tossed back into the sea of lies. Poppy had always said her two sons *hated* each other. Tommy, she'd said, was very like his father. Stubborn and bad-tempered. '*Nasty*,' was the word she'd used, spitting it out with venom. While the younger one, Neil, was sweet-natured. '*Like me*,' she'd added, visibly preening herself while Claire had hoped he was not *too* like his mother.

'Yes,' Zed responded, not understanding her query. 'They were out together. Clubbing.' He was watching her for a clue which word had sparked her surprise. 'They both said, independently, that she'd lent them money to have a night out.' He seemed to sense that he needed to repeat the word. 'Together.'

Claire was frowning and shaking her head. This didn't sound like Poppy either. Like many single mothers, she had been frugal where money was concerned.

'*Can't afford fancy evenings out. Not a penny to spare, Claire.*' She'd giggled at the inadvertent rhyme.

So had this tale of two brothers with opposite personalities who hated each other been just another of Poppy's fables? Like her poverty? Were they, in fact, friends . . . allies even?

Who knew? Claire felt the full frustration of not being able to rely on the veracity of even one of the blandest of Poppy's claims.

'You don't believe this version?'

'It doesn't fit with the picture Poppy painted of the relationship between her two sons. That's all.'

He watched her silently for a moment before resuming his story. 'The daughter, Holly-Anne, was on a sleepover with a school friend.'

'Really?' And this was the daughter Poppy had claimed was *clingy as ivy. Paralysingly shy. No friends. No social life outside school. Never goes anywhere. Sits in her bedroom. On her own.*

Another fable.

Zed Willard watched her for a further moment, and then he must have picked up the gist of this Poppy story. Maybe he was beginning to get it now.

'So, I gather Poppy had arranged it that she was alone in the house?'

'It seems like it.'

Claire leaned back in her chair and absorbed the facts. She had long ago realized that nothing happened by chance where Poppy Kelloway was concerned. There could only be one reason behind these circumstances. So maybe her guess at a deranged partner *hadn't* been so far from the truth after all.

Poppy had had largely heterosexual, butterfly-like romances which she described as 'dalliances', laughing when she'd described fancy dates, dinners, outings, weekends away. Fact or fiction, this looked different. Arranged. And had ended in murder which put a different tilt on the plan, to put it mildly. For once Poppy had not been in control. Instead, it looked as though her habit of invention had, this time, resulted in fury. Claire flipped through a few more of her stories, wondering which one had resulted in her murder. She had a wide repertoire to ponder. As well as deceit about her own life, there had been allegations against others of sexual predation, an assault and some mocking references to sexual prowess which might or might not have been true. The fact that she'd looked attractive, petite and potentially vulnerable added authenticity to her stories. She was easier to believe than to doubt.

Maybe DS Zed Willard sensed the way Claire's mind was tracking because he asked, 'You have a record of previous events?'

'Oh yeah.' She could hear weariness as well as cynicism in her voice.

'We have plenty of documentation about minor infringements and a few court cases. Lots of potential leads.' His face changed. 'She was a pretty adept shoplifter.' He was testing the water. 'But so far we haven't connected any of her minor criminal activity to her death.'

'I take it she wanted the house to herself that night?'

'Looks like it.'

'She was up to something then.'

He nodded.

'Have you interviewed Poppy's children? Do they have a clue who she was expecting?'

He nodded again, very slowly and thoughtfully. 'We've interviewed them under the usual constraints, appropriate adults, counsellors. The whole singing, dancing team.' He looked bored now, and frustrated. 'The boys . . .' She was aware he was scrutinizing her for her reaction to what he was about to say. 'They never asked whom she was expecting that night.'

'So?'

'They arrived home at around one a.m.' His eyes were still trained on her, watching for her response, testing the water, wondering how much detail to give her.

She interrupted. 'Together?'

'Yes.' He frowned. 'Still together.'

'How?'

'Taxi,' he said slowly, pausing his story.

'Knowing they'd be late, she'd given them money for a taxi?' This didn't make sense either for a mother who was struggling to make ends meet.

'*Even Tommy has to be in by ten. At the latest. I'm a strict mum.*' Said with a certain amount of self-satisfaction. '*They do what I tell them.*'

But all Claire could think was that this was another anomaly and found herself shaking her head and frowning. 'Were there signs that she'd had a date? Made dinner?'

DS Willard shook his head very slowly. 'No dinner.'

'*I'm a cordon bleu cook. Love to cook for my friends.*'

Zed Willard was still speaking. 'Just two glasses and an almost full bottle of wine. No more than two half glasses had been poured. One glass had been rinsed clean.'

He gave a wry, twisted smile which was accompanied by a heavy frown.

'Forensic evidence?' She'd asked the question almost hopefully, but DS Willard shook his head. 'Nothing. Only signs of Poppy herself, her mum and the three children.'

And Claire realized. Because no part of Poppy's story could be relied on, this was going to be a much more difficult case than DS Willard anticipated. It was dancing on thin ice or trying to keep your balance on a yacht in a choppy sea. Her frown had registered with Zed but, as she said nothing, he picked up his narrative. 'When the boys got home they found their mum.' His face twisted.

Which was when Claire stared at him and shared some of his

horror. He had been at the scene, she had not. They had filled in their own details and were both silent. Pictures flashed through Claire's mind – she saw two boys, shivering with shock, wrapped in grey NHS blankets inside the yawning brightness of an ambulance, rescued from a scene which would haunt them all their days.

So what picture did DS Willard see?

'She'd put up quite a fight. There was blood in the kitchen, some on the stairs. She'd tried to escape. She finally died in the lounge.'

He continued, 'The knife was taken from a block in the kitchen and that's where the initial assault took place.' He put his hands flat on the coffee table as though he was preparing to stand and then he sat back again, still refusing to meet her eyes.

'And you have no DNA evidence from the crime scene?'

'We're working on it.' He continued with a tired sigh and a limp, impatient gesture. 'We think it's like this. They shared a small drink, as indicated by an almost full bottle of wine. She said something that made our killer mad. She went to the kitchen – possibly to weaponize herself with the knife. Maybe to get her mobile phone which was found on the floor in the kitchen as though it had been kicked underneath the table. The killer followed her into the kitchen, which is where the first blow was struck. Non-fatal stab wound to her shoulder.' He tapped his own left shoulder.

'Knife blocks.' Something of his old energy was emerging. 'Hate those bloody things. Why can't knives be locked away in some sort of drawer?' He gave a twisted smile. 'Have you ever noticed, Claire, in any film that shows a knife block, the camera homes in on it and either victim or villain picks one out. Usually the longest, sharpest one, and proceeds to—'

'Yeah,' she said, 'of course.' She waited, dreading more detail.

'She got to the bottom of the stairs. Maybe,' he mused, 'thinking of locking herself in the bathroom, but she only got halfway up.' Again, he tried out a half-joke. 'Like the Grand Old Duke of York's men.' He looked nauseous. 'That was when the real, planned attack took place. She was dragged back into the lounge and . . .' He drew in a deep breath. 'Our killer poured a corrosive substance over her genital area.' Now he looked like he really would heave. 'And after a while her throat—' He swallowed. 'Her throat was cut.'

Claire held up her hand. He didn't need to go any further. She got it.

They were both silent for a minute.

'How long?' Claire hardly recognized her own voice. It sounded small and frightened. Zed's eyes drifted towards the evidence bag.

The words burst out of him like a lanced boil. 'He'd drenched her knickers in a powerful caustic soda gel. Drain unblocker. Her skin was . . . she must have suffered terribly. She'd tried to pull them off. Her hands . . .' His eyes dropped downwards.

'Her genital area?'

He nodded and she understood the message only too clearly. *'Liar, liar, pants on fire,' she muttered.* 'Poppy Kelloway was a pathological liar.'

SEVEN

9.30 p.m.

'This was a specific punishment.'

He nodded. 'I think so.'

She had the feeling this would be a long night. 'Another coffee?'

'Thanks.'

She used the time while brewing his drink to think about what this meant. Trying to erase the image of her patient screaming at the punishment being meted out to her.

When she returned he was sitting, staring blankly at the wall and, by the expression on his face, his thoughts were equally dark. He took the mug from her, evading her direct gaze.

She prompted him, but gently. 'And you think the link with Greatbach is enough to send you spinning round here? To warn me?'

He lifted his eyes to hers. Warm, brown, toffee-coloured eyes which held an apology. 'Well – yes. Partly. Obviously the appointment card. That was why I wanted to speak to you . . .' He looked around the room. 'Privately.' He took a long sip of coffee – a delaying tactic she recognized. 'I don't have to spell it out to you, Claire. It puts you – and Greatbach – in the picture. This guy is dangerous.'

'If it is a guy,' she responded automatically.

'I can't see it being a woman, Claire. Poppy was petite but she looked as though she could have defended herself from a female attack.' He was silent, still watching her.

'You really think it's a patient?'

'It's one of the possibilities we're considering. It could even be a member of staff.' His reply was cautious. 'We're considering all possibilities . . .' He broke off. 'She was a minor criminal. Nothing more. So why?' It had burst out of him, almost uncontrolled.

'Revenge.' And she recalled the impassioned hatred of Harry Bloxham's sister. 'Her lies could lead to people losing their jobs, marriages disrupted, even suicide.'

'Yes,' he said. 'Motive enough.' And he fell silent.

She filled the gap.

'I take it you've spoken to the ex-husband, Robbie?'

'Yeah.' He gave a brave attempt at a chuckle but it fell flat. 'First place we looked. Except in this case he was in Cardiff for a rugby match.' He managed another smile. 'We've located him on some TV footage. He stayed down there on the Wednesday night, drunk as a skunk, in a hotel.' Now his expression was rueful. 'Where he knocked up a mighty bill for whisky plus two bar stools demolished because of a ref's poor decision.' He couldn't prevent himself from angling his next comment. 'He doesn't seem to have played much of a part in either her or her children's lives.' His eyes flicked up in query.

Claire simply shook her head. This version would suffice for now but maybe the tale Poppy had spun had been just that. She had always claimed that Robbie, her ex and the father of her three children, played no part either financially or socially in their lives.

'*I do it all by myself.*' Truth? Or another of her lies?

'So, what leads do you have?' She watched him curiously. 'CCTV anywhere near Poppy's house?'

'Not on that street. Unfortunately. Not angled towards the houses. Only over the central parkland area.'

'Neighbours' video cameras?'

'Not so far. We're still checking.'

'And there's no DNA evidence of an intruder?'

'Not yet.'

'Does that mean the perpetrator was forensically aware?'

'Possibly.' He wasn't willing to go further. Instead, he asked, 'Did she have relationships?'

Claire took her time before responding. 'In the loosest sense of the word. Poppy was always up for what she called "dalliances".'

He was frowning. 'You mean romance?'

'Not romance. I never heard her express affection. The "dalliances" were to suppress boredom or to see what she could get out of them. When a relationship didn't live up to expectations she could get quite inventive.' She chose the next word carefully, but it was the most appropriate one. 'Vicious. And when her behaviour had a result, she was triumphant.'

She recalled a few of what she'd termed Poppy's victims: a teacher who had lost his job; Harry the gasfitter who had committed suicide. And Darren Rawlins who had broken her arm when she had mocked him. So she claimed.

Poppy had taken vengeance, reporting him to the police, hounding him on social media, adding an allegation of sexual assault against minors, which was never proven, and which she confessed to Claire had been made up, *'To teach him a lesson.'*

Darren had been a sports coach. Another one who'd lost his job.

Any female acquaintances heard stories of their husband's groping as well as sightings of them with other women – even men. Poppy could be inventive. But any of those ex-husbands who had lost their homes, wives, families, she mused, would hate her too. Even the ones whose relationships had held up.

She met DS Willard's warm brown eyes. How could she get him to understand the pernicious nature of Poppy's stories, the sheer spite behind them, spreading an ink blot of poison through all her relationships – except the one with her mother which she didn't dare lose. Her mother was too useful to her. He would know the facts, maybe, but not the sheer malice behind her lies.

'I think she was on a dating website. She tended to stick to guys who were local.'

She could tell by DS Willard's pursed lips that he understood perfectly what she was saying. 'We've got her phone and her laptop and realized she was – erm – active in that area. We're trawling through her contacts.'

'You say you believe this was pre-planned?'

Zed Willard nodded, wondering where she was going with this.

'Then it was out of character,' she said. 'Poppy tended to be spontaneous. This was someone she knew . . . well.'

'Yeah, we're on to that.' He was looking a bit irritated.

'What do her boys say? They must know something.'

'We're having to tread very carefully there. All three children are, naturally, traumatized. Particularly the boys. They were the ones who found their mother's body. In that state.'

So had he, she thought, reading the distress in his face.

'Where are they now?'

'With their maternal grandmother, Lynne Shute.' A pause. 'She's looking after all three of them.' He picked up on something. 'You know her?'

'I've met her a few times over the years. If I remember correctly she's either divorced or separated from Poppy's dad, lives in Newcastle-under-Lyme. She's a feisty woman. Tough, but a stabilizing factor, someone the children can trust and rely on.'

'Tell me more about the relationship between mother and daughter.'

She was transported back to the time when she had first met Lynne, the noisy arguments between mother and daughter outside her clinic room which had escalated as Lynne screamed out, '*You shouldn't have let him go. He was too good for you. And the boys need a dad.*'

To which Poppy had responded in that quiet, dangerously soft voice. '*I do a good job on my own. I don't need him. I don't want him. He's bad for them.*'

She'd moved closer to her mother and Lynne had seemed mesmerized by the proximity, leaning back in her seat, away from her daughter's poison.

'*When Robbie and I were married he tortured me, made me do things I didn't – want – to – do.*'

Lynne had remained silent and then, after a few moments, she had regained her voice. '*Well, you had three kids with him.*'

At which point Poppy Kelloway had smiled. '*That's what you think.*'

After a moment Lynne Shute had recovered herself. '*Well, whoever the father or fathers are, those three would be better off living with me.*'

And Claire had realized she'd meant it. For a moment she'd thought Poppy might attack her mother. But her eventual response was muted.

'*Don't you dare say that.*'

But it was Lynne who now had the upper hand. And her expression was almost a mirror image of her daughter's.

Claire left the memory.

DS Willard was probing her. 'I've got the impression that she's quite supportive – has helped with the children?' He made it a question and was watching her, trying to gauge her response. When she made none, he added, 'She was quick enough to step up to the plate and take on the kids.'

'She's certainly the only adult family member Poppy is still in contact with. I believe their relationship . . .' here she paused, '. . . wasn't without its difficulties.'

'They seemed perfectly happy to go with her.' A hint of a smile sneaked out. 'So that's one problem we don't have to deal with. Placing two teenagers and a—' He stopped. Then: 'Can I confide in you?'

'Of course.'

'Rely on you to keep this to yourself?'

'Of course.'

'Poppy made a lot of complaints to the police.'

Claire's ears pricked up.

'Of stalkers and predators, people hanging around outside her home. Nothing ever substantiated. Nine-nine-nine calls saying someone followed her home. In short, she used up a lot of police time with unsubstantiated allegations. We never found a thing. So she was labelled . . .'

'A timewaster.'

Zed nodded, his expression shame-faced. 'She rang early that evening, around six o'clock, saying someone was hanging around outside. A PCSO called round and didn't see anyone. Then Poppy said she'd made a mistake. The PCSO called it in and . . .' He was chewing his lip. 'The next thing was . . .' He paused. 'So now there's bound to be an investigation,' he said gloomily. 'And if it's leaked to the press . . .' He took a while to say it. 'God help us.'

'But it opens up an alternative possibility.'

He nodded. 'That she did have a visitor – not the person she'd prepared for.'

'Yes. But it could also have been another display of her attention-seeking behaviour.'

They were both silent.

'About the two boys and Holly-Anne. I think I might be able to help.'

Zed Willard looked up, a gleam of hope in his eyes.

'There's a new guy in post,' she said thoughtfully. 'He specializes in paediatric forensic psychiatry, treating children who have been subjected to traumatic events. He's worked for some time with Médicins Sans Frontières and the Red Cross helping children from war zones. I think – maybe . . .' She paused and then changed that to, 'Would you like me to speak to him . . . perhaps pass him your number?'

Willard gave a slow nod. 'That might be . . . Yes. Please. I think that's a good idea. It might help.'

'Consider it done,' she responded, but then she sensed that DS Willard hadn't quite finished.

'Ummm.'

She had an idea she knew what he was asking. The list.

'I don't think knowing all my patients' names is going to point you in the right direction. You'll need to narrow it down somehow.'

'Well, if you could describe in general terms their personality types . . .'

'I'm not into profiling,' she said coldly.

But DS Willard waited, sensing she could and would do just that. 'So are there any of your patients who are capable of this?'

She sighed and shook her head. 'No one that instantly stands out.'

Willard drained his coffee – cold now – and stood up. 'It was worth a try,' he said, smiling now. 'But thanks for the coffee and the suggestion about the child psychiatrist. Can I leave it to you to talk to him?'

'Of course.' She hesitated before asking quietly, 'Do you have anyone in your sights?'

He shook his head and started to speak. 'I sort of hoped you might be able to point us in the right direction.'

'I'm sorry,' she said. 'Let me think about it. Maybe a name will pop up.'

'Yeah.'

She saw him to the door, noting as she let him out that he had come in a marked squad car. That should set the neighbours talking.

No blue lights, thank goodness. But as he reached the car he opened the door and stood, looking at her with an intensity that made her shiver. 'Be careful, Claire. And watch out for your patients.' It was all he said, but he'd set her nerves jangling.

EIGHT

10 p.m.

C laire couldn't bolt the door behind him because Simon was out, but the house felt ominously empty when Zed Willard had left and she'd heard his car reverse down the drive before accelerating on to Waterloo Road. She was disturbed by the fact that her own home, her haven, now felt unsafe. She hoped Simon would be home soon.

She sat for a while, in the dark, disturbed by the pictures Zed Willard had painted. Not only of that deliberate assault on her patient, but also by the question he'd planted in her mind, that maybe Poppy's assailant was one of the patients she saw in her various clinics. That she would be alone, talking to someone who had committed such a premeditated, cruel act, watching Poppy's skin burn while her hands had tried vainly to wipe it away. And then that terrible final act of slashing her throat. She was trying not to dwell on it, but she could picture the scene only too well. Poppy had been small and slim. Her appearance had always been well maintained – neat make-up, nothing too brassy or bold, curly blonde hair, nails and clothes immaculate. She had, on the surface at least, an attractive personality – vivacious, outgoing, a good listener. Some might say she had a flirtatious personality. It was only when you dug deeper that you realized truth and fiction were not aligned.

Because she didn't stick to facts, she could rustle up a fantastic past. Not a teaching assistant, divorced with three children, but probably an investment trader or a model or an ex-Olympic athlete. When you don't have to tell the truth your entire life story becomes a work of fiction. And yet behind this work of fiction there had to be a truth. Because just as it was possible that the killer had resented one of Poppy's lies, it was also possible that in that lie, Poppy had stumbled on an uncomfortable truth. While Claire had taken a history, when Poppy had first been referred, she had mentally ticked off the points she could verify. And Lynne Shute, Poppy's mother, had been an important and credible witness. And so, piece by piece, Claire had verified what 'facts' were truth and what fiction. Some were obvious, such as a rich aunt leaving her money, or that she'd won on the lottery, or lived in New York for some years, or been the head of a prestigious girls' school. But others were less so: that she'd been sexually abused by an uncle when she was ten years old (the uncle had died without ever being charged), her mother had forbidden her from ever contacting her father, and she'd been involved in a road accident which had resulted in a head injury.

Poppy was bright enough to give some of her stories a convincing turn, but they were no more than skin deep. And there was another flaw. She had a poor memory. So when you first met her she might claim to be a retired actress, but somehow on the second or third encounter she would meld that into an 'investment banker who'd made enough money to retire in her forties'. She rattled off the accounts quite airily, almost as though she didn't even expect to be believed. What made Claire so cross was that there was no point to them. No end benefit except for the downfall of the victim. They were just hollow stories. And sometimes when Poppy had attended the clinic she had sported a black eye or a bruised arm, once or twice wincing as she'd lowered herself into the chair. But the person who had inflicted these injuries had remained a secret.

One of her patients? Or . . . No. Claire shuddered.

She had warned Poppy of the consequences of making someone feel a fool, but it had made no difference and Poppy had continued with her wild stories, on one occasion telling Claire's secretary, Rita, that she couldn't attend her appointment because she was 'currently visiting the Grand Canyon'.

'She'd rung from a local number,' Rita said in disgust.

And that was the point. Claire had realized a year or so ago that something strange and twisted in her patient had wanted her lies to be transparent. Recognized. The usual psychiatrist's explanation to such behaviour was to class it as 'an appeal for help', but Claire rejected that explanation and tried to explore other interpretations. Poppy hadn't cared or made any attempt at engaging with her, though. She'd simply smiled throughout Claire's explorations.

And it had ended in this.

Bugger it, Claire thought, and went to bed. But she didn't sleep until she heard the sound of Simon's key in the door, the bolt finally being shot across and his soft footsteps ascending the staircase, passing her bedroom door and on up to the top floor.

NINE

After a restless night haunted by vivid dreams, Claire had woken early. She headed downstairs and made herself a coffee to take back to bed, still disturbed by the fallout from DS Zed Willard's visit and the details he had given her. She sat up in bed, opened her iPad and drank her coffee, but instead of logging on to any particular site, her mind drifted back to one particular day and one particular story which had snagged at the time but now seemed to hold burgeoning significance. She had been holding a clinic some-time in . . . November. It had been one of those depressingly cold, dull grey days when one could almost believe the sun never would shine again, that it wasn't even there behind the tumbling, billowing cumulus clouds that almost blanked out the light completely. In the dungeon of the clinic fluorescent lights were switched on and that had given the entire area a subterranean feel, airless and blue as a cave. One of the patients on her list that day had been Ranucci. Tony Ranucci, who had been suffering from guilt and flashbacks after a road accident in which his wife and baby daughter had died. Ranucci had been driving recklessly, witnesses had said, and he had tested positive for cocaine and alcohol at the roadside. Some might have judged him harshly, but that wasn't Claire's remit. He had 'got away' with a hefty fine from the courts and a worse sentence from either deity or justice depending on your religious beliefs. He was haunted by guilt. She had been seeing Ranucci, whose family came from Naples, for almost two years, and was about to discharge him as the flashbacks had reduced both in number and in severity. And he was clean – of drugs at least. In fact, he had reverted to the swaggering show-off he really was. There was no sign of the frightened, cowering person who had first walked into her clinic, unable to sleep because the moment he closed his eyes he was tortured with visions of his dead wife and their baby daughter, bloodied and accusing as a Shakespearian character. So, some might say, his treatment had been successful, the result of drug therapy which had now almost completely been withdrawn, combined with numerous hours spent with Edward Reakin. Others might say he deserved a lifetime of suffering after his crime. That dark November afternoon she had walked out to the waiting room to call in her next patient. And there she had spotted them. In animated conversation was Poppy, dressed in a flashy silver anorak over skin-tight red jeans, doing that thing she did when her lies were climbing unbelievable heights: throwing her head back, blonde curls tumbling down her back, laughing, mouth wide open, every white tooth in her head on display. Claire had recognized the body language. She was spinning a story. She could tell from the movement in her shoulders and Ranucci's open-mouthed, incredulous stare. And from the look of Ranucci's bright eyes, body tilted towards her, practically pelvic thrusting, he was drinking it all in. Whatever her story. For a second she had stood watching them, two of her patients interacting, manifesting their worst characteristics while feeling a slight frisson of apprehension. Both had their dangers. Ranucci's family were violent criminals. This encounter was a dangerous, toxic mix.

Sitting up in bed she felt clammy, trying to shake herself free of the memory, but it clung to her like a spider's web she'd blundered into. And as she revisited that memory she wondered.

Ranucci had all the male arrogance of an Italian stallion. And she'd studied Poppy's animated act, all the stops pulled out, talking rapidly, body language animated and sexy, rippling laugh, eyelids flickering; the story she was spinning was one of her best. Ranucci was drinking it in.

But she'd chosen the wrong one this time.

When Poppy had sauntered into the clinic room fifteen minutes later, she'd sat down carefully, elegantly crossing her legs and still tossing her bleached blonde hair. Claire had tried to warn her. Not in words or information but obliquely. Gently and subtly. 'The gentleman you were talking to out there. He has a past, you know.'

It was as far as she dared go.

But Poppy's manner was nonchalant. She combined a toss of her head with a throwaway remark. 'I guessed that. It's OK, Claire. I know his type.' She'd been so confident, so arrogant, so sure of herself and her power to enchant. Claire might have known her patient would take no notice.

And when Ranucci's turn came she also recognized that to try and warn him would be a waste of time.

'Nice girl, that one,' he'd said, jerking his thumb towards the door.

And she had responded. 'All my patients have a past, Tony.'

He'd met her eyes with an understanding of his own. Then they had proceeded to his consultation.

Sitting up in bed, Claire was chilled by the thought. Should she mention the encounter between Ranucci and Poppy to DS Willard? Was Ranucci Poppy's murderer?

Wait, a voice in her head advised. *Wait.*

But revisiting that moment now, she remembered something else. As she'd ushered Poppy into her consultation room, Ranucci's darkly hooded gaze had followed her right up until she'd shut the door behind her patient. And she remembered something else, something Ranucci had tossed into one of their initial consultations when she had been exploring his family history. 'Renowned, even in Naples,' he'd smirked, 'for their artistry, Dr Roget.'

Would that creativity include an acid assault on a woman who'd tried to deceive him? A poetic reference to a childish nursery rhyme? She hadn't taken up the comment but, remembering it now, she still felt the chill.

And there was another thing which she hadn't attached enough significance to. At her next consultation, a couple of months later, Poppy had said, 'Tony not here today then?' And she had given one of her secretive, speciality smiles, which usually indicated she was dreaming up another story.

Claire hadn't told her that she'd instructed Rita to make sure these two particular patients never crossed paths again.

So, as she'd picked up Poppy's notes that day, she'd simply said, casually, 'Not today.'

'Shame,' Poppy had said. 'I thought he was rather nice. And at least he's not married,' she'd volunteered, watching Claire out of the corner of her eyes. 'Anymore.'

And for once it wasn't one of Poppy's stories that Claire was wondering about, but what tale Ranucci had spun.

'Snazzy dressers, aren't they, Claire, the Italians,' had been her next comment. While her blue eyes had watched for a response, it had been on the tip of Claire's tongue to warn Poppy away.

But she hadn't, and Poppy hadn't mentioned him again.

So, in answer to her own query as to whether she should alert DS Willard to the encounter between two of her patients: not yet. There were more names for her to consider.

It was time to get up.

TEN

S imon caught her as she was about to leave the house. 'So,' he
said with a wide grin, 'you had a visitor last night?'

'How on earth did you know?' Zed Willard had left a good
hour before she'd heard Simon creep in, like a man with a guilty
secret.

He tapped the side of his nose in the age-old gesture. 'Next-door
neighbour. I was putting the rubbish in the bin and she caught me.'
He winked at her. 'The police, I gather. Hope you haven't been
doing something you shouldn't?'

Irritatingly she felt her face grow hot. 'He just wanted to fill me
in and get my opinion.'

'On the Poppy Kelloway case?' He looked alarmed.

She nodded.

'Why?'

'Why what?' But she knew what he was asking. Why had the
police come to her? And she knew the answer. But . . . 'I can't
really tell you, Simon. I'm sorry.'

He stared at her for a moment before turning away without
comment.

She'd wafted the exchange away, hoping she hadn't introduced
any awkwardness between them. But the conversation had exposed
how little she actually knew about DS Zed Willard's personal circumstances. Married, single, divorced, long-term partner – male or
female? She had absolutely no idea. All she actually knew for certain
was that he had a sister. She knew that because she'd spoken to her.

Claire drove herself into work.

The rest of the day passed slowly with no word from DS Willard
and the local news had passed on to another subject, the upturn of
one of the local football clubs, Port Vale, the club beloved of the
Potteries' favourite pop star son, the completely wonderful Robbie
Williams. Smiling now, Claire forced herself to focus on her half-
brother's rapidly approaching wedding, picking up the phone,

connecting with Gina Aldi, and arranging the shopping trip for her
wedding outfit with her and her partner, GP Julia Seddon. Claire
and Julia had been at medical school together in Birmingham and had
remained close friends ever since. Her relationship with Gina had sealed
the bond between the three of them and they met frequently.

Saturday 16 April, 10 a.m.

On the train down to Birmingham, Claire tried to give them her
ideas. 'Nothing too flowery,' she warned. 'Something classic but
not frumpy.' Her two friends, sitting opposite her, listened to her
instructions while exchanging amused glances. God only knew what
she'd come home with if they had their way. Gina Aldi, artist, slim,
lively, with dark hair curling down her back, always dressed with
flair, and today was no exception – a pair of grey trousers and a
shocking pink, oversized jacket with huge shoulder pads. Julia
Seddon, her partner, couldn't have been more different. She was
what her mother would have called homely. She dressed sensibly,
in brogues and tweeds, which suited her plump figure. Claire guessed
she fell somewhere in between. In character too, the two women
couldn't have been more different. But they were a perfect foil for
each other, Gina with her imaginative flights of fancy and Julia with
her grounded common sense. And again, Claire guessed, she rated
somewhere in between. They were the perfect trio, complementing
each other by their contrast.
   'OK,' Julia said comfortably, 'we hear you.' But at the same time
she was giving Gina a broad wink and a look which told Claire they'd
already discussed the day's requirements in some detail. 'We get the
idea and will sit through hours of changing-room watching . . .'
   'And no hat,' Claire growled.
   Gina was smiling, tossing her dark hair behind her shoulder.
'How about a fascinator?'
   'Maybe.'
   'Or a padded headband?'
   Claire felt awakened. 'Now those I *do* like.'
   'I know the shops to take you to, Claire,' Gina said as they left
the train and walked along the platform of New Street Station,
dazzled by the bright lights of the shopping complex constructed
around it. 'But then you must let us take you to lunch.'

So it was a deal. Taking the train down had avoided the congestion charge and then they'd treat themselves to a fancy lunch. That was the plan.

But throughout the morning Poppy's murder hung in Claire's mind like a recurring bad dream. And, even though she'd been looking forward to the day out with her friends, she was finding it hard to focus on shopping for her wedding outfit. Clothes shopping – difficult enough in normal circumstances – was twice as hard now. Her mind felt polluted with the knowledge that she might have input into the final solution. She might actually know the killer.

Because, like Zed Willard, although she tried to deny it, she suspected the torn-up appointment card did mean something. Directed against her. The killer would have anticipated the police would confront her with it. And, as he'd torn up the card, the killer would also know she would extract her own inference. It had been a deliberate action as well as a message.

She would read that message and understand it. *She's not going to need that appointment now.*

And whoever this torturer/killer was, he was smart enough to leave no forensic evidence.

So her mind was only half on the shopping trip as they leafed through racks of outfits, Gina tut-tutting as she looked over one after another, taking hangers off the racks, pursing her lips as she appraised the garment, only to replace it back on the rack while Julia watched, amused but playing no active part in the selection. Part of the trouble was that the shops were full of spring/summery flowery outfits in pastel colours: pinks, pale greens and, worst of all, lavender, which, with her colouring, would make her look anaemic and washed-out. One dress seemed to call out to her, reminding her of her duties. A cream background splashed with bright, scarlet poppies. She didn't even pick that one out. She needed no visual reminder. And as she, Julia and Gina cast their critical eyes over the clothes, the three of them found themselves for once in agreement, shaking their heads.

'This won't do,' Julia finally decided. 'And besides, your mind isn't really on clothes, is it?'

Claire shook her head. There was no getting away from her appearance: light brown hair, pale skin and a very slim figure bordering on too thin. She knew that but, however much she ate, her weight remained stubbornly the same. She was of medium height with steady grey eyes, and she knew that when she tried on several outfits, whereas other women might have one distinguishing and lovely feature they could call to the fore, she didn't. Her physiognomy was almost abstract. A negative, a wallflower. Plain. Her mother's description of her fitted only too well. She was a negative who would be happy not to attend the wedding at all. But she had to. Even if only for Adam and Adele's sake. She knew they would notice her absence and be terribly hurt by it. But what she really wanted from an outfit was to be able to fade into the background, blend into the wallpaper so her mother and stepfather would hardly notice her at all, meaning she would be able to walk straight past them causing hardly a ripple in their consciousness. She wanted something quiet and unobtrusive while every outfit she looked at would feel like dressing up, playing a part badly. And her mind seemed intent on recalling Poppy Kelloway's flamboyance and flair in that department. Whatever outfit she had worn, she had carried it off convincingly.

When she finally tried an outfit on, emerging from a changing room in a calf-length magenta dress which flared around hips she didn't have, Gina had her hands on her own slim hips, looked critically at her and shook her head. 'You need some highlights in your hair,' she decided. 'I'd get those done first and then we'll come again. And Claire, whatever it is that's upsetting you, it's really not helping.'

Claire returned to the changing room and her own clothes, to study her hair in the mirror. Maybe Gina was right, both about the hair and her distraction. Perhaps it was time to come clean.

Julia watched her emerge from the changing room, the dress draped limply over her arm, to be returned to the assistant with a shake of her head. 'What is it, Claire?'

'I'm sorry,' she said. 'I'm being a damp squib.'

'It isn't just the wedding that's getting to you, is it?'

Claire shook her head. 'No.'

When they were seated at the restaurant, Claire finally unburdened herself and watched her own horror mirrored in her friends' faces. 'Dear God,' was Julia's response. 'No wonder you're not exactly running through the alternatives for a wedding outfit.'

'Do the police have any idea who . . .?' Gina didn't need to finish the sentence, give voice to the words.

'Well, I'm not exactly privy to the investigation . . .' Claire was aware she was hesitating. 'So far I don't think they do.'

Gina was silent. It was left to the practical Julia to ask, quietly getting to the heart of the matter, 'And the appointment card? Do they attach much significance to it?'

Claire shrugged and tried to avoid the truth.

But it screamed at her.

ELEVEN

Monday 18 April, 10 a.m.

It was a shame that the hairdressers were closed on a Monday. But before she changed her mind she left a message at her salon that she wished to make an appointment to have some highlights put in. 'Some time later in the week,' she said, and left her mobile number.

She could work out a few hours away from Greatbach when they gave her an appointment time.

Next, she took the bull by the horns and asked Rita to cross-reference patients whose appointment dates and times had coincided with Poppy's attendances and pass her their notes. 'Men only,' she said.

Thinking about Ranucci had focused her mind. If the killer's clue of the torn appointment card was an attempt to draw her into the case, she would do her bit, fight back, and pull up the notes to scrutinize them. The hunted could become the hunter. She was convinced that, knowing her patients inside out, all the hidden crevices of their minds they tried so hard to hide, she would be able to find this clever, cruel killer before the police.

In her office Claire began to think rationally. Poppy liked men. In a way that could translate to disliking women, seeing them as a threat to her influence. So, could the killer be a woman? She sat and thought. Though Poppy was petite, she was strong and wiry. As Zed said, she looked like she could defend herself. It would have taken some strength to have overpowered her, even more to restrain her while tipping the corrosive gel over her and holding her while she struggled. Besides that, in the years since Claire had first known her, Poppy had never once mentioned any sort of friendship or relationship with a woman. She had no real female friends.

Friendships with her own sex might begin warm and open but women soon found out the cost. Even the relationship between Poppy and her mother was taut. Another point which convinced Claire that this was *not* the work of a woman was the preparation Poppy had made, making sure all three children were out of the house. This hadn't been for a woman but a man. Poppy was flirtatious to the opposite sex. She enjoyed their attention and the scene at home had been carefully planned by her. A male ego had erupted that night. Or had it? Had the act been premeditated? And had she read the torn appointment card wrongly? Was the real message blame for failing to cure Poppy of her lying?

She tried to console herself with the sop that the hours spent with her and Edward Reakin had kept her patient out of the courts. So it hadn't been completely futile.

It wasn't even a consolation prize.

But the fleeting thought of Edward Reakin reminded her of his suggestion that she review the notes he had made around a month before Poppy's murder. She'd already scanned them but now she wanted to really study them further.

She opened them to that last consultation with the clinical psychologist to see if she could pick up on something she'd missed.

A little like Edward's quiet, unobtrusive nature, his writing was regular, neat and small.

I saw Mrs Kelloway at 11 a.m. She said she was in a hurry and didn't have much time. I reminded her that part of her course of treatment was a half-hour session with me every eight weeks.

I asked what was so pressing. Her reply was that she had to be somewhere.

'Where?' I asked.

Her response was surprising. 'Put it like this,' she said. 'If I don't get there I'm in trouble.'

I asked her, 'What sort of trouble?'

I was aware that this might be one of her stories but she seemed sincere and more than a little disturbed.

Claire was tempted to underline the word sincere. Poppy always seemed sincere. That was the trouble.

She read on.

'I've sort of fallen foul of someone.' She quickly changed that to 'some people'. 'If I don't pay up . . .' And she dragged her index finger across her throat.

Claire smiled at Edward Reakin's precise, pedantic description. Index finger. But the action brought it all back and she shivered and touched her own neck.

I asked her if it was money and her response was unexpected. 'More than that,' she said.

'I am being watched, stalked, threatened and I feel . . .' She touched my arm. 'Frightened.' I felt sorry for her. She really was terrified.

Now Claire was staring into space. Poppy had been a consummate actress. But Edward Reakin was a psychologist with years of experience. Surely Poppy couldn't have fooled him with an am-dram performance?

In the end I let her go. I asked her whether I could be of any help . . .

Again, Claire found herself staring into space. Edward was a skilled, gentle man, with a wealth of experience, expert at asking probing questions in such a polite, soft voice that he lulled his patients into a feeling of safety so they forgot they were, actually, being gently interrogated. This was an examination they had to pass. When Claire had started at Greatbach, Edward had been married, one of the quiet ones. But slowly rumours had begun to circulate that his wife had had lovers – not one but a succession of extra-marital affairs. And Claire had witnessed the metamorphosis as a tall, slim, fair-haired man had turned into a thin, balding, middle-aged man with a stooped back. One day he had entered her office, closing the door quietly behind him and told her, in a softly apologetic voice, as though it was his fault, that he and his wife were divorcing. She'd never forgotten the moment, the sad, embarrassed look on his face as he'd spoken quietly and with dignity while his bent shoulders and anguished expression revealed his true feelings. He had looked so sad and vulnerable then that she had been tempted to fold him in her arms and try to console him; his anguish had been so palpable and it was obvious that whatever the true circumstances of his marital break-up, he blamed himself.

Edward Reakin seemed to have fallen for whatever it was that Poppy had been playing at. But then, in Poppy's eyes she would have seen him as a man, a soft touch. Even she could almost see him pulling out his wallet and handing over some notes. Because that was the way Poppy worked, wasn't it?

But she said she'd work it out – somehow.

Rita arrived, interrupting her thoughts, her arms heavy with sets of notes which she dumped on Claire's desk. 'This enough for you to be getting on with?'

'It'll do. Thanks, Rita.'

By accident or design, as though Rita had made him chief suspect, Ranucci's notes were at the top of the pile. Claire opened them and read through the letters she had addressed both to the courts and to Ranucci's GP. Some phrases stood out: manipulative, *controlled violence*, and the old chestnut, *substance abuse*. Blamed for so many crimes, but in her opinion it simply uncovered the darker you. Let the beast out. Ranucci was reckless and had many of the elements of psychopathy. He could also be subtle.

Come on, Claire. Think.

Analyse.

DS Willard had described the crime scene as devoid of forensic evidence. Did that mean cleaned? She thought about what he'd told her. The assault had taken the killer from the lounge to the kitchen, halfway up the stairs and then back to the lounge where he had mutilated, tortured and finally killed Poppy, taking the trouble to leave two messages, one to Claire – the torn appointment card – and the other to Poppy: *Liar, liar, pants on fire.*

She was tapping her finger on the desk, trying to decide if Ranucci was a likely candidate. And now she wasn't sure. It was too subtle for him. Ranucci wasn't clever. He was boastful. If he'd wanted to say something he would have carved it into her chest. And yet . . . and yet. He had the requisite male ego. That put him back in the frame.

But if she was going to pass this information on to DS Willard she had to at least have a grounded suspicion.

She put Ranucci's notes to one side. In many ways he fitted the bill. She knew he was attractive enough to have aroused Poppy's attention. She also knew they had met and noticed each other.

But something else was missing. It was the moral judgement element. The punishment for lying. Ranucci had none. He wouldn't have cared that Poppy Kelloway told lies – unless it had been about himself and the wife and daughter he had professed to love.

Worth investigating, she decided.

She picked up another set of notes.

John Ryder. At thirty-eight years old, John Ryder's marijuana use over a number of years had resulted in extreme paranoia. He was divorced from his wife who claimed he had threatened her. Tick number one. As a result of her complaint he was not allowed unaccompanied access to his eight-year-old daughter, of whom he was obsessively fond. His wife Georgia's claims were unsubstantiated and Claire had always wondered whether the threats had really ever happened. It had certainly given Georgia Ryder some control over her daughter and ex-husband. Ryder's obsessive adoration of his daughter made the threats extra cruel. Georgia Ryder could not have hurt her ex-husband any more, and her behaviour had resulted in his pathological resentment of women – all women. Claire had even sensed it directed against herself. The poor child, whose name was, ironically, Joy, was torn between her two parents, and more than once Ryder had expressed his hatred of his ex-wife. He would, he'd said, kill her one day. But then, Claire reasoned, returning to Poppy Kelloway, Georgia would have been his target – not Poppy, another patient who cared for her own children. Ryder had no actual history of violence but his upbringing had given him a strong sense of justice and in that way he fitted the bill. Had any of Poppy's lies contributed to his restricted access to his daughter? Or to put it another way, was that what he believed? Had she possibly toyed with his only too visible weak point?

It was possible. The last time she'd seen Ryder he had seemed even more agitated than usual. When she had questioned him on this he had muttered, 'Something to do with my . . .' The rant had been against his ex-wife. No mention had been made of Poppy. One might believe they didn't even know each other. But Claire had seen her, sitting behind him in the waiting room, tapping his shoulder to gain his attention. And when Ryder had turned there had been an eager expression tightening his facial muscles. Maybe Poppy had been telling him of a way to circumvent the court's ruling and his wife's venom and see more of his daughter, which was the only thing Ryder appeared to want.

If he'd swallowed that fable only to be disappointed, she could imagine him wanting to punish her. Cruelly.

The next set of notes she picked up were those of Tre Marshall. Again, she hesitated. Marshall was a complex character. Thirty-four and of above average intelligence, he had been diagnosed as a paranoid schizophrenic when he'd been in his early twenties. And he was classed as well controlled. It was a few years since he'd had any delusions or psychotic events and he attended clinic regularly, never having missed an appointment. Tre even had a job helping out at a local hospital as a porter. He was a model patient – quiet, punctual, polite. So why was she still holding his notes so tightly?

Because . . . Tre had been training to be a priest. He had a degree in Theology from Oxford and had planned to enter a seminary but had been turned down when he had given details of graphic visions he'd had of the Devil. He had been referred to her 'for assessment'. And when she had examined him as a new patient he had displayed scars on his back from self-flagellation. Occasionally he used the words 'self-destruct'. Marshall was deep. Deep and highly intelligent. But not quite deep enough to conceal any emotion he might feel. Nor intelligent enough to hoodwink the professionals who treated him. She'd often met his eyes, initially bold and challenging, before he'd dropped his gaze, concealing something he couldn't quite hide. Shame for his condition. She recalled also seeing him and Poppy in the waiting room, Marshall sitting behind Poppy this time. Normally he would be holding a book – often the Bible – but that day he had been staring fixedly at her, his lips moving in what looked like supplication – or a curse. Until he'd blinked, looked up to the ceiling, slowing his breathing. She'd watched the pair of them, realizing that because Poppy was only pretending to use her little mirror to apply her lipstick, she was perfectly aware of Marshall's scrutiny. She would probably consider a religious man a challenge. She was tossing her head and scrunching her shoulders – putting on her lipstick with extra care, small movements, which drew attention to her – and it registered with Claire that Poppy was making Tre uncomfortable, an instinct which had been born out later by his fidgety demeanour and palpable tension during the consultation.

She sat still. Tre Marshall fitted the bill only too well. He had no history of violence except against himself, but his sense of right and wrong – of a punishment severe enough to fit a crime – fit only too perfectly. Maybe Poppy had considered his religious zealotry a challenge.

Her hand rested on Tre Marshall's set of notes. She should see him, question him and decide for herself. There was certainly no need to alert the police at the moment because she had nothing to give them.

Like the rogue callers who unintentionally mislead the police during a major investigation, she would only make things worse.

She returned to the pile of notes Rita had selected for her.

She focused on men under sixty but over twenty-five. And the pile was getting smaller as she discarded various patients.

She hesitated over another set. Professor Rotherham. Age sixty-one. Just outside her parameters. And why, she questioned herself, are you even thinking this?

Because. She realized she'd come full circle.

Because his OCD had given him a side effect of desiring right, justice, fairness. And that strange instinct for the punishment to fit the crime was bugging her. Had he been on the receiving end of Poppy's deceit, he would have *hated* it. At the same time, he would have suppressed his anger. So had *he* fallen victim to one of her stories? She couldn't quite see it. But there was something in his perspective that snagged her. A certain rigidity in his thought processes. That was what led to the bleeding hands and sore knuckles which he presented at every consultation. She visualized his sparse, wiry frame and strange, compulsive habits. He was a classicist who related, with relish and a certain amount of just deserts, the punishments of the Gods in classical literature, in particular the tortures, the subjects of which he had frequently introduced during previous consultations: Tantalus, who could never *quite* reach his food or water; Sisyphus, whose name was forever connected with a hopelessly unattainable task. Erysichthon, Medusa, Marsyas – the list was endless and cruel, the tortures inventive. And Poppy's punishment? Claire sat up straight as she recognized something. Poppy's torture had *not* been classical but connected with a childish ditty. So should that realization let Professor Rotherham off the hook? Tempting. But her hand hesitated over Professor Rotherham's set of notes as she remembered him relating stories of the punishments of the saints – graphic details that many people would find too horrific.

'These,' he'd said, with professorial dignity, 'were the main contents of my lessons. Until . . .'

Until what? Claire thought now. The professor was sixty-one years old. He'd loved his job. In fact, he'd once said to her that he could have gone on and on and on working.

So why had he retired?

It was something she'd never explored in spite of his response when she'd once asked him why he'd retired early.

Now his response struck her as significant and relevant. 'I did not retire,' he'd said with dignity. 'I was retired.'

And for once Claire had been struck dumb.

And now, despite her arguments to the reverse, she was still troubled by the fact that she could well imagine him working out what might be a just punishment for lying.

Surely cutting out a tongue? Or slitting a throat?

She kept the professor's notes on the pile of suspects.

She went through the remaining names, excluding the older patients, some of whom were being treated for dementia. The pile was getting smaller. More manageable. Luckily she had a good memory for faces so each patient was accompanied by memories.

In the end she had her list: Tony Ranucci, John Ryder. She put a question mark by Ryder's name because his diagnosis was officially depression. But there was a sinister aspect to his deep depression. His marijuana smoking had left him with paranoia and some psychosis. When he had first been referred, eight years ago, at his first consultation he had backed into a corner, eyes terrified and obviously hallucinating. Even the police had recognized that this was a psychiatric problem with a sinister aspect to it. The event had taken place outside the school where his own daughter was a pupil. He had grabbed her mother and produced a knife. His ex-wife had been injured with a superficial cut to her neck which could have proved fatal had it reached either the carotid artery or the jugular vein, both of which are unprotected by either muscle or bone. When John Ryder had been referred to her, something about him had troubled Claire. Something manipulative and fully aware which he tried his best to conceal. The assault on his wife indicated an unforgiving nature and now she was thinking about him she remembered something else too, another encounter maybe a year after the time she had seen Poppy tap him on the shoulder.

Poppy flopping into the chair during an outpatients' clinic, jerking her thumb towards the waiting room where John Ryder was still sitting. 'He,' Poppy had said, '*is a right weird one. If you ask me, he's proper nutty.*'

Which had struck Claire as funny. She'd had trouble suppressing her laughter. One could apply that epithet to practically everybody in Greatbach – even her at times. But Poppy had a point and Claire was not laughing now.

Now she recalled her response to Poppy's words. Noncommittal to a throwaway remark but she had shelved the moment away, perhaps sensing its portent. She tapped her finger on the set of notes and put them to one side, picking up the next.

This was another anomaly. Jarrod Stonier, thirty-four, was a little easier to understand. Diagnosed with a narcissistic personality disorder, she saw little of him. His condition was intractable and untreatable. There was little she could or needed to do. She put his notes to one side. His appointments might have coincided with Poppy's but she couldn't see any connection. Jarrod would sit in a far corner of the waiting room until his name was called. And then he would respond, carefully, making no eye contact with any of the other patients waiting, keeping his distance from them, walking as near to the wall as possible as though mental conditions could be deemed contagious. She hadn't seen him making any connection to Poppy. He was too careful. In fact, she ruminated, he possibly recognized a similar character to his own and gave her an even wider berth than the others. One could say that Jarrod Stonier was a success story. There had been no problems with him for more than two years. She might not need to see him again. But maybe he was worth talking to.

Likewise, Ed Sutcliff, who had bipolar disorder, currently well controlled with carbamazepine, and Kris Deppner, who had suffered from an eating disorder but was now well controlled with a BMI of twenty-one – just about acceptable. She'd discharged him back into the care of his GP. In the intervening years Edward Reakin had spent some time interviewing both men and no red flags had been raised. She could trust his judgement.

Then she came to Erik McKenna. Now here was a problem. In a way Erik was not unlike Poppy. They had more in common than perhaps they might realize, but while Poppy sought attention by dramatic lies, Erik was quite simply loud. He had the subtlety of a steamroller, shouting, talking over others, volubly disagreeing with anyone voicing a different opinion and this had cost him job after job. He was unpopular but he couldn't see it. Rhino hide. She had even noted Poppy shifting from a seat near him when he had started voicing one of his opinions. And she had seen the look he had given her in return. Pure poison. But there was no way Poppy would have cleared her evening for Erik McKenna. She consigned his notes to the pile at her feet to join Kris Deppner.

Her mind flipped back to a couple of occasions when Poppy had attended the clinic, wincing as she sat down, sporting a black eye or a bruised arm. Poppy would never have cleared the scene for a man who had assaulted her. She could never have been that stupid, could she?

But then, she mused, or rather hoped, maybe Poppy's killer was not one of her patients? Perhaps she and the police were paying too much attention to a torn appointment card. Maybe there had been no message implied. Maybe even Poppy had torn it up herself. She might have come to the conclusion that Claire – and Greatbach – were not doing her any good.

But the fact remained. Poppy had been murdered because she had pissed the wrong person off.

TWELVE

Tuesday 19 April, 10 a.m.

T he hairdresser rang with an appointment for four o'clock, which suited Claire as she could manage a full day's work before her 'transformation'.

And then she did something that she'd vowed not to do. Even at the time, she was well aware that it was a mistake. Somehow her fingers had found Grant's number on her keypad and somehow she had pressed 'call'. Big mistake because he answered almost at once. And he listened to her halting concerns about her patient's murder and the muddled, possible connection to herself. He made no comment until she'd finished. Then he said, 'You want me to come and stop with you for a while?'

And she realized, with horror, that it would be so easy to slip back into that comfortable arrangement where she would feel safe. 'No.' She had to stop his flow. 'No. Really, I'm fine. And, Grant . . .' Too late, she realized the pit she was falling into.

Grant cleared his throat, a sure sign he was uneasy, and she heard his silent question: *So what are you ringing for?*

And, for something to say, some excuse or reason other than the fact that she still missed him, she diverted into a rambling explanation of her failure to find a suitable wedding outfit, somehow including Gina's advice about highlights, and she could almost see him smile before he spoke. 'So you want me to come and help you find a wedding outfit?'

She let out a relieved breath. 'Something that'll let me keep in the shadows.'

'With highlights in your hair?'

This was the trouble. They were on the same wavelength. She was smiling too.

'Hmm,' he continued, pretending to consider the option, before commenting with an insightful, 'Family, eh?'

Nailed in one, she thought, before something else struck her. *Who would ever know her so well?*

He came back to her, breaking up her thought. 'Any chance you can take Friday off? I have a really quiet day.'

She felt humbled. After they had broken up, sort of, Grant had started an interior design firm, and while it had been slow for a year or two, partly due to the pandemic, it was now, apparently, taking off. For him to take a day off to come shopping with her was, probably, quite a sacrifice. He followed up his offer with a suggestion. 'I know a few shops in Chester,' he said casually. 'How about we spend the day there?'

Her relief was tangible, though hopefully only to her. 'Yeah. That'll be good.' Because she didn't know what to say next or even how to end the conversation, she made a clumsy statement. 'Thanks for your . . .' And then she was stuck. Did she mean opinion, concern, help, support, listening ear? A bit of all of those.

'You're welcome.' His response sounded cool now, mere politeness. She was about to respond with a warning, something like, 'Any outfit we choose won't transform me or make my mother like me,' but she didn't get the chance because a woman's voice cut in.

'Grant.' It was sharp, peremptory and proprietorial, a voice that held ownership and command.

Claire was stunned, knocked off balance, particularly when her on/off boyfriend ended the conversation with a hurried, 'Got to go, Claire. Sorry.' Which left her staring stupidly at her phone screen which now displayed only the time. Who the hell was that? she wondered. Grant had never mentioned employing someone. Was she a client? She'd picked up on something else. Grant's hurried response had made it plain he didn't want this woman to know to whom he was talking. She replaced her phone in her bag and headed for the wards.

Simon was busy at the nurses' station, peering at some blood results on the screen. A set of notes was in his hand. She drew up behind him and read the name. 'Dana?'

He nodded, his eyes still fixed on the screen. 'Yeah. She's reached therapeutic levels of her sodium valproate. I thought she was less psychotic when I saw her yesterday. I noted some improvement. And Edward says he's seen an improvement too. Fewer hallucinations and an acknowledgement, at least, that little Lily Rose is her daughter.'

This was good news. 'Any mention of the resident ghosts?'

He shook his head and she began to hope. In most cases of puerperal psychosis there was a moment when the patient showed signs of recovery. Could this be it? A new beginning? 'Good,' she responded.

'So when can we start bringing Lily Rose into visit her?'

'This is the critical phase. We'll have to move cautiously.' She paused for a moment. 'In a day or two, if Dana continues to improve, we can start accompanied visits. It's a bit of a tightrope walk, getting the timing and balance right. But let's hope that soon we can reunite mother with daughter and progress towards bonding.' Then she fell silent, drowning in her own experience with her mother.

Her silence must have alerted her registrar because he wheeled around. 'You all right there, Claire?'

'Yes.' And when his eyes remained stubbornly on her she admitted, 'No.'

'So . . .?'

'Two things really.'

'Poppy Kelloway,' he guessed.

She looked around her. No one was watching or listening.

'I didn't tell you earlier because I couldn't.'

'The policeman?'

'There might be a link between the murder and here.'

'Greatbach?' His astonishment was intense.

She then told him about the appointment card.

His response was predictable. 'Shi-it.'

'The police are treating it as potentially significant,' she said. 'That's why Detective Sergeant Zed Willard called round the other night.'

Simon was skewering her with a glance. 'There's something more, isn't there?'

She tried to sweep it under the carpet. Blow psychiatrists with their searing perception and uncomfortable insight.

She described the assault on Poppy, following that up with, 'I'm looking at patients whose appointment times coincided with Poppy's or who might have had some contact with her.'

'Is there anything I can do to help?'

She felt herself relax. 'I'm just glad you're around, Si.'

He was frowning, picking up on her vulnerability. 'And the police think this . . . person might feel some animosity towards Greatbach – towards you – personally?'

Again, she hid behind the phrase. 'It's one of the theories they're exploring.'

He was silent before coming up with a suggestion. 'What about Grant, Claire? If you want to move him back in that's fine with me. If you'd feel safer with him around.'

She was chewing her lip, considering, until she blurted out, 'I think he's met someone.'

'Really?' He stood back and folded his arms, smiling now. 'Well, I can't say I'm surprised. Not really, considering you keep him on a very long leash and quite apart from the fact that you've let me move in as your top floor tenant for a few months. Gives him a bit of a hint, don't you think? Edged him out?'

Annoyingly she felt her face heat up.

Mercifully he moved on. 'What makes you think there's someone else in his sights?'

'I was talking to him on the phone . . .' She could hear a wobble in her voice and felt furious with herself. What on earth was wrong with her? *Psychiatrist*, she lectured herself, *stabilize your mental state*. 'I heard a woman's voice – sort of – summoning him.'

Simon shrugged, unimpressed. 'Maybe just a work partner.'

'Sounded as though she was ordering him around. He rang off pretty snappish. Besides, if he was employing someone he would have told me, I think.'

'Yeah. Right. I guess. Maybe a customer.' But she couldn't fool him or pull the wool across those perceptive eyes only partly concealed behind thick-rimmed glasses. 'And you care?'

She shook her head and after a brief pause he returned to Poppy Kelloway.

'So have the police got a suspect in their sights?'

She shook her head. 'Unfortunately, no.'

'That detective,' he said next. 'I think he's sweet on you.' And for the second time in as many minutes she felt her face warm.

THIRTEEN

3 p.m.

I t didn't help matters that when Claire returned to her office, DS Zed Willard was waiting for her outside the door.

He took a step forward looking only slightly apologetic. 'Your secretary said you'd be back soon.'

'Right.' Then anxiety took hold. 'Have there been any developments?'

He motioned towards her office door. 'Better we speak in private.'

He followed her into her office, and once she'd closed the door behind him, he sat down opposite her. 'We have picked up some DNA,' he said, 'but it doesn't match anything on the database.'

She knew what he wanted to ask and shook her head. 'Have you any idea of the red tape we'd have to cut to subject a number of my patients to a DNA test? With no more corroboration than a torn appointment card? You're going to need more than that, Zed. However, I am making progress with the list. If you can wait a little longer, you might not need to test my patients. Certainly not *all* of them.'

His face flushed slightly as he seemed to consider what she'd said. He looked around him, through the window out into the corridor where people were passing, a few peering curiously in. 'Not really any security here, Claire.'

'No. It's a hospital, not a police station.' She knew she'd sounded waspish but she had to deflect this attempt to rush names or records out of her by disturbing her with concerns about her safety.

'You need to take care,' he said next, confirming her suspicion.

'You really think I'm at risk?'

'I think you might be. Do you want a police presence here, Claire? Just for the time being. Just until we . . .'

The missing phrase was *make an arrest*. 'No.' She followed that up with a firmer, 'Absolutely not. The patients here trust us *because* there is no sign of a police presence.'

'Right. But . . .'

She read concern in his eyes. 'But what?'

'This man is a cruel monster. The post-mortem showed second-degree burns in the . . .' he hesitated, '. . . panty area and on her hands. It would have been horribly painful. The sooner this killer is caught, the sooner you'll be safe. I saw her mutilation with my own eyes, Claire. This man is on the periphery somewhere. You might already know him. And he might know that. Which puts you in prime position for . . .' He stopped there.

And for once as she watched his face redden, Claire didn't know what to say.

He spoke next. 'What do you know about Poppy's family?'

'As far as I know she was an only child with warring parents – a violent father.' She qualified the statement. 'So she said.'

'And her ex-husband?'

'Robbie? I met him a couple of times when Poppy was first referred. They were already divorced.'

'*Why* was she initially referred?'

'Her GP picked up on her personality traits and thought she'd benefit from a referral to Greatbach. There were a couple of shoplifting charges which stayed under the radar as the stores dropped the prosecutions in the face of some of her outrageous allegations against the store personnel. Then fraud. She worked in a bank and started stealing money. She was prosecuted then but pleaded all sorts of extenuating circumstances including the fact that she was sole parent to three children. I got dragged in on account of her "fragile mental state" and the agreement was that she remain under my care, and so avoided a criminal record. And I'm sure that most of the other victims who had been on the receiving end of her alternative truth never involved the police. Quite honestly, I think they mainly weathered the storm she'd created.'

Apart from poor old Harry Bloxham, she reflected.

'Ah,' he said. 'I did wonder how she got through the CRB check.'

'She wouldn't have been a danger to children.'

DS Willard looked sceptical.

'No. That was the anomaly with Poppy. Look at her own children. Balanced, nice kids.'

'I haven't met them.'

'Well, I have. In the school holidays she'd bring them with her. They'd sit, quietly reading or playing games on their phones or something. They were – are – nice children.' She waited, struggling to put into words the instincts she'd felt. 'Poppy had two sides to her. That was what made her lies so . . . convincing.' After a pause, she added, 'Potentially dangerous.'

DS Zed Willard waited.

'Caused mayhem. Absolute pandemonium, but you have to realize she didn't – couldn't – actually distinguish lies from the truth. What we might perceive as wishful thinking was, to her, an alternative version of events.'

Zed Willard was watching her. 'I don't understand.'

Claire shrugged and looked away, frowning. 'It's an unusual phenomenon,' she said, 'which started when Poppy was very little. She came from a violent household. Her father assaulted her mother multiple times so her mother made up elaborate fairy stories in which her father was kind, really, but he had had a curse put on him so he was sometimes taken over by an ogre. Poppy repeated this to herself when her father was violent and on one occasion she put herself between her mother and father and screamed to let the devil out. It so shocked her father that he stopped what he was doing and he left soon after. So her little outburst had the desired effect. Thereafter her mother continued with fables, presenting them as the truth, turning a boiled egg or another cheap meal into a posh restaurant, a second-hand dress from the charity shop as a couture frock made just for her. It was a habit that Poppy adopted but with more imagination and success . . .' She paused. 'And it had a dark side. If there was someone she didn't like, usually men – however tenuous the contact – she would invent a story about them, that they had touched her inappro-priately or said something. Sometimes she would claim they had made a racist comment about another person. And of course, because Poppy was pretty, petite and convincing, she was believed. Which led to her lies becoming more damaging, and conversely, more convincing.' Claire's frown deepened. 'And she stuck to them.'

'Because?' Zed interrupted.

'Because to her the fantasy was simply an acceptable alternative version of the truth.'

'Why fantasize at all?'

'Because she preferred her own version.'

Zed Willard was still struggling to find a rational explanation. 'Spite? To get even?'

Claire shook her head. 'Because she could.'

Zed blew out an irritated breath and frowned. 'I know her

behaviour, even though we might think of it as minor in the wider scheme of things, has harmed many individuals.'

'Oh yes. I'm sure you know about some of the victims. Three or four cases where people lost their jobs . . .' She hesitated. 'Marital break-ups. And one suicide, of course.'

'Harry Bloxham.'

'She accused him of sexual assault. There was no evidence, as there wouldn't be. He was . . .' She smiled. 'A very good-looking guy but not very bright. He worked for the gas board as a fitter and came to her house to fix the boiler. The children were at school. She accused him of assaulting her, saying he'd touched her breasts, put his hand on her bottom. Absolutely no evidence at all. Nothing. But the poor guy hanged himself as she was believed and he lost his job.'

'And your private opinion?'

'I don't think any of it happened, but as they say, mud sticks.'

'Did he have any close relatives who might have wanted revenge?'

'He did. A sister, Lisa. She wrote me very angry letters.' She hesitated before furthering her narrative, which took her to the ugly side of Poppy's stories.

Bloody Lisa. Sitting outside my house shouting stuff at me. As though she blames me for her stupid brother going and hanging himself. Stupid bloke. He must have known it was just a tease.

Claire's response had been: *'But you involved the police, Poppy.'*

'Yeah, but they should have known it was just . . . fun.'

She never could quite press this point home. That relating a malicious tale about someone – was – not – fun.

'Not to him.'

And for the nth time she had tried to persuade Poppy to see the end result of her tales. That they left behind a wake of unhappiness, destruction, fear and mistrust.

At the same time she'd known that she was wasting her time – and effort. In the years since she had first met Poppy Kelloway she'd had no effect on her behaviour.

The thought struck her like a thunderclap. If she had made a breakthrough, Poppy might still be alive, caring for her children and doing her job. Not lying on a mortuary slab until the coroner released her body for burial.

She became aware that DS Willard was watching her and to her surprise and relief he changed tack. 'I'll tell you what I don't understand, Claire.' His tone was more relaxed, simply enquiring.

'Go on,' she prompted him.

'She was married long enough to have three children. What are they – seventeen, fifteen and eleven? So that's a span of at least six – seven years?'

'Yes. That was one of the good periods in her life.'

'So was this a break from her lies?'

Claire was thoughtful for a moment. He had a point, one which perhaps she hadn't explored enough. Why the hiatus? Or rather, *how* the hiatus? Robbie Kelloway might be off the hook as far as being a suspect for his ex-wife's murder, but maybe he did have some answers. They had been together for around seven years – if he was the father of all three children, something which Poppy had hinted might not be the case. But that little hint, dropped carelessly into one of the consultations, might well be another one of Poppy's little tales. Now she was more curious about her and Robbie's relationship. Had it been tranquil? Unbeknown to him, DS Willard had brought someone to her attention who might give some hints towards Poppy's psyche.

But first she wanted to be sure of something. 'You are absolutely certain his alibi holds up?'

'Yes. We've checked all the footage. It's him all right and the CCTV footage is dated and timed.'

'Have there been any similar crimes committed?'

He shook his head. 'Nothing like this.'

'Ever?'

He shook his head.

'So it is all about Poppy.'

'It seems so.'

He was watching her.

'Did she ever use her lies for gain?'

'You mean blackmail?'

Again, she was plunged into the past, face-to-face with the ugly side of her patient.

'*Told him if he didn't pay up I'd blow the dirt on him. I'd cover him in shit so completely he'd look like a tar baby. Old bugger gave me what he called a sweetener.*' Her mouth had been twisted in derision. '*A little gift.*' Her voice had been heavy with malice. '*I knew what it were, all right. Hush money.*' And then that almost insane peal of laughter.

Claire had tried to warn Poppy that this was a dangerous game.

And what good had that done? Her words had had no effect whatever.

She thought of something. 'You said that the night she died, Poppy rang saying someone was outside her house?'

'Ye-es?' He was uncertain where this was leading.

'Did she give a description of the person?'

'Yes, but it was so vague. Medium build, medium height.'

'Man or woman?'

He gave another sigh. 'The usual hoodie pulled up. Could have been anyone. In fact, the whole debacle was a complete waste of time.'

'And the enquiry into whether the police failed her?'

For the first time that afternoon DS Willard managed a twisted smile. 'Will take months,' he said slowly, dragging the words out as though keeping time with the pace of the enquiry.

She was silent for a moment, thinking how often what seems like a useful and significant breakthrough can result in nothing more or less than the sand pouring through an hourglass. Then she finally capitulated and told DS Willard of her plans. 'I thought I might have a "refresher" clinic. I've cross-checked a few patients whose appointments coincided with Poppy's. I plan to interview them and assess their current mental state. I think I can pick up on any animosity directed towards her.'

DS Willard looked appalled. 'No. No. It's too dangerous. If you've narrowed the list down, you can just give us the names.'

She leaned across the desk. 'It's my job,' she said quietly, 'and my training.'

But she read something in his eyes. In the evasion, the troubled look, and she watched as he winced at the memory. He tried to smile but it didn't reach the troubled look in his eyes. She realized he was frightened for her, seeing Poppy's torture superimposed on her.

'Zed,' she urged, 'I think I might be able to uncover something. I might be able to help. It could be the last service I can perform for her.'

'No.' It burst out of him, shocking her with its ferocity.

She was about to argue but, with perfect timing, his mobile phone rang. He read the caller ID, stood up and in one smooth movement he was out of the door, simultaneously telling the caller to hold on while apologizing to Claire. He was back moments later. 'Sorry – there's been a development.'

And then he was gone.

FOURTEEN

W hen Zed had gone her office felt small, claustrophobic, the air heavy from the recent conversation. It also felt empty and too quiet. And she was acutely aware that in this pile of notes there lay, perhaps, a killer. DS Zed Willard's thinly veiled warnings had firmly placed her in a vulnerable position. From one of her patients? It was a sickening thought.

Mentally she added another name to her list to follow up: Lisa Graham. She hadn't been Poppy's mystery caller that night, but she had shared the contents of her brother's suicide note with her social media account and that note had, fatefully, put some of the blame on the doctor who was failing to stop her patient's lies. Lisa had been furious. She had contacted Claire and, even though it was far too late to clear his name of Poppy's allegations, she had begged her to testify that her brother was innocent and that any stories spread about him by Poppy Kelloway were lies. But Claire had refused to make any public statement. She hadn't been asked to appear as a witness at his inquest and so she had kept silent. And Harry's sister had never forgiven her. The letters slowly dwindled to nothing, and Claire had been glad to try and forget about this tragic chapter. There had been no point in raking over the dirt. Harry had committed suicide. There was no doubt about the coroner's verdict. Any testimony she might have given wouldn't have made any difference. But when she had spelt this out to Lisa, her fury had compounded. 'You might at least have the decency to clear his name,' she'd shouted down the phone. 'My brother was no sexual predator.'

But although the last thing Claire wanted to do was to have *any* contact with Harry Bloxham's sister, she wondered whether she might have some valuable information. Had Lisa Graham sought revenge on the woman she claimed had destroyed her brother? Could the hatred she had had for Poppy Kelloway have been so intense she had convinced someone to commit that horrible crime on her behalf?

The trouble was that Lisa was the only person Claire knew for sure really hated Poppy. That hatred had transmitted itself in the numerous letters addressed to her at Greatbach.

She didn't even know what excuse she could possibly have for contacting her. And she certainly wasn't willing to pass her details over to the police, but she did know Bloxham's sister felt she had good reason for seeking vengeance on the two people she held responsible for her brother's death.

Claire remembered the phone call and the letters – every word of them.

> He was just one of those doltish, handsome fellows without a bloody clue. He had no chance of saving himself from her story. She knew what she was doing. She bloody enjoyed it. Clever little bitch. And I hold you responsible. You're the doctor. You should have come forward with the information about your patient, made it plain she was not to be trusted and that it was lies. All of it LIES. And yet you didn't come forward and testify at his inquest. You're a coward. You bloody coward. Why do you have to defend a guilty, malicious woman and let my poor, stupid brother die with a legacy of her lies? Clear his name, for goodness' sake, even if it's too late to save his life. Expose her. Do something decent for once instead of sitting behind a desk in your pointless bloody clinic listening to patients without a bloody clue how to cure them.
>
> Pointless, Dr Roget. You are pointless. Why didn't you tell the court that your patient was a pathological liar . . .?

And so on. The words had stung and the sentiment behind them – that her work was pointless, her achievements meaningless – chimed in too true with the appointment card ripped into pieces.

She shook herself free of the memory of Lisa's fury and the sting of her words, realizing only now the full depths of the legacy Poppy had left.

Then she glanced at her watch. She should be leaving for her transformative hair appointment. Maybe, she thought, harking back to Lisa Graham for a split second, she needn't worry about contacting Harry Bloxham's sister. If she knew anything about Lisa

Graham, she would soon contact her – even if it was only to gloat – or to warn her.

If she hurried and could find a place to park, she'd only be a few minutes late for her appointment. Before she left, she hesitated only to add another name to her list.

Robbie Kelloway. He might have the perfect alibi, but he'd known Poppy better than any of them. She was the psychiatrist but she'd bet he held some answers. And she had the perfect excuse to contact him. She could offer her condolences, check him out, interview him to provide 'insight'.

And now she really must go.

FIFTEEN

4.25 p.m.

Having highlights put in your hair is a form of medieval torture, Claire decided, as she flicked through *OK!* magazine, seeing the latest pictures of the royals and gossip from Brooklyn Beckham's post society wedding fallout. Foils, bleach, incessant chatter, facing a mirror and, at the end, being expected to admire one's new look, back (with the help of a mirror) and front. Watched by an anxious hairdresser, she stared at her reflection as though seeing a stranger. Steady grey eyes looked back at her, her eyes studying a face she never really did study. And she was expected to admire herself, another foreign stance.

Truth? She didn't recognize herself.

Sylvia, the hairdresser who had wrought such a transformation, noting her client had apparently been struck dumb, prompted her anxiously. 'All right?'

'Yes. Yes. Thank you.'

She didn't really know what to say, so she opened her mouth and thankfully found a few spare clichés.

It looks great. Wow.

But the woman who looked back at her was someone she didn't know. Shoulder-length hair, tiger-striped, a half fringe swept across her face, her eyes looking larger, her skin paler, her lips fuller. She licked them while the assistant brushed the cuttings off her shoulders. The bill was a shock, particularly when Sylvia suggested she have the whole thing done all over again in a couple of months' time. Pen hovering over her appointment book. 'Hair grows, you know.'

She muttered something about having to check her diary, paid the bill, and stepped out of the salon.

Hours later she stared at herself again in the mirror. Who would have thought having blonde streaks put in her normally fine, mousey, nondescript hair could have transformed her appearance so much?

Well done, Gina, she thought. The artist was right. She looked . . . different.

Wednesday 20 April, 11 a.m.

A week since Poppy's murder, Claire's morning was spent peppered with compliments about her hair, before she attended a multi-disciplinary meeting together with Edward Reakin, the clinical psychologist, Simon and Salena Urbi, her Egyptian registrar, as well as Astrid the clinical lead nurse and representatives of various other disciplines. At the back, hovering near the door as though he was anxious to leave as soon as possible, was Saul Magnusson, the paediatric forensic consultant she'd mentioned to DS Zed Willard. He was the epitome of a Viking: tall, blond, powerful looking. But his physiognomy belied a soft personality, hands that were gentle with the children whom he pinned with a pair of ice-blue eyes, and a quiet, kindly voice speaking in barely accented English. Claire had hoped he would stay at Greatbach; he was a real asset to their status as a forensic unit and his experience with MSF and the Red Cross had given him valuable experience with traumatized children. But she sensed that this powerful man with his magnetic personality was a wanderer who would soon be moving on to some war-torn location where, arguably, his talents would be needed even more than here, in Stoke-on-Trent, where his caseload consisted of the children suffering deprivation or the fallout from absent, alcoholic or drug-addicted parents, as well as children suffering other mental illnesses.

She caught his eye and he read a request in her raised index finger. He nodded but she sensed his reluctance, his impatience to be doing something more with his life than spending time with children with ADHD, advising their parents (more frequently just one parent) to encourage sport and a healthier diet for the children whose malnutrition manifested itself in obesity rather than beriberi, kwashiorkor or marasmus. He was a restless man, she'd realized quickly, during their first few encounters. He would soon be off, back to Africa, Afghanistan, Syria or maybe even Ukraine where children who'd had a previously happy and safe life had been plunged into confusion, injury and terror, the rug having been pulled from under their feet in the cruellest of ways. Saul spoke several languages fluently and could make himself understood in most. He was also a talented mimic as she'd realized on the few occasions when she and her colleagues went for a night out. He was even a fairly profi-cient belly dancer, which had had Salena Urbi, her Egyptian registrar, screaming with laughter.

When the morning meeting had finished Claire drew Saul aside and he gave her an almost apologetic smile which she registered with a sinking heart. *Please, not so soon. Don't leave yet.* He had brought an exoticism to the slightly drab psychiatric unit, blowing a fresh wind along its dingy corridors. And his energy had energized them. Not just with his belly dancing, but with his can-do attitude. It seemed that sometimes no task was beyond him.

'So,' he said, grinning now and focussing all his attention as well as that boundless energy on her. 'What is it you want me to do this time?'

She glanced around the room. The others had left so no one could overhear. 'Did you ever meet Poppy Kelloway?'

He shook his head, blue eyes flashing across the question. As succinctly as possible she outlined the situation as well as the role she was asking him to play, to interview Poppy's three children, the two boys, teenagers Tommy and Neil and eleven-year-old Holly-Anne. He listened very carefully before making observations of his own.

'And you want me to find out the true story behind their night out, how was it that the brothers went together, when their mother claimed they were not friends?'

'Exactly. She actually said they hated each other.'

'They will be traumatized by finding their mother in such a situation.'

She bent her head. 'Of course.'

'But you think they might have noted something that they, maybe, have omitted to tell the police?'

Again, she nodded.

'And the girl, Holly-Anne, you say, she was having a . . .' He hesitated over the phrase, separating the two words: 'Sleepover with a friend?'

'A friend her mother claimed she didn't have.'

Saul looked serious. 'And the boys are not really children, are they?'

She thought about that for a moment. Responding slowly. She hadn't seen them for almost five years – not since she had taken their mother on as a patient. Of course they would have grown up in the meantime. Tommy would be around seventeen now and Neil, his younger brother, must be fifteen.

'Yes, I see. I think I am getting the picture, Claire. You think Poppy's children might know something that, perhaps, they do not realize they know?'

'Or they do know but are not sharing.' She drew in a long, slow breath before letting it out in a sigh. 'It's worth a try, Saul.'

'Of course. Where are they now?'

'Well, here's the problem.'

He listened carefully, his expression bland except for the frown that was deepening. And to her surprise he focused then on the grandmother. 'And she is Poppy's mother?'

'Lynne,' she supplied. 'Lynne Shute.'

'She is truthful? Yes?'

'I think so. I've only met her a couple of times. But yes, as far as I know, she is truthful.'

Claire was silent for a moment, stumbling over something that had bothered her ever since her convent education. *What is truth?* Pilate had asked rhetorically, as though it could not be defined. But surely it could? It was . . . And there her mind ran dry.

Saul Magnusson was watching her patiently, only very slightly puzzled at her abstraction. She shook her head, unwilling to enter into a philosophical point halfway through the day.

'So, Claire, what exactly is it you want me to do?'

'Talk to them, Saul. Find out the truth, how their mother suggested they go out, what reason she gave? I'm curious. And the police really aren't up to this. Maybe you could find out whether Poppy lied to her children.'

'What exactly did she say *about* her children? How did she describe them?'

'She said that they were . . .' She smiled, wondering what the Danish equivalent was. 'That the two boys were chalk and cheese. That Tommy, the older one, was grumpy and difficult while Neil was sunny-natured. Like her.'

Saul frowned. 'Not too much like her if that meant he liked her . . .' he stumbled over the word, '. . . inventiveness.'

'You could put it like that.'

'Anything more?'

'She said they had huge arguments and hated each other.'

'She used that word? Hated?'

'Yes, though even at the time I thought it was a bit strong.' But then she herself had experienced sibling hatred – for a time. She forced herself to leave that moment. 'And yet we have this picture of the two brothers having a night out together. Very pally.'

'Brothers frequently quarrel and then make up.'

Claire frowned. 'That wasn't the picture Poppy painted. She used the word hate.'

'But you say she was prone to exaggeration and more,' he said politely. 'So two boys who occasionally argued might be elevated to two boys who *hate* each other?'

He had managed to inject a certain amount of scepticism into his voice, which made Claire smile and acquiesce. 'Possibly.'

'And the girl – Holly-Anne, her name is? How did her mother describe her?'

'Poppy told me she's shy. Has no friends and is very isolated. So how come she's suddenly at a sleepover?'

'An idea might be to speak to the friend and find out how this' – again the pause as he stumbled over the phrase – 'sleepover came to be.'

'Yeah.'

'So what you want from me is for me to find out any truth about their mother's death from the point of view of these three children?'

She smiled. 'That'll do – for a start. Oh, and here's the number for the SIO on the case.'

He gave her a warm smile then put his head on one side. 'Is there something different about you?'

She was startled. 'What?'

'I know.' He looked pleased with himself. 'It is your hair.'

She touched her head self-consciously. 'My brother's getting married in a few weeks' time. I wanted to look . . .' Her voice trailed away before she stumbled out the phrase *my best* but Saul Magnusson's eyes were sparkling.

'It looks very nice,' he said formally. 'Very . . . umm . . . glamorous.' He was looking mischievous now but she was anxious to return to the subject.

'So, you'll see them?'

'Yes. Of course. You know, Claire.' He put a hand on her shoulder. 'I did wonder about coming here to Stoke.' He'd said the word in an abrupt fashion as though it was some far-flung foreign place instead of here, the Potteries, home of Spode, Wedgwood, bottle kilns and oatcakes. 'I thought of it as a backwater,' he confessed. 'But I had heard such good things about you and the work you do here.'

She responded awkwardly. 'Thank you.'

He continued to embarrass her. 'I read the article you wrote about women who form relationships with "Lifers". It was good. It taught me many things and showed great insight into these . . . unusual liaisons.'

She held her hands up to stop him and he laughed. 'So, when you ask for my help with three children who must have had an interesting time with such an inventive mother, I am glad to help.' He accompanied his words with a slight bow which made Claire feel even more awkward. But she smiled and thanked him then gave him Lynne Shute's details so he could summon the children himself. She wanted to distance herself from this action.

She suggested if he had any relevant information he could liaise with the police, but he waved the suggestion away. 'No,' he said. 'I will report to you. That is best, I think.'

And he strode off, his steps long and quick, covering ground as quickly as a pursued deer.

SIXTEEN

1.45 p.m.

She found Edward Reakin in his office on the top floor. He was a sensitive man, balding, in his forties, though with a stoop that suggested a much older man. His divorce a few years ago had resulted in a loss of confidence – and he had probably never been a man blessed with an exalted ego. Now he was shy and quiet, with a hidden depth of knowledge and penetrating insight. Over the years Claire had worked closely with him she had developed a huge amount of respect for him – as well as deep pity. He had a mild, intelligent manner, was prone to taking his reading glasses on and off when he was agitated, and his perception was legendary.

'Edward.'

As always, he was polite and questioning, waiting for her to open the conversation. 'Claire?'

'Poppy Kelloway.'

He nodded. 'Yes, I thought you might want to talk about her.'

'That last consultation. How much credence did you attach to it?'

His response was cautious. 'You know Poppy,' he said, drawing in a long, regretful breath. 'She just loved the drama.'

'But you felt this was authentic?'

Again, that puff of regret. 'Who knows?' he said, dropping his shoulders. 'Maybe she was being a better actress than usual.'

'But if . . .' Claire prompted.

'If it was true, I would suspect a moneylender, though usually they simply lump on the interest. They don't usually threaten. They just make sure their "clients" are in debt to them for the rest of their lives.' He paused, thoughtful as ever. 'If not a moneylender, considering her precarious finances, then I would have said drugs.'

'When did we last test her for drugs?'

'Not more than a month ago. We've kept a watch on that.'

'So a moneylender or a fantasy.'

'It would seem so.'

Claire registered his expression of apology as though he had personally failed his patient. It was as though he was hardwired to always believe he was the one at fault even though the converse was true. Edward had spent hours trying his hardest to unravel Poppy's psyche, delving into her past and reasoning with her, trying to persuade her to recognize the fallout from her lies, which she didn't even recognize as lies. It had been an uphill task, one in which he was bound to fail – and fail again. And this was another fallout from Poppy's lying, the damage she did to anyone who tried to help her. They were left feeling a failure as Edward did now. Sometimes, he'd confided in Claire, he'd even thought he'd reached her only to be disappointed when she produced some other fantasy the next time he interviewed her. Or, even more cruelly, she mocked him for having swallowed yet another fable. It had taken him years to finally reach the realization that Poppy's lying was in her DNA. 'In the end,' he'd said, 'I gave up. Like you, I decided it was a waste of time. I listened, I commented, and it was as though she drew me into her game because now I was the one who was being dishonest, pretending.'

'The police think her murder was the result of one of those lies. I just wondered if this moneylending thing had some truth behind it, whether she really was frightened. She certainly rang the police saying she was being watched.'

'And the police think they can get to the bottom of this?'

'I certainly hope so.' Claire was recalling the torn appointment card together with the implication the police were drawing, that she was the one who was vulnerable now.

But Edward was intuitive. He put his head on one side, frowning as he looked hard at her. 'Claire, what aren't you telling me?'

She hedged. 'I'm probably not supposed to tell you. It hasn't been made public.'

He waited and she told him about the torn appointment card, trusting it would go no further. He looked concerned. 'So, it puts Greatbach – and possibly you – in the picture.'

Reluctantly she nodded. 'I just wondered, Edward . . .'

Instinctively he guessed what she was about to say. 'If she dropped a clue? Said something?'

'Anything?'

Edward Reakin pursued the subject with some passion. 'Haven't they got someone in their sights? Her ex, possibly?'

She shook her head, reminding herself again that Robbie Kelloway might be a useful person to talk to – even if the police were certain he was out of the picture for his ex-wife's murder.

'He was away and has an unshakeable alibi.' But now she recalled the phrase Poppy had used. *He tortured me.* Prescient? Or again, one of her fables?

Edward gave her one of his rare smiles. 'Doesn't that automatically put him in the picture?'

'This isn't fiction, Edward. Besides, there was no real acrimony between them.' She couldn't suppress the smile that was forming. 'In a way – and surprisingly, considering Poppy's weakness and her dramatic claims – I saw an amicable divorce. I don't know how they managed it, but they did. In spite of her tales, I actually thought him a likeable character. Quite open, in complete contrast to her. To me she took the line that they both wanted their freedom.'

Edward Reakin looked dubious. 'With three children? How did she manage – financially?'

Claire simply shrugged. 'There seem to be two different versions. The newspaper report implied that she had no help from him financially. But she lived in a lovely house and seemed to manage OK, so I think that version is yet another of Poppy's inventions, something she put around to make her appear a victim.'

'That fits. And her current partner?'

'She doesn't have one.' Claire felt compelled to add, 'As far as we know. She was like a butterfly, moving from one paramour to another. I don't think she had a steady partner.'

Edward simply stared at her with his steady grey eyes which displayed puzzlement, his glasses held loosely in his hand. 'But I saw him,' he said. 'There was a man with her when she attended last.'

Claire was stunned. 'That's news to me. I've never seen her attend clinic with a man. Who was he?'

'I don't know, but they seemed . . . close.' He pictured the scene, heads close together, sharing secrets, scanning the patients in the room and sharing a private joke, almost certainly about them.

'When was that?'

'Just a month ago.'

'I never met any partner,' Claire said again.

Edward's look was understanding. 'I wouldn't have believed in him either,' he said sympathetically, 'if I hadn't actually met him in the flesh.' He gave one of his rare grins. 'I even shook his hand to make sure he was real and not another fantasy. I think I've turned into a doubting Thomas.'

The biblical phrase struck a chord in Claire's mind. Every time they heard one of Poppy's stories, they were all turned into doubting Thomases.

'Have you told the police? Given them a description so they can follow this mystery man up?'

She knew at once that she'd wrong-footed him. 'I-I-I didn't think.'

'I told them she didn't have a regular partner,' Claire said. 'Maybe her mother knows who this guy is, but they haven't said anyone's come forward.' She reflected on this new fact before curiosity took hold. 'What was he like?'

'Fit. Maybe late forties, early fifties. Looked like he worked out. I wouldn't like to have crossed him. He looked tough. Medium height, gingery hair a bit sparse. He had a tattoo on his right arm. Jeans, but a very clean-pressed blue shirt and he smelled clean, of aftershave. Smokers' teeth. Slightly casual, confrontational manner. Brummy accent.'

'Did he give a name?'

Edward Reakin frowned. 'Something beginning with D. Dan? David? Darren? Something like that. I didn't catch his surname.' He brightened. 'Maybe he didn't give it. After all, *Poppy* was the patient – not him.'

'He didn't come into the interview room, did he?'

'Oh no.' He paused, looking anxious. 'You think I should have told the police?'

'Yes, I do. I'm surprised you haven't already.'

He was defensive. 'I hadn't realized there was this connection with Greatbach. I thought it . . .' He looked apologetic and she felt she'd been a bit sharp with him.

He followed up with a quiet statement. 'I'll speak to the police at once.' Then he paused, hesitated. 'Her children should know who he is, surely?'

'I've roped Saul Magnusson in to interview the children – though Tommy's seventeen. Hardly a child anymore.'

'Saul? That's a good idea. If anyone can talk to these poor kids, I'm betting Saul will be able to.'

'Yes.'

Edward hadn't finished. 'This man. He seemed a bit rough round the edges, but I can't believe . . .' His voice trailed away until he added miserably, 'I thought I'd hear about an arrest any day. I'd better speak to the police. Do you know who the senior investigating officer is?'

'Our old friend, DS Zed Willard. I expect someone senior to him is overseeing the case, but he's the one I've spoken to. I'll leave it to you then, Edward.'

He nodded and as she left his office she acknowledged that she wasn't anxious to get in touch with DS Zed Willard again. He had asked her out for dinner once. She had turned him down, but the request had left residual awkwardness between them and she didn't want to send any wrong messages. As far as her private life went, she had enough on her plate with letting go of Grant strand by strand. She was about to visit the canteen and pick up some sandwiches when, right on cue, her mobile phone sang out a contact from the very man.

'Hi.'

'Hi.' He sounded – as ever – jaunty. 'You OK, Claire?'

'Yeah. Fine, thanks.' She waited for him to tell her why he was calling.

'You had your highlights done?'

'Yes.'

He laughed at that. 'Can't wait to see them.'

He still hadn't said why he was ringing and she was foot-tapping impatiently. 'I am at work, you know.'

'I realize that.' Now he sounded hurt. Still waiting to hear why he'd called her, and she gave out a gentle prompt. 'So—?'

'I was thinking about our shopping trip on Friday. I'll come and pick you up, shall I?'

'Yeah. Thanks. That'd be nice. Save me driving.'

'Around ten OK?'

'Yes. That'll give us a full day.'

Finally, he blurted it out, failing to make his tone casual. 'Fancy stopping out somewhere?'

Woah. She felt a rush of – excitement? Adrenaline? Hormones? Whatever – it was quickly followed by guilt.

Instead of prompting her he waited, silently, patiently, wisely.

And she threw caution to the wind and caved in, just managing to keep her response casual. 'Yeah. OK. That'd be nice.'

Unwise, Claire. Very unwise.

'Great.' He couldn't keep the excitement out of his voice. 'And Claire . . . really looking forward to seeing those highlights.'

She closed him down. 'See you Friday then.'

'Be ready for ten.' His voice was light, carefree, happy. He knew he'd won. This round anyway.

And she had just made a very unwise decision. But she savoured the moment before looking at her watch.

Time to head to clinic. And the first on her list of potential suspects.

SEVENTEEN

C laire faced Tony Ranucci across the room and spent some time studying him. He was one of the first she had called into the office with either an extra appointment or a regular appointment brought forward in connection with Poppy's murder. The tests she had pre-ordered had all come back negative. No drugs and no alcohol. It appeared that Tony Ranucci was being a good boy. But she didn't think so. It just wasn't something they could test for. As Poppy's lies were hardwired into her character, so Bad Boy was in Ranucci.

She watched him carefully. And was relieved when, after the polite preamble which opened most consultations, including congratulations on his 'clean' screen, he was the one to open the subject. 'You hear about what happened to one of your patients, Doctor?' There was a note in his voice, which mocked her.

She looked up from her notes.

'I did.'

He shifted forward in his chair, his face animated and eager. 'I knew her, you know.' She realized he was anxious to get something off his chest, so she put her pen down.

'Yes,' she said quietly.

'We hit it off, you know.'

How much of this was the braggart speaking?

'She'd been a spy, you know.'

Claire simply lifted her eyebrows and suppressed any hint of doubt. 'Really?'

Ranucci was ahead of her. 'And if you believe that . . .' He finished with a chuckle and folded his arms.

'So . . .?'

'Yeah. But she had a way with her.'

'You know I can't comment—'

He was watching her with a wicked gleam in his eyes. 'Yeah, I get that, Doctor.' He stood up to lean across the desk. 'If you're interested – or wonderin' – we went out a couple of times.' He paused. 'And I *have* spoken to the police.' His eyes narrowed so he looked sly. 'Not sure where they got my name from, but there we are. The police are clever at unearthing secrets, aren't they?'

She wasn't sure where this was heading and limited her response to a brief nod.

'Well, after this extra little chat it'll be six months before I see you again, eh?' he finished jauntily and swaggered out of the room.

She stared at the door still vibrating from his exit and scooped in a long breath.

It was five o'clock. She could have gone home but she wanted to spend some time with Dana Cheung. Her patient suffering with delusions after giving birth had caused her to wonder. A month from now she would be facing her mother, her stepfather, her half-brother and his fiancée. The weekend with Grant would be taken up with finding the right outfit to wear to the occasion. Anticipating what for her would be an ordeal made her wonder why her mother was so hostile towards her. All her life Claire had put the strained relationship down solely to her father's abandonment of his wife and baby daughter. But now she wondered. Was it possible that her mother, possibly only partly as a consequence of being abandoned by her husband, had suffered from post-natal depression? Even puerperal psychosis, like Dana? The irony was that, although she was a psychiatrist, supposed to have an almost supernatural insight into the workings of the human mind as well as understanding the mental state behind pathological behaviour patterns, it had taken a patient to make her recognize what might be the truth.

She climbed the stairs to the top floor, hoping to find a clue to either support or refute her theory.

When she peered in through the window, Dana was lying on her bed. She looked calm. Sleepy but peaceful. There was no sign of the baby. Claire pushed open the door and Dana looked up to greet Claire with recognition and a questioning expression. 'Dr Roget?'

Claire settled down in the armchair by the window. She glanced out at the quadrangle, peaceful and quiet in a chilly bout of rain. Today it looked drab and empty.

She turned her attention back to her patient. 'So?'

Dana shook her head. 'I can't understand what happened, Doctor,' she said. 'I'm still very confused. It was as though my mind was taken over. I remember having thoughts about . . .'

She was still avoiding speaking the baby's name, Claire noted.

'Terrible thoughts. Frightening thoughts. But now they are melting away.'

'How do you feel about Lily Rose now?'

Dana frowned at the mention of her daughter's name and didn't respond straight away. 'I . . . I . . . Can I be honest with you?'

Claire nodded.

'Well then. I am confused.' She leaned in. 'Someone put these thoughts in my head. I don't know who and I don't know how or why, but they *were* planted in my head – somehow. And there is a connection. I just haven't found it yet.'

Claire could have pursued the topic but she had already made her judgement. *Not quite there then.*

Instead she watched Dana for a moment, deciding which of her medication to adjust. Before she left she tried to reassure her patient. 'We're getting there, Dana. And soon you will be in a better place. But this is going to take just a little more time.'

Dana Cheung closed her eyes in a passive gesture of submission.

Outside Claire met Salena Urbi. 'We need to keep Dana in,' she said. 'And she's not ready for visits from her daughter.'

Salena opened her dark eyes wide. 'Not even accompanied?'

'I think we'll wait a bit longer. Increase the sodium valproate. If we're still getting nowhere in a couple of weeks we might have to try an add-in medication. Maybe a benzodiazepine.'

To herself she was voicing a doubt, wondering whether her patient would ever really bond with her daughter. So, was her relationship with her own mother similarly doomed? Permanently?

Reality told her: yes. It was irretrievable after all this time.

So shut the door, Claire, and stop clamouring to be let in.

And yet she continued to hope.

Salena loosened her hijab. 'Claire,' she said, 'we know it takes time.' Her smile was wide, showing white regular teeth. 'Even what we term normal new motherhood is hard enough. But when you don't even know what's real and what isn't . . .' She put a hand on her shoulder. 'Even more difficult. For some women who miss out for one reason or another on the early bonding process, it never really recovers. But for others the bonding heals.' It was as though she was talking about her, Claire thought, listening to her registrar's wise words.

'We can wait, we can hope and we can use medication and counselling together with CBT. Let's be hopeful.'

Claire nodded her agreement but inside she felt depressed. Salena's words were sunny and optimistic but she knew the truth and the statistics.

For some the bonding never heals.

She and her mother would almost certainly have this great impassable chasm between them for ever.

But, as she tripped back down the stairs to her office, she swore. *One day I will find my father and I will speak to him. And maybe then I will have some perspective. Maybe then I will understand. And I will have the truth in my hand.*

But for now, she simply had that hollowed-out feeling one has when deprived of a mother's love, a loss that seemed greater as she grew older and saw how her mother treated Adam.

EIGHTEEN

Thursday 21 April, 9.15 a.m.

She heard nothing from DS Zed Willard during that day or the next, though she listened out for news, hoping there would be an announcement of an arrest. But the radio and Internet remained stubbornly quiet.

The only phone call she did have was from an increasingly excited Adam, with his soon-to-be-wife, Adele, chiming in with every minute detail of The Big Day. At least three times. And whooped when Claire described her new hair colour. Their excitement and enthusiasm were infectious, and Claire almost found herself envying them. It all sounded so magical. Such a fairy tale. The dress, the bridesmaids, the flowers, the church service, cars, music, everything geared towards the froth of romance. And these two really loved each other. It was pulling Claire towards something elusive that was fantastical, magical, a fairy tale. She was suddenly glad she would be on Grant's arm to attend this day, which might have its princess and handsome prince but, for her, also had its dragons. Though maybe that was unfair. Adam's father, Mr Perfect David Spencer, had never been horrible to her. He had tolerated or simply ignored her, taking his cue from his wife. This was the way she'd always read it, though treating Dana Cheung had given her some insight into her mother's treatment of her and that insight was leading her down the path of forgiveness. But there was one fact which placed an obstacle in this neat and tidy theory. Puerperal psychosis tends to re-emerge in subsequent pregnancies and births. *Not with Adam*, the voice whispered in her ear. No depression there. No horrid dreams or psychotic evidence. Nothing but joy.

So, was she deceiving herself, clutching at straws?

Friday 22 April, 10 a.m.

Claire woke early, with plenty of time to get ready. Simon had already left for work so the house was quiet and empty when the knock came on the door. Grant was in good time.

It was one of his traits, always to arrive on time, or even, occasionally early. He stood on the doorstep looking achingly familiar, in well-pressed jeans and a denim jacket, its sleeves pushed up to the elbows. He took a step back and studied her. 'Claire,' he said, 'love your hair.'

She immediately felt embarrassed, patting it self-consciously and wondering if she looked as though she was making a vain attempt at stepping back into being a teenager.

But he was grinning at her, his face friendly with that warmth that epitomized him. 'It looks amazing,' he said, his voice husky and without a hint of sarcasm. 'You look amazing.' That was when she realized she knew him well enough to respond with honesty. 'Really? You really think so?' She heard the note of surprise win over the doubt in her voice.

He moved forward, holding his arms wide, and it seemed the most natural thing in the world to let him fold them around her. With his index finger he tilted her face up to his and touched her mouth with his lips. Softly at first before upping the pressure and she drew in a deep breath. This was what she always remembered when she thought about him. Grant couldn't help himself. He was sexy.

Later he drove them to Chester, periodically smiling as he glanced across at her as though to reassure himself that she was still there. That was another thing about Grant Steadman, perhaps in his favour, maybe not. He made you feel special, like the only person who mattered to him in the whole wide world. That was why his mother and, in days gone by, his sister, Maisie, who'd died, found it so hard to let him go. He gave you a hundred per cent of his attention. It was like an addictive drug because when he was not there you missed it and the missing became an ache.

The traffic was light, the weather cloudy but bright, and they were soon parked outside a hotel right in the centre of Chester. It was a black and white property which overlooked the crooked, two-tiered walkways known as The Rows. On the way over they'd made desultory conversation, he talking about his latest assignments (no mention of a 'partner' or a 'customer'), while she made observations about various patients, discussing the diagnosis of puerperal psychosis and its impact on mother and child, but without mentioning the possible relevance to her own mother.

And then she did. 'I wonder if my mum suffered from that when I was born.'

He gave her a long, searching look. 'I thought you believed the . . . difficulties' – he'd chosen the word well – 'were more to do with your father leaving.'

'I'd always thought so but treating one of my patients has sort of made me wonder.' Her voice was small when she followed that up with, 'I'd like to know.'

'Ask her.' That too was typical Grant. He would blunder into a question which was delicate, seeing a direct way through to the truth.

'Yeah.' But she knew she never would. That level of honesty and frankness had never existed between them. She took a brief moment to imagine the scenario. *Mum, did you suffer from postnatal depression or even psychosis when I was born?*

And her mother's response: *A stony, hostile stare.*

'How sad,' Grant commented. 'And how ironic that you treat women with the condition, yet it's taken you all this time to recognize it in your own mother.'

'It's just a theory,' she responded sharply, and Grant fell silent, but she could see a little smile twitching his lips. He wasn't going to take her on. That was for sure.

He changed the subject. 'Talking about your patients . . . have they arrested anyone yet for that woman's murder? I haven't heard.'

'How did you know she was one of my patients?'

He looked confused. 'I think you must have mentioned it.'

She was shaking her head. 'I don't normally discuss my patients with you – certainly not by name.'

'Then I must have read it in the paper,' he said.

It disturbed her. 'Are you sure Greatbach was mentioned?'

He shrugged, starting to lose interest. 'I must have seen it somewhere.'

Not good, she was thinking.

But he must have a thread. 'Are they asking you to help?'

Now she felt alarmed. If Grant could work this out then so could others. She tried to put him off. 'It's just a theory.'

They'd pulled up in the hotel car park. She turned to him. 'I'm doing what I can, Grant. What I should. I have a duty.'

And he nodded, knowing he should back off now.

They climbed the steps to the hotel foyer. 'Drink in the hotel bar?'

Her mood lifted. 'Oh no. We have serious work to do, Grant Steadman. No slacking here. We're not here to idle and get drunk.'

'Really?' And she knew he was laughing at her.

The moment felt good.

They checked into the hotel, leaving their overnight bags at reception and headed out to the streets. Grant seemed to have a nose for finding unusual shops, small retail outlets for clothes the owners had designed themselves, but nothing seemed right. She held dresses against her and stood critically appraising in front of full-length mirrors but wasn't tempted to try anything on. Some seemed too theatrical, others were not flattering, in spite of her jazzed-up hair. Until they reached a small establishment in a back street. It was early afternoon and the sunlight was golden, lighting the way.

From the outside the shop looked uninspiring, a narrow window with nothing dressing it but a bolt of material artistically draped. But even the material was enough to draw the eye. It was fine silk, a shimmering, royal blue, and it held her gaze. Grant held the door open and she entered a shop which, like the TARDIS, seemed much bigger on the inside. A single mannequin stood in the centre and her eye was caught by the outfit. It was a silk suit, in grey, with a floor-length magenta, butterfly-strewn net overskirt billowing out behind. She took a step closer, watched by a woman of around thirty wearing tight jeggings, a black T-shirt and numerous piercings on her ear, nose and through her lips and eyebrows. The woman said nothing but watched her with eyes heavy with black make-up. No urging her to try it on or flattering her with suggestions of how glamorous she'd look in it; not trotting out the clichés that it was 'meant for her', that it was her size or quoting the price. Instead, she simply watched her with a critical eye. And Grant was also quiet. It was like a conspiracy. If either of them had poured words into the silence the spell would have been broken.

Claire took a step forward, reached out and felt the silkiness of the suit and the sharp rasp of the overskirt's lace. She felt drawn towards it, imagining what it would feel like to slip inside that jacket, fit each button to its buttonhole, feel the skirt ripple against her legs. She stepped back and let the woman unbutton the jacket. Almost in a dream, Claire stripped down to her bra and pants in the changing room while Grant handed the garments in through the curtains.

It could have been tailor-made for her. She didn't need to stand back and study her reflection; neither did she feel the need to parade outside. It *felt* good, the silk sliding over her legs when she moved, the overskirt teasing her with its insubstantial lightness. It felt perfect.

She didn't even bother looking at the price tag but restored it to the hanger and handed it back to the shop owner through the curtains. She could finish the outfit with a fascinator or a jewelled headband and would soon find some suitable shoes. Stilettos, she decided. When she came out of the cubicle she read Grant's crooked smile of approval and the warmth in his eyes. He moved towards her. 'Success?'

She nodded. He hadn't really needed to ask. He'd seen it in her eyes. They chatted a little with the woman in the shop, who had designed and stitched the outfit herself and had, wisely, stayed in the background without fussing, letting Claire and Grant decide for themselves. Some minor alterations were needed, the waist taken in and an extra fastener on the jacket. Claire wasn't anxious to have her cleavage on show. She arranged to pick it up in a week's time and they left the shop, looking at each other, one thought in both of their minds.

It was early evening before they emerged from their hotel room. And now they really were hungry. They linked arms and headed out to the city.

NINETEEN

Monday 25 April, 8 a.m.

The weekend had left Claire even more confused about Grant than ever. They had extended their stay to the Saturday night too, spending Sunday meandering, hand in hand in sunshine, along the River Dee, watching boats and ducks, swans and families. Claire had felt relaxed and contented.

Let the feeling wash over you, she'd lectured herself, *without questioning why and where and what it is all leading to. In particular what the cost of continuing might be. Will be*, she corrected.

Grant had said nothing when he'd dropped her off back at Waterloo Road. They'd parted with a long kiss but he hadn't pressed her. He'd driven off with a wave and a quick blast of his horn. And was gone.

But at her Monday morning clinic she came back to earth with a bump with some unwelcome news. It was barely eight o'clock and she had just arrived at her office, early, because she felt guilty at having taken the Friday off and wanted to put in more than a full day's work, when her phone pinged with a message.

Hi, it's Zed here. Can you ring me on this number asap please.

She rang it straight away. 'Zed?'

'Claire.'

'What is it? I thought you—' She changed that to: 'Did Edward Reakin get in touch with you?'

'He did.'

She was confused. 'He told you about the man Poppy was with?'

'He did.' He wasn't leaking any detail here, but she'd heard no note of triumph in his voice.

'But surely . . .?'

'It's her brother.'

Instant deflation. 'I didn't know she had a brother.'

'Well, a half-brother.'

'So . . .?' She wanted to ask whether this brother was a suspect but the question seemed a little blunt so she left it swinging in the breeze like a creaking pub sign.

Zed filled her in. 'His name is Drake Shute and, while he does have a criminal record, he also has an alibi. He was with their mother.'

Claire felt cheated. 'Poppy never mentioned him. Neither did Lynne when I asked her about the family.'

'I wonder why,' he mused. Then added, 'We haven't struck him off the list. We are still looking into him.'

They were both silent, Claire wondering whether this had been the reason for the urgent appeal.

'Has Saul Magnusson been in touch?'

'We've yet to hook up.'

He paused and got to the heart of his phone call. 'I wondered how you're getting on interviewing any patients you might have seen who could have known Patricia.'

So, they were back in that mire of uncertainty, the ball returned to her side of the court. Back to checking outpatients who might have known Poppy, back to searching for one of her patients who had not only had appointments coinciding with Poppy's, but also the necessary diagnosis that could have shoe-horned them into violent crime. At the same time as she was aware that the focus had shifted back to her – both as psychiatrist and, at least in DS Willard's eyes, a potential victim, and her mouth felt dry. Also, thanks to Lynne's failure to mention she had a son as well as a daughter, plus the fact that it was she who had given this 'half-brother' an alibi, she felt out of the loop.

Was she now seeing demons behind every tree?

'You still there?' DS Willard broke into her thoughts, sounding tetchy. Perhaps he was losing patience with her failure to produce a likely suspect.

'Yeah.' And to her shame she sounded sulky.

'Well?'

'I'll get back to working through my list, Zed, but it takes time. And it's an inexact way of finding a killer.' She was wondering how to point out to him that actually she did have a full workload of needy patients. Instead, she turned the conversation. 'Did you have any luck identifying the DNA you found?'

'No.' He must have felt he needed to add something else. 'I don't want this happening to anyone else, Claire. Whoever did this is unbalanced. Dangerous. Cruel. We know he has you in his sights. We have to identify him before . . .'

Though maybe he'd only meant to put her on her guard, he was scaring her. Her mind paused for a moment while she shifted through patients, mentally trying them out for a fit. And then her focus shifted back to Poppy's mother and this half-brother she'd never even mentioned. DS Willard had mentioned a record. Now she was wondering what the nature of this record was.

There was no sound on the other end of the phone so she felt she needed to prompt the officer. 'Was there anything else?' She wished she hadn't sounded quite so crisp.

'No – except . . .' There was a softening in his voice. 'Please be careful.'

And then it burst out of her. 'Why do you keep saying that, Zed? I don't understand why you're so sure I'm in imminent danger.'

She wanted him to see things *her* way for once. And she needed to defend herself from this unseen threat, even if only to justify her role – to herself.

'He identifies you with Poppy.'

'But I'm not anything like her. *I* don't go around making things up about people, destroying lives, making things worse, taking pleasure in others' suffering. If anything, I'm trying to put lives back together again. Help people see a way through.'

'I worry he doesn't see it like that. And . . .' He paused before blundering through. 'You failed with Poppy.'

Her temper was rising. 'Not for lack of trying,' she said coldly. 'We carried out all the treatments and advice that is standard in such cases. Poppy was resistant to therapy. That's not our fault. We did what we could.'

Maybe DS Willard had belatedly woken up to the faux pas he had just committed. His response was chastened. 'I realize that, Claire. I'm asking as a friend. The answer is somewhere inside Greatbach. Take care. Please?'

And then the line went dead.

She sat, staring at the phone in her hand. If the telephone call from Zed Willard had been to warn her, all he'd actually done was alarm her.

Unease lay like sludge at the base of her mind, mixing with guilt because she'd spent the weekend focussing on a wedding and side-lining the murder of a patient when DS Willard had probably been immersed in it. But maybe the answer was resting right beneath her hands. The notes she'd picked out were still in a pile on her desk.

Inside lay all the consultations she and the other health professionals had had with each patient. If DS Willard's hunch and fears were correct, her hand rested on the history and inside story of a killer's life together with the machinations of his mental state. Psychiatry tries to explore every dark corner of a patient's past, using their experiences to try and effect a cure or else, if that was not possible, to predict the trajectory of the future: who would reoffend, who would stay on the right side of the law, who was clever enough to disguise their crimes, who was a danger to society, who was vulnerable, who should be locked up. But a cure in psychiatry cannot be proven by a simple blood test or scan. It is an inexact science which firstly depends on an accurate chronicle of events. Zed Willard had said their killer had left no clue of his presence. That was too devious for a spur-of-the-moment crime. But the planning of such a crime belonged firmly in the path of the intelligent sociopath. That was where she needed to look.

If Poppy had met her killer here, in the very place where she should have been safest, then it was up to her doctor to follow the signs: the torn appointment card, the punishment, the history, the diagnoses, the coincidental appointment times.

Liar, liar, pants on fire.

She shuddered and pressed the buzzer for her first patient, planning out her day. When her clinic had finished she would head upstairs and reassess Dana Cheung. She was anxious to reunite mother with daughter before it was too late and the damage irreparable.

But she was in for a surprise. The day would not work out the way she'd planned it.

TWENTY

11.20 a.m.

The clinic had started predictably enough, with three or four patients with varying diagnoses. Not one of them was likely to be Poppy's killer and they weren't in her sights. They were in for routine checks. She pressed the buzzer for the next patient: Douglas Pryde, known as Duggie.

He lumbered in, a heavy, thick-set man in his late forties, who had suffered paranoia and psychotic episodes following prolonged substance abuse. He had been a heavy user of marijuana and inhalants which had had a detrimental effect on his cognitive function, and that had not been high in the first place. He dropped heavily into the chair and waited for her to begin. Duggie was a typical patient. He was unfailingly polite – as many of them were. He always turned up on time for his appointment. Never missed. And while he could not be cured, he no longer abused substances, although some cynics might say he was just as dependant on the benzodiazepines she was prescribing for him as he had been on his cocktail of illegal drugs. He would never work again; instead, he was issued with long-term sick notes citing 'Effects of substance abuse. Mental instability'. She watched him, wondering. Poppy's killer? She discarded the theory without giving it much serious thought. Duggie wouldn't have got near her. Poppy was smart and instinctive. She would have recognized the signs of a hopeless case and backed off pretty quickly. And Duggie was no oil painting to tempt her in other ways. Claire went through the routine questions, asking about behaviour, feelings, adherence to his therapy regime, attendance at the group psychotherapy sessions and the day centre, and received routine responses. It was a ritual they had to go through for her to continue authorizing his certificates. And some measure of supervision was necessary. Psychosis can easily translate to unpredictability which in turn can provoke violence – from others. People are uneasy around unpredictability. And this can make them lash out. But one thing heartened her. Duggie was clean and had been for years. His blood tests had come back negative to all illegal substances. These days Duggie indulged in little more harmful than a pint or two of cider and the drugs she prescribed. She signed him off for another six months and he stood up, hesitating. 'I 'eard about Poppy,' he said awkwardly.

She was taken aback at the use of Poppy's pet name rather than 'Patricia' as the newspapers were calling her. 'You knew her?'

'Oh aye,' he said. 'Met her here, Dr Roget. She were nice. Chatty. Pretty too. Sorry to hear she was . . .' He gulped and couldn't say the word.

She knew she had to phrase her next questions very, very carefully. 'Did you ever meet up with her apart from here?'

Duggie stood, frowning. Then, 'Can't say as I ever did.'

She'd turned to wash her hands at the sink. 'So you didn't really know her well.'

Duggie shuffled his feet as though he was uncertain how to answer. 'I talked to 'er,' he said, still awkward. 'We went for a coffee but . . .'

'But . . .' she prompted.

And then he boiled over. 'She made out I'd nicked a chocolate bar from the canteen. Said she'd seen me do it. Laughin', she was.'

She could see his face in the mirror over the sink. He was still angry, his face flushed at the false accusation. Claire dried her hands carefully on the paper towel.

'I 'adn't.' Duggie was still protesting his innocence.

She turned around. 'I'm sure you hadn't, Duggie. When was this?'

'Last appointment. S'pose it were six month ago.'

His face was flushed with the injustice of it all, his breathing hard as an elephant charge, his chest heaving. She was suddenly aware of his physical bulk.

It was all registering. 'Have you seen her since?'

Duggie puffed out his chest. 'Wouldn't want to.' He spoke proudly. 'Not too fond of liars, Dr Roget. When I were a lad I went to church. Regular,' he added. 'Liars will perish, it says in the Bible. Destroy those who speak falsehood.' His face was impassioned, lit up with a religious memory bordering on fanaticism. 'It do say in the Psalms the Lord abhors the man of bloodshed and deceit.'

'Do you still go to church?' she asked quietly, disturbed by this new insight into a patient she'd thought she'd known so well.

Duggie looked evasive. 'Not so often now,' he said, then, gathering strength, he continued his rant. 'Lying just to get me into trouble and laughin' at me. Nasty, I call it. Cruel. Above cruel.' He was shaking with the unfairness of it. 'Lucky for me the WRVS lady serving in the shop wouldn't have none of it. Didn't – believe – a – word. But I can't go in there any more out of embarrassment. It's a shame. I used to enjoy my cup of coffee after I'd seen you. Now I just go home.'

Home to his bedsit in Bucknall.

He hadn't quite finished. 'You know what really shocked me, Doctor?'

She shook her head though she could have made a stab at an answer.

'It was 'er laughin'.' His sense of outrage was palpable. 'Fit to burst. All the time I was embarrassed she – was – just – laughin'. I was nothin' more than entertainment. That's all. Wicked, ain't it?'

She could only nod, but decided to follow the outrage. 'So when you say that liars will perish and those who speak falsehood should be destroyed, who do you think will do that?'

Duggie exhaled with a whistling breath combined with a movement of his facial muscles so he looked less bovine, almost cunning as he circumvented the question. 'That can be left to the good Lord.'

She nodded, partly to display sympathy, but she was realizing perhaps she and the team should have spent more time exploring Duggie Pryde's religious convictions.

When he'd left she spent some time testing the theory that Duggie Pryde had murdered Poppy before she rejected it out of hand. Poppy hadn't made elaborate arrangements to have the house to herself for the man she'd taunted with the theft of a chocolate bar in the hospital coffee shop. But he could have been the one she rang the police about, she reminded herself, possibly recognizing someone she'd taunted in the past, someone who was, like her, mentally unstable.

She couldn't have found a more graphic illustration of the fallout from Poppy's lies, even one as petty and pointless as this.

But Douglas Pryde's story had reinforced her instinct that one of her patients *could* be involved in her murder and one of her patients *could* be resentful enough to want to harm her. She made a vow to herself to be watchful. This teasing little episode had taught her that Poppy took her entertainment when and where she could – opportunistically. She visualized the waiting room on some of the days Poppy had attended, talking to anyone and everyone as they waited to be called through, moving chairs, turning around, animated, unbridled dialogues, loud laughs, while other patients sat quietly in corners, motionless as dummies and hoping they would *not* be noticed. Poppy had wanted the opposite. To be seen. To be noticed. To be listened to. The pile of notes was a little lower now, but it was still possible the killer hid in there. She recalled DS Zed Willard's face as he had described Poppy's injuries, his warning to take care, and wondered if she should leave it to the police. Give Zed a couple of vague pointers and let them find the killer. After all, they were the one with the resources to do just that. Her job was to see patients *whatever* their past and *whatever* crimes they might be capable of and theirs was to identify a killer. She tried to shore herself up. Surely Zed Willard was over-emphasizing the risk? She'd been seeing many of these patients for years.

And when she picked up the phone to check with Rita that the rest of the appointments had been sent out and current appointments rescheduled, she was faced with another problem.

'I'm glad you've rung, Claire,' Rita said, sounding hassled. 'I've had Lynne Shute on the phone. She wants to speak to you.'

And I want to speak to her, Claire thought.

She told Rita that she would ring Lynne.

TWENTY-ONE

1 p.m.

Her mind was still combing through possibilities as she climbed the stairs to the top floor, her thoughts focused on Poppy rather than the patient she was heading for.

Dana Cheung was sitting on her bed when Claire entered the room. She looked calm and wide awake, perfectly cognizant to all that was around her, turning her head and smiling when Claire walked in. She had been reading a magazine which she placed back on the bed. Another good sign. There were no signs of paranoia: no sudden, jerky movements, no intent listening to inaudible voices, no fixed attention into a corner of the room where spooks might be lurking. She met Claire's gaze with a steady one of her own, even managing a smile as she'd put the magazine down. Claire sat down, still carefully watching her. Hopeful.

'How are you feeling?'

Dana nodded, drew in a deep breath and sighed. 'I'm all right.' But her voice was flat and unemotional. Possibly a side effect of the drugs she was on. The usual benefit/cost equation being one of the many battles in medicine.

Claire tiptoed around the periphery of the subject she wanted to broach. 'Graham has returned to Qatar?'

'He went yesterday.' Dana's voice was still flat. She was avoiding looking at Claire and looked vaguely in the direction of the window instead, upwards into the sky as though she sighted the very plane her husband had jetted off on.

Claire pushed. 'How do you feel about that, Dana?'

Dana shrugged. 'He has to go.'

It was a strange way to describe the exit of her husband from a taut situation.

'And Lily Rose?'

Now Dana did turn her head, meeting Claire's scrutiny fearlessly. 'My mother-in-law is visiting her daily,' she said steadily.

'How does that suit you?'

Dana's shrug held even more of the *don't care* attitude.

'Dana,' Claire began, 'do you want to take care of your baby yourself, eventually?'

That was when her patient's anger bubbled up and boiled over. 'My mother-in-law hates me. She doesn't want me to have my daughter. She's . . . plotting to keep my baby for ever.'

There was an element of truth in this. On the brief occasions Claire had met Fangsu Cheung, she had recognized an element of possessiveness in the Chinese mother-in-law. Maybe she should approach this case from a different angle. She pushed a little further. 'Lily Rose is not your mother-in-law's child, Dana. She's yours.'

Dana's face changed, taut with emotion. 'Of course I *want* my baby. I *want* to love her. I want to *know* her. But . . .' She held out her arms, as though for the child. 'I'm afraid I'll hurt her.'

'Why?' She'd asked the question in such a low voice she wouldn't have been surprised if Dana either hadn't heard it or chose to ignore it but, to her credit, her patient didn't try to duck the question.

'Because . . .' And then Dana dropped back into the fantasies she'd hidden behind. 'E Gui, the hungry ghost, the one with the small mouth pulling and sucking the life out of me.' Her voice was low, as though she dreaded being overheard. 'And then Baigujing will take my bones.'

'Dana,' she said gently, 'that simply isn't true.'

Dana shrugged. And that was when Claire made the connection. Dana's psychosis had not improved itself for a day and a half after delivery. Midwives frequently encourage breastfeeding in the hours following delivery, sometimes straightaway. It helps the uterus to contract and minimize postpartum bleeding. 'You tried to breast feed?'

Dana's face was pure anguish. 'I felt her sucking.' She was

breathing hard now, fast and gasping. Beginning to rock to and fro. 'She wanted to . . . She would have sucked my life out of me.'

That was when Claire made another connection. 'How did you hear about E Gui?'

Dana looked confused. 'I don't . . .' Her voice trailed away in a misery of confusion. Her eyes scanned the room as though searching anywhere, everywhere for an answer. Finally she gave up, shaking her head.

'Dana, you don't have to breast feed. In fact, Lily Rose is apparently managing perfectly well with a bottle.'

Dana put her head on one side, swivelling to scrutinize Claire suspiciously, weighing up whether to trust her. For a moment doctor and patient were connected as they surveyed each other, each trying to get the measure of the other. 'I had milk,' Dana said softly. 'But they gave me something to stop it.'

Claire nodded warily. Something still wasn't right.

Then Dana smiled. 'So she won, in the end.'

Not yet, was Claire's thought as she left the room. *Not safe yet.* It was still too soon. Dana's mental state was still unstable in spite of her superficial recovery. The next step would be brief, supervised visits with her daughter, but not yet.

She walked away.

One day she would ask her mother questions. Were you depressed after I was born? Did you imagine weird things about me? Were we separated following my birth? Was I breast or bottle fed?

And as she descended the stairs back to her office, Claire pondered Grant's insightful comments about her relationship with her mother, pointing out the irony that she could recognize it and treat it in others while failing to see it for herself. It could be true. One day, she vowed, she would find her father and question him. And maybe then the moniker, *French Frog*, that her mother had given her, would no longer feel like an insult or a punishment but a connection with him. She would find out – finally– why he'd gone.

Back in her office she closed the door behind her and sat down to think, while realizing how impossible it was for her to shed any light on a situation that had developed when she'd been too young to recognize it or affect it.

Minutes later she picked up the phone. She should return Poppy's mother's call.

Lynne sounded agitated when she picked up the phone. Almost confused. Drunk? She must be in her sixties, Claire reflected. But she sounded older with a smoker's croak. Maybe it was the shock of her daughter's murder and having to care for three children, two of them teenagers, all of them damaged. She remembered that in her first sentence. 'Lynne,' she said, 'how are you coping?'

'Oh, you know, Dr Roget.' She was determinedly putting a brave face on it, trying to shrug off the obvious difficulties of her daughter's murder as well as her current domestic situation. 'But thank you so much for asking and thank you for ringing me back.'

'It must be difficult looking after the children.'

'Not really.' Lynne's answer surprised her.

'But they must be traumatized, particularly the boys after such—'

Lynne cut in, her voice sharp as a knife as she repeated, 'Not really.'

Claire was astonished, struck dumb. Had she read this wrong? She picked up the thread. 'So, what can I do for you?'

'I wanted to thank you for all you did . . .' She changed that to a more truthful, 'For all you *tried* to do for Poppy. We did appreciate it.'

We? Who were *we*? Poppy certainly hadn't appreciated Claire's opinion, advice or intervention and had never modified her behaviour as a result. She had recognized that these consultations had been insisted on by the courts. 'I hadn't realized Poppy had a brother.'

'Half-brother,' she snapped. 'Different fathers.'

'Right. But they were . . .?' She'd been about to say *close*, but again Lynne cut across her.

'I could do with having a chat with you.'

'Of course,' Claire responded politely. She owed Poppy's mother that.

'I can see you on Wednesday,' she said. 'It will be good – for both of us – to have a talk.'

'There's things . . .' Lynne hiccupped, hesitating, before ploughing on. 'There's things I should tell you.'

'Fine.' Claire wasn't quite sure how to respond to this. There was a brief silence while, perhaps, they both reflected. Then Lynne said, 'I was wondering about this psychiatrist.'

Claire knew instantly to whom Poppy's mother was referring. 'Dr Magnusson?'

'Yes . . .' Again, the hesitation. 'Why has he asked to see the children?' It sounded like an accusation. She followed that up with a slightly more polite, 'The police told me it was *you* who suggested he might be called in?'

'Yes.'

She felt she should qualify her suggestion. 'Dr Magnusson is a renowned child psychiatrist who has experience dealing with children who've been traumatized or bereaved. And your grandsons, in particular, have suffered both.' And then she picked up on the subtext. 'You're worried he might make things worse? Upset the children?'

'They were terribly upset when the police spoke to them so I . . .'

And then Claire realized Lynne Shute really was worried about a specialist child psychiatrist interviewing Poppy's three children. It was perfectly natural for her to feel protective of her three grandchildren. She was, after all, acting in *loco parentis*. But equally natural must surely be a desire to want to identify her daughter's torturer and killer? And if the boys, in particular, could pass on anything that might help, surely she should want that?

She moved on to question another aspect.

'Lynne,' she said, 'what about Robbie? Surely as the children's father, he has some rights?'

It was as though Lynne had expected the conversation to take this turn. Her response followed smoothly. 'I've talked to Robbie,' she said crisply. 'We've decided that, as Tommy has exams coming up and Neil has his GCSEs soon and all three of them are used to spending time with me that, for the time being, they'll stay with me. We'll let the future take care of itself.'

'And you're all right with that?'

'I am.' She did not enlarge.

Claire moved back to an attempt to allay her fears about the effect seeing a child psychiatrist might have on her three charges as well as the result.

'Dr Magnusson will deal with them delicately, I promise.' She felt compelled to add, 'But if any of the children do have something, some tiny detail, that will lead the police to your daughter's killer, it could really help.' She waited for Lynne to agree but there was nothing.

On the other end of the line there was complete silence as though Lynne Shute was holding her breath. Claire was tempted to fill in the void by urging Poppy's mother to cooperate with Saul Magnusson, but she held back, sensing any intervention or persuasion could have the opposite effect. She reminded herself that this was a *police* investigation – not hers. She needed to stay on the outside. In neutral territory.

All the same, she followed that up with, 'So I'll see you on Wednesday?'. She glanced at her diary. 'Three fifteen?'

'Thank you.' Her voice was chastened. But as Claire ended the call she wondered what Lynne Shute's real agenda had been. She puzzled over this. Lynne's daughter had been tortured and murdered, yet there had been no hint of grief or anguish. Maybe all her emotion was tied up with minimizing the trauma to her grandchildren. The other point that now seemed irrelevant was that uncomfortable memory, the throwaway comment Lynne had made which now haunted her, that Poppy's three children would be better off living with her, as though she had engineered this situation, implying that her daughter had been an unfit, unstable mother. But although, in some ways, Claire could empathize with this view, it went against the image she had of those three quiet, polite children, sitting, waiting for their mother to emerge from the consultation room.

Poppy hadn't made sure her three children were out of the house just for her mother.

Her office window overlooked the corridor and when she looked up Saul Magnusson was watching her, his tall blond outline framed by the corridor lighting which was dingy – a tiny cost-saving exercise for the NHS. *May I come in?* he mouthed, with a small gesture of his hand. She nodded. Maybe his expertise would throw a light on this troubling case which continued to confound her.

He sat down. 'The three children of your patient, Claire. I've been in touch with the police and I have agreed to spend some time with them. They gave me the details. I wondered if there was anything in particular you wanted to mention?'

She relayed the content of the conversation she'd just had with Lynne Shute.

'So . . .' He'd quickly picked up on her concerns. 'Often a certain numbness sets in,' he explained. 'Denial. Emotional paralysis. The facts are too much for young minds and the scene they returned to that night was horrible. I have seen this effect in children traumatized by violent scenes, by war, kidnapping. Outwardly they appear calm. Inside all is turmoil.'

It was a good explanation and Saul had more experience than she of the aftermath of children exposed to extreme violence.

'I will let you know when I intend to see them,' he finished politely.

It was another link in the chain.

TWENTY-TWO

S aul had no sooner left than Rita knocked on her door.
'Claire,' she said, looking troubled, 'I've got Tre Marshall on the phone. He sounds agitated. He's asking to speak to you.'
Her anxiety transferred to Claire. 'Will he have received the appointment we sent out?'

Rita nodded. 'I put him in for next Monday.'

'OK. Put him through.'

She knew there was a problem the moment Tre started to speak. Like rapid gunfire. Staccato, aggressive. 'Why have you brought my appointment forward? I'm not due until September. Someone told you to make it next week and I want to know who it was. Who was it, Doctor? Who's telling you things about me? I haven't done anything. I haven't done anything wrong.'

She knew she'd stirred a hornet's nest by moving his regular appointment and tried to soothe him. 'No one is telling me anything about you, Tre. And you've done absolutely nothing wrong. I have some spaces in my clinic and thought you wouldn't mind my bringing your appointment forward.'

Silence as he absorbed this. Then, 'Are you sure?' She could feel his suspicion melting away but sensed he was not one hundred per cent convinced.

She tried again. 'Absolutely, Tre. In fact, we're really pleased with your progress. I thought it would be nice to check up on you a bit sooner.'

The silence felt abrupt. He was evaluating her response. 'Well, that's all right if . . . I suppose . . .' That was followed by another silence, then he spoke again. 'But I *have* to see Teresa. She's my community nurse. She's the one who keeps an eye on me and she might come when I'm not there and then she'll be worried and then—'

He was still speaking quickly, agitation speeding up his words so they tumbled out of his mouth, his thoughts jumbling up as he spoke. She tried to cut him off, to placate him about Teresa, the community psychiatric nurse. 'I'll tell Teresa that you'll be coming to the clinic so don't you worry about that.' But she hadn't quite allayed his fears.

'Soon. Too soon.' She could hear his fingers tapping on something. A quick, panicky sound. *Rat tat tat, rat tat tat.* Then, again, silence.

'Well then, I suppose it'll be longer between appointments next time, won't it?'

Surely by then they would know who had murdered Poppy?

She injected what was meant to be a comforting jollity into her response. 'It certainly will. Tre . . .?'

More silence. Then, 'Yes?'

'When did you last see Teresa?'

'A week. Two weeks. I don't know. I can't remember.' And then a suspicious, 'Why do you want to know? Anyway, she can't help.' He was still speaking quickly, but it was the silences in between that alerted her. That could be when he was listening to another voice.

And this was confirmed by his next utterance. 'Stop speaking. Stop bloody speaking. I don't want to hear you. I'm putting my hands over my ears to block you out. Hands over ears.' He started to sing. 'Liar, liar, pants on fire. Tra la. Tra la.'

The words hit her with a hammer blow. He wasn't speaking to her.

'Where are you, Tre?'

'I'm at the train station. I'm watching trains.' It was a favourite haunt of his. But she had to be sure.

'Stoke station?'

'Yes. I like being here. The sound blocks out his voice, you see. The trains help me.'

'OK,' she responded calmly. What never failed to touch Claire was the suffering her patients experienced when these psychotic episodes were in full flow. The anguish in Tre's voice was very real – as was the voice which would not stop speaking to him.

'Tre,' she said, 'I'm going to ask Teresa to find you and bring you here. Is that OK?'

Silence.

'Tre.'

'Yes?' In contrast to his previous responses this was in a whisper; he was afraid of being overheard.

She kept her voice low and calm. 'If Teresa can't make it, it

might have to be the police. But they will still bring you here, as
I'm asking. They will bring you to Greatbach. To me. Stay where
you are.' She heard the tone as well as the pace of her speech –
slow, monotonic, calming.

His response was still rapid and panicky. 'Make it quick.'

'I'll see you soon then, Tre.'

'Goodbye.'

His voice was sounding timid now. Maybe he was calming down.

But the image pasted behind her eyelids was of Tre Marshall
'embracing' those trains, jumping off a bridge.

And she was puzzled. Tre Marshall had been well controlled. He'd
even managed his part-time job with no problems. There had been
no complaints. But she hadn't realized how finely balanced his mental
state was. He'd been edging along a tightrope. And making the
appointment earlier had been enough for him to fall. Or had it not
been the appointment but something else? *Liar, liar, pants on fire.*
His words rang in her ears.

It was no coincidence.

She contacted Teresa immediately. Teresa worked closely with
an emergency response team, headed by Ryan Davies, another
experienced psychiatric nurse employed by Greatbach. Teresa was
with another patient and was surprised when Claire related Tre
Marshall's mental state.

'He's been good,' she said. 'I've had no worries about him for
ages.'

'Has he ever mentioned Poppy Kelloway?'

Teresa was quiet for a moment. 'Not directly,' she said.

'Indirectly?'

'Stuff about sinners being punished. Nothing out of the ordinary
– for him,' she finished limply. And then Teresa promised she would
head for Stoke station as soon as she could, where, hopefully, she
would find Tre Marshall either on the bridge or else cowering in a
corner.

But the psychiatric emergency response team relied on police
support and she wouldn't be there for at least half an hour. A
police presence was the last thing Claire wanted. If anything could
easily tip Tre into a blind panic, it was the sight of police uniforms
heading towards him.

And she didn't have a spare bed.

TWENTY-THREE

7 p.m.

As it turned out, she didn't need it.

The telephone call came when she was in her office. She should have left hours ago but she'd decided to wait until Tre arrived. Even so – she looked at her watch – it was taking an inordinately long time.

And when DS Zed Willard's number appeared on her phone screen she felt the first jolt of misgiving, recognizing something else. It was taking too long.

'Claire?'

His voice was subdued, hesitant, and there was another element. Reluctance. And an apology.

'Zed?'

'I'm truly sorry.'

She already knew what he was sorry for. Another patient who wouldn't be making their appointment.

'You have – had – a patient called Tre Marshall?'

She wasn't going to nitpick over the tense. 'Yes.'

'I'm sorry,' he said again before saying it a third time. 'I'm really sorry. He jumped.'

'What happened?'

'Your nurse . . .'

'Teresa.'

'Yeah. That's the one. She was with a patient. She was having difficulties reaching us because of the roadworks so contacted us.' He was speaking carefully and precisely, as though he was in a court, giving evidence.

She knew how unfair this was. The police had only basic training in dealing with patients with mental health problems. They had plenty of other problems to deal with and this was not their primary role. Their remit was dealing with crime, something tangible. Not invisible enemies. Their training tried to persuade them to be calming and understanding. They tried but it wasn't enough.

'I'm sorry.' She knew the officers who'd dealt with the situation would feel they'd failed.

He paused, giving her time to absorb his news. Though she didn't need it. From when she'd heard him speak earlier in the day, she'd half expected something like this. Tre had had a strong sense of justice and injustice. And his training to be a priest had prepared him for punishment. They'd had many philosophical conversations on this very subject, cut short by limited appointment constraints. Punishment had been one of his most popular subjects.

More than once he had quoted the Bible to her.

Though shalt not bear false witness.

The memory flashed through her mind as she realized something else. Zed Willard was SIO on the Poppy murder investigation. Why was *he* the one ringing to tell her about Tre?

Liar, liar, pants on fire.

She kept the phrase to herself.

'Zed,' she began, and he read her mind.

'We're looking into it, Claire. That's all I can say at the moment.'

The feeling of dread covered her with black gauze.

'I'll keep you up to date.' His voice was still sharp. It was as though he'd accused her. *Another one of your patients, Claire.*

She thanked him before exploring a thought she'd been pushing away ever since she had first heard of the circumstances surrounding Poppy's murder.

Was it possible that Tre's voices would order him to punish Poppy for her lies? Flagellation and flaying had been part of their discussions. Had he been a victim of her lies? Was this crime not the result of cold revenge but mental illness?

Had it not been her summoning him to an early appointment which had tipped him over the edge but a guilty conscience? A punishment deserved?

Whatever the truth, like Harry Bloxham, Tre Marshall was another fatal result of Poppy's lies.

And she was angry that she had been drawn into the role of facilitator.

TWENTY-FOUR

Tuesday 26 April, 9 a.m.

Claire had spent the night worrying over Tre's death, the question filling her mind. Was it possible he had killed Poppy? She could not ignore his words, which felt now like a final appeal. But she had never known Tre to commit a violent act, let alone one which involved a cold-blooded torture before the final killing. His discussions around the subject had been purely theoretical, philosophical. But she knew from experience that it could be hard to understand a distorted mind. One cannot pin rational thought to such damage. Any logic remains unbalanced, off-kilter. A mistake. If Tre had had nothing to do with Poppy's death, why did he refer to that particular rhyme?

And the fact remained: now two of her patients had died in chilling circumstances. She would be drawn into the inquest, asked to make a statement about Tre's mental state. At some point a line might be drawn between these two patients and she would be expected to respond. Honestly. For now, she awaited a call from Teresa.

She too wanted answers.

She climbed the stairs to the top floor and walked along the corridor to Saul Magnusson's office. He stood up politely when she entered and waited for her to speak. He never wasted words and was not a natural communicator, except when he was interviewing children. Then he seemed to come alive, smiling as he teased out their actions, uncovering thoughts and opinions. She had watched him work and read his notes. He was like a magician in his own field. Children responded well to this giant of a man with his bleached eyebrows, hair the colour of sun-ripened corn and eyes that were the clear icy blue of a Norwegian fjord.

'Good morning, Claire.'

'I wondered when you were seeing any of the Kelloway children.'

'I am seeing the two boys this afternoon. I wasn't sure whether to see them together or separately. What do you think?'

'Possibly together?' she ventured.

'Maybe.' He frowned. 'But of course, that does have certain . . . drawbacks. There can be a certain amount of collaboration.'

'Collaboration? They've been through a terrible experience,' she reminded him.

'True.' He was still frowning.

'And they're not under suspicion.'

'No. But I am anxious that any small thing they might have noticed individually could be crucial to the police investigation.'

'Surely they'll be able to draw strength from one another? Support each other.'

'That is true. But I am very interested in the fact that Poppy said they did not get on as brothers.'

That drew a sigh from Claire. 'Saul, we can't rely on *anything* Poppy said.'

'I realize that. Did *you* see any sign of antagonism between the boys?'

'I only met them a couple of times a couple of years ago when they appeared to be on their very best behaviour. I didn't really see them interact. They just sort of sat there, quiet, polite.' She smiled now. 'I think Poppy had them well under control.'

Saul was thoughtful. 'Ye-es.'

'And what about Holly-Anne? When are you seeing her?'

'I'm leaving her until later. She wasn't at the house and she is younger. I suspect she will have little to contribute by way of information.'

She liked his precise way of speaking, the way each word was weighed.

'You may sit in, if you like.'

'I would like to,' she said slowly, 'but I think it's better if I'm not *seen* to be there, don't you? This is *your* interview, Saul. The boys don't really know me. They last saw me a couple of years ago with their mother. And they stayed outside the clinic room so wouldn't have witnessed any exchange between us. They will wonder why I'm there. Seeing me watching you interview them might inhibit their responses.'

'Very well. I agree. If we use the main interview room there is a two-way mirror.'

'If it's OK with you. I don't want to tread on your toes.'

Saul smiled at her and took her idiom literally, as was his way.

'That would be quite painful, I agree. Very well then, Claire. This afternoon.'

'I'm also hoping to speak to the children's father, see if I can get to the bottom of why he had so little to do with them. Check up on Poppy's claim that he refused to support his family financially.' She didn't add that this was another fact that didn't square up. Poppy had never really displayed any sign of financial hardship. 'And I'm talking to Poppy's mother tomorrow. She asked to speak to me.'

'We do what we can,' he observed. 'You are going to be busy.'

'Yeah.'

She left his room knowing she would enjoy watching Saul Magnusson's skilful interrogation of the Kelloway boys this afternoon. And she was curious to see how the boys were turning out. What had the effect of their mother's strange condition been? How had it affected their growing up?

Tre's fate still troubled her, but she also knew that the statistics of patients with severe mental illness dying a violent or early death were horrifyingly high. She also recognized that such events often had a trigger. What if, somewhere in Tre's poor, tangled mind, he had heard some detail about Poppy's murder and made a connection? Either something she or someone else had said or he'd thought they'd said? Fantasy? Fiction? It didn't even have to be factual but could be imagined or fantasized. Part of the primordial soup contained in a troubled mind.

And that was what made this case so difficult.

TWENTY-FIVE

9.40 a.m.

As she was already on the top floor, Claire thought she would see how Dana Cheung was progressing and check with the ward staff that there were no immediate concerns. She hoped at least one of her patients would have a happy outcome.

Sometimes a chink of light beams in with perfect timing.

Watched by Astrid Carter, one of the senior psychiatric nurses, with years of experience at Broadmoor and other major psychiatric units, Dana was breastfeeding Lily Rose. She was stroking the dark, downy hair of the tiny baby's head, completely absorbed in her daughter. Astrid met her eyes and smiled, her finger unnecessarily on her lips, the message clear: *Don't break the spell.*

Claire's heart leapt. For once this was going to turn out well. She felt a smile crease her own face and moved away from the window, but with a tinge of regret. Dana's case might have resonated with her because of her own relationship with her mother, but there was no happy resolution on the horizon for Claire. Had her mother had the skilled support Dana had received, maybe things could have turned out differently between them.

She felt robbed.

2.30 p.m.

Saul must have decided to see the boys separately in the main interview room. He ushered in Neil, the younger of the two boys, as Claire watched through the mirror. She was sure he would be fifteen years old now. Lynne sat in the corner, seemingly indifferent to the proceedings, fiddling with her nails and looking around the room, even glancing once or twice at her mobile phone, rather than at her grandson and the psychiatrist. Claire noted Saul's easy way with the boy as he gestured Neil Kelloway to a chair adjacent to him. The room was shuttered with vertical blinds. It was small, square, painted in neutral colours, a sort of mushroom. The colour scheme and decor had been deliberately selected so there was nothing to distract the mind. Claire focused on Poppy's son, studying him, the son Poppy had claimed was sweet-natured, like her. In his navy and yellow school uniform Neil looked small and young for his age, plump, with his mother's pale feathery hair. He had a sort of agitated, anxious to please manner, slightly bouncy. He was bent forward in the chair, holding good eye contact with Saul Magnusson.

'Good morning, Neil. I am Dr Magnusson.' Saul spoke English with only a trace of an accent but something in the stilted construction of his sentences, combined with his unmistakably Nordic looks, gave his nationality away.

'I don't want you to feel there is a right or a wrong answer to my questions. You understand?'

This drew a nod from the boy, who seemed mesmerized by the

paediatric psychiatrist and very anxious to please. Eyes wide open, he listened intently as the psychiatrist spoke.

'Only the truth matters, you understand?'

The phrase was ironic with its cloaked reference to the boy's mother, but Neil did not appear to pick that up. He gave another eager nod. Lynne glanced across briefly, perhaps alerted at the word 'truth'.

As she watched the boy, Claire was reminded of his father. Robbie was a tall, determined man with a hefty build like a rugby player, bulky and very sure of himself. The type of man who would dogmatically lay down a rule and expect it to be followed to the letter. He and Poppy had split up not long after Holly-Anne had been born, but the marriage had survived seven years so something must have been right at one point.

She made a mental note to chase up Robbie Kelloway soon, partly to refresh her impression of him.

Had he really completely abandoned his three children? Was he such a neglectful father? Or was that another of Poppy's tales?

If so, why? She had never had the impression Poppy felt aggrieved against her ex-husband. When the subject had cropped up there had been no underlying spite. Claire had rejected Poppy's claims of torture as belonging to her dramatic fables.

And now his son sat, eagerly trying to answer Saul Magnusson's skilful questions, his brown eyes fixed on the child psychiatrist's face as Saul teased out the truth.

'Tell me, Neil. Was it usual for you and your brother to spend time together?'

The boy shook his head. Looked at the floor, breaking eye contact.

'Are you and your brother close?'

Another shake of the head, followed by a timid comment. 'I get on better with Holly-Anne.'

'Is there a particular reason for that?'

A shrug. 'I just do.'

Saul waited until Neil responded to his silence as though it had been a prompt, a startled, anxious lifting of his eyes.

'Tommy can be quite mean.'

Saul put his head on one side, inviting a little more detail.

And Neil responded. 'He punches me – a bit. Sometimes.' He looked down at the floor, ashamed.

Saul smiled. 'And it was not usual for you and your brother to have a night out together.'

That drew a vigorous, determined shake of his head and a puzzled look. 'Never.'

'So, tell me about that night. How did it come about? Who suggested that you go out together?'

Neil frowned. 'We had some money from Mum to go to the club in Hanley. She said it was OK.' He added quickly, 'As long as I didn't drink.'

'So, it was your mother's idea?'

'Mmm.'

In the corner Claire was watching Lynne, who had stiffened at the direction of the psychiatrist's questions. Her mobile phone was sliding from her lap.

'Which club was it?' Saul's voice was casual but Claire knew these probes were, in reality, needle sharp.

'Four Crosses,' Neil mumbled.

'You had been there before?'

'Once.' The boy gave his grandmother a swift glance, perhaps anticipating a telling-off, but he needn't have worried. Lynne gave him a nod of encouragement.

'So, what did you do there?'

Neil looked puzzled at the question. 'We just sort of hung around. Got a drink. Tommy chatted to a couple of mates.' He stopped as a memory intruded. 'He kept looking at his watch.'

'All night?'

Neil nodded slowly, correctly, deliberately. 'And then sometime after half twelve we got a taxi home.' He got that out quickly, like a racehorse on the home front.

At the same time Lynne shifted noisily in her chair and Neil looked directly across at her.

Saul noted the contact and gave a swift glance towards the two-way mirror, checking Claire had heard.

'And that sort of evening had never happened before?'

Neil shook his head. Less bouncy now, less eager, more anxious.

'Was your mum expecting a visitor that night?'

'I don't know. Maybe. I think she was.'

'Was she dressed up?'

Neil shrugged. 'Don't know.'

Claire was remembering DS Zed Willard's description of the clothes Poppy had been wearing that night. Jeans, a sparkly, low-cut top, high-heeled mules. Make-up, matching purple underwear.

'Do you have any idea who she might have expected?'

Without warning the boy's eyes filled with tears. Lynne half rose in her seat as though she wanted to put a stop to the questions, but she fell back when Saul lifted his hand.

'No.' The word came out of the boy's mouth like a bullet.

And suddenly the atmosphere in the room was charged.

Then the storm broke. Neil nodded miserably, as though breaking a confidence.

'She didn't want us there.' He aimed a swift look at his grandmother and muttered, 'She just wanted us out of the way. And when we got home . . .' He stopped speaking, his face frozen.

Lynne sat rigidly now. But all Claire could picture was Zed Willard's description of Poppy's clothing. *Heavily bloodstained.* How much had Neil taken in before fleeing from the home and ringing the police? The boys had been found standing outside, in the rain, according to Zed Willard.

Saul nodded and his eyes warmed. 'Thank you, Neil. You have been most helpful.'

The relief in the boy was visible as he let out a breath and his shoulders dropped. Saul nodded. 'You can go now.'

Lynne stood up, anxious to leave, but Neil hovered at the door. 'Should we have stayed in, do you think?'

'No.' Saul's voice was reassuring. 'Your mother wanted you to go out. She arranged it and you went. Whatever happened and why it happened is not your fault. I don't want you ever to blame yourself. Bad people find a way to be bad. Just remember that.'

Neil made an attempt at a smile and was gone.

TWENTY-SIX

3.15 p.m.

Teresa was waiting for her back at the office. She looked pale and shocked. Claire sat her down and Rita brought them both a coffee.

Teresa sucked in a long, slow breath. 'Everyone's nightmare,' she said. 'He had a habit of heading for the train station. He'd been there so many times. And he'd been so well lately. But I should have . . . I was with someone else,' she said. 'I can't be in two places at once. The roadworks were awful. They held me up. And Ryan was tied up in Biddulph. Miles away. Sometimes . . .' She ran her fingers through fine dark hair. 'I think this job is impossible.'

Claire did her best to comfort the nurse. 'I know the feeling. It is impossible.'

Teresa sniffed.

'Tell me about the last time you saw him.'

Teresa consulted her diary. 'Just over a week ago,' she said. 'Monday the eighteenth. It was around six o'clock in the evening.'

Five days after Poppy's murder.

'I'd called round to his flat for a routine visit. Just to check up on him. No particular reason.'

'Unannounced?'

Teresa looked at her sharply. 'Well – yes,' she said, obviously wondering where this was leading. 'He was making himself some cheese on toast.' They both smiled at that. Tre had practically lived on cheese on toast. Teresa tossed her long dark hair back. 'He seemed . . .' She spent some time considering her answer. 'He seemed slightly more agitated than usual but nothing concerning.'

'Was there anything in particular?'

'I don't know . . .' Teresa gave out a long sigh. 'I don't know. Nothing obvious. He didn't say anything that made me particularly concerned. Except . . .' she added slowly, '. . . there were some drawings. On the kitchen table there was a sketchpad. He'd been trying to draw a face.'

'Anyone recognizable?'

Teresa shook her head. 'He wasn't much of an artist.'

They both wanted to be able to smile.

But instead moved on.

'So, when you got my call?'

'I thought it was the same as it had been on numerous occasions before.' She looked at Claire. 'How many times have I been to Stoke station in the past five years? I thought it'd just be a matter of talking him down again, maybe bringing him in if he was in an obvious crisis. But . . .' She put her hand over her eyes, trying to block the scene out. 'I was too late,' she said. 'He'd already – he was lying . . .' She tried to gather herself together. 'The police were there, and Ryan. All of us – too late. Oh, God, Claire, I feel so responsible. I should have . . .'

They'd all been there at one time or another, blamed themselves for what they perceived as their personal failure. Claire badly wanted to reassure Teresa, to say it wasn't her fault, that there was nothing she could have done, that statistically traumatic events happened to people with mental health problems, that her workload was far too heavy. All these words passed through her mind but she knew, whatever she said, Teresa Coren would always search back to that last contact she'd had with a patient she had watched over for years and find one tiny detail that should have alerted her. Instead, her mind slid over these pleasantries to the heart of her questions. 'Did Tre say anything out of the ordinary?'

Teresa's shoulders stiffened and there was a shard of glass in her response. 'What do you mean, Claire?'

Claire reached out and touched her hand in a gesture meant to reassure, but she wasn't sure it connected. Teresa was still frowning.

'Two patients have died.' Claire knew she had to recover the equilibrium, remove any hint at suspicion or finger-pointing. 'Both Tre and Poppy have been our patients for years.' And she repeated her earlier question, not wanting to steer Teresa in the wrong direction. 'Did he mention Poppy?'

Teresa shook her head. 'No.'

'Was there anything that might have alerted you? Was anything different?'

That made Teresa stop defending her position and think. 'You know how he used to rabbit on,' she began. 'Say things.' They both knew. Words had gushed out of Tre's mouth uncontrolled, like a waterfall after heavy rain pouring over a ledge. Teresa's frown deepened. 'He did say something odd,' she said slowly. 'Something I've never heard him say before.' She smiled. 'Almost philosophical. Something about . . .' She frowned. 'Biblical.'

'The exact words?' Claire prompted.

'What is truth?' She smiled. 'Actually, he said it in Latin – *quid est veritas* – but I understood. I did Latin GCSE. It's rhetoric, isn't it?'

Claire recognized the words. As for their relevance to Tre – and Poppy – she wondered.

Tre, with his diagnosis, was a convenient person on which to hang a crime. It could all be so nicely and neatly wrapped up, pleasing everyone. Except somehow she didn't believe it was the truth.

TWENTY-SEVEN

4.15 p.m.

Tommy Kelloway's interview had been arranged for when his school day had finished, so just after four o'clock she headed back to sit behind the mirror to watch.

Poppy's older son would be seventeen. Quite changed from the boy she had met two years ago. She was curious to see what he was like now. How scarred was he by his recent experiences?

The difference between the brothers could not have been more obvious. While Neil was shy, quietly spoken and unsure of himself, his brother was the opposite. Tommy strode in, truculent as a boxer entering the ring for a prize fight. His chin was up, his mouth a straight, stroppy line. He was tall, well built and would be an intimidating opponent.

After a swift appraisal, Saul's manner was perfect. He stood up, topping the boy by three or four inches, and held out his hand.

'Thank you so much for attending, Tommy. You mind if I call you Tommy?'

Tommy gave a quick, jerky shake of his head and muttered something. His eyes were watchful. He was measuring up an opponent.

As with his brother, Saul was mannerly and formal. 'Thank you,' he said with a small bow of his head.

He began by offering his sympathy, which Tommy brushed aside with a dismissive shake of his head, reminiscent of a cat shaking a mouse. He was giving Saul a long, surreptitious stare while saying nothing. And Saul began his interview as though he had not picked up on the boy's rudeness.

At first, he asked opening questions, about how he was settling back at school, checking that he was happy living with his grandmother (who was sitting quietly, in the corner). However, as Saul continued his seemingly casual, directionless wanderings, Claire realized he was veering off-piste, drilling down to relevant facts.

'Had you been to the Four Crosses before?' The precision of the question startled her.

The boy's eyes were still wary, his hands tucked underneath his thighs. His grey uniform trousers were a little short for his long legs.

'Yeah.'

'Many times?' Saul's voice was gently reassuring, non-threatening. Lulling the boy into a sense of security. It was a professional device which Saul must have honed over the years. Gentle, probing, extracting answers as skilfully as an animal extracting grubs from a tree trunk.

'Three or four.' Tommy's eyes were shifting around the room, searching for a safe space to rest, and he was frowning, having to focus hard on his responses.

'With your brother?'

'No.'

'With school friends?'

Oddly enough, Tommy Kelloway wasn't quite sure how to answer this. He was blinking fast while thinking. Saul waited, patience combining with a bland expression. He made no attempt to provide an answer for young Kelloway. Just waited, a half-smile making him appear a benevolent, listening friend.

'Once, with a friend from school. And I went a couple of times on my own.'

Both Claire and Saul recognized this as an odd answer. Saul had lifted his head, momentarily turning it a fraction in her direction.

But instead of pursuing this avenue, Saul changed tack.

'Tell me about your relationship with your mother.'

Tommy started to shrug, but then words burst out of him like an angry tide. 'How do you think you'd feel when someone makes up stories about you, makes you out to be a failure, makes a fool of you? Tries to ruin your life?'

That, too, had been unexpected.

'So?' Saul prompted, and waited.

And, under the quiet focus of the psychiatrist, Tommy calmed down. Saul shifted forward in his seat, his eyes trained on the boy. 'Tell me about that night, Tommy.'

The boy was wary. 'What do you mean?'

'When was it that your mother suggested you and your brother had a night out together?'

'The day before.' He'd had his answer ready.

'So that would be the Tuesday?' Saul asked.

'Ye-es. I suppose so.'

'And how did that come about?' His tone was paternalistic, friendly, but Claire knew his skin would be prickling with watchfulness.

'She said that . . .' Tommy was finding the words difficult. 'She said that she had a friend coming round.'

'Did she say male or female?'

Tommy shook his head vigorously, certain of this answer – at least.

'So did you have a guess?' Saul was giving him a friendly, encouraging smile.

Tommy was still blinking fast. 'I thought it was a bloke . . . probably.'

'Right. That had happened before?'

'Not like that.'

'You mean . . .?' Saul was being careful to prompt without suggestion.

'Making sure we were out of the way.'

'So normally?'

God, he's so good at his job, Claire was thinking.

'We'd just stay up in our bedroom.'

'Ah, yes.' As though he'd just thought of this. 'Did you and your brother share a bedroom?'

A wary nod.

'And that worked well?'

Another wary nod.

Saul moved on seamlessly. 'So, who were these friends?'

'It wasn't often.'

'OK.'

Tommy shrugged. A *don't know, don't care* gesture.

But Saul persisted. 'Male or female?'

'Both.'

'And did this happen often?'

Tommy shook his head. 'Maybe four or five times.'

'I see. So let's get back to *that* night, shall we?' He didn't wait for a response. 'You left at . . .?'

''Bout eight,' Tommy said warily.

'She gave you money.' Saul smiled. 'That was kind.'

Tommy's eyes flickered over the psychiatrist with something like disdain. 'Yeah,' he said. Then added, 'Not so kind if it's a bribe.'

'How much?' Saul rapped out the question.

'Twenty quid.'

'So enough for a drink and a taxi home.'

Claire sat back in her chair. She could see exactly what Saul was doing. He was laying a trail of breadcrumbs, finding the facts that could be checked. Her mind wandered through. The police could check the CCTV of the Four Crosses, interview taxi drivers. And would the brothers collude when, according to witnesses, they were not good enough friends to trust each other? She hadn't realized that Tommy had disliked his mother. And Neil?

She wasn't sure. She'd watched the interview with him, feeling more had been left unspoken than uttered with the younger boy. She revisited Poppy's murder, trying to pick up clues. It had been carried out with revenge and hatred at its core. Not the boys, she thought, her mind flipping back to the quiet, subdued trio of well-behaved children, sitting quietly, while she interviewed their mother. But she had to remind herself that was two years ago.

She focused for a moment on Lynne who, so far, had sat motionless in the corner, not intervening or showing any emotion as Saul Magnusson teased out the boy's version, her only movement glancing down, periodically, at her phone screen. But she had picked up on the subtext of her grandson's responses, had stopped looking at her phone now and was watching the proceedings, twisting her wristwatch in a gesture that looked agitated.

Right through the interview Tommy's stance had remained unchanged. His chin was still up, his body rigid, his eyes wary. But the wariness had increased in intensity. It struck Claire that he was a very determined character. Tommy had moved his hands from under his thighs and now they were stuck in his blazer pocket, elbows splayed out, but even through the material Claire could see his fingers clench and unclench. His hands, she was realizing, were his 'tell'.

'Did you love your mother, Tommy?' Saul's tone was soft, coaxing.

It was as though he had asked a trick question and Tommy's response was swift, instinctive – and heartfelt. 'Not always.' It had burst out of him, unstoppable.

And Saul nodded, understanding. 'Yes,' he said. 'I think I understand. Sometimes she was . . . difficult to love. Yes?'

Tommy nodded, looked down, ashamed, his fingers now out of his pockets, claw-like.

Claire saw exactly what Saul had done – slid the two of them on to the same side, the opposite side to Poppy. And Tommy Kelloway didn't even realize what had just happened. But his wariness was slowly melting. He was appraising Saul now, maybe wondering whether he could trust him.

'Do you have any idea whom she was expecting that night?'

Tommy shook his head, the aggression sucked out of him. He looked tired. Exhausted.

'Had you met some of her boyfriends before?'

'No one that counted.' His voice was sharp. 'The minute they'd left she'd start taking the piss. No one really mattered to her.'

'Except you, perhaps?'

Tommy looked at Saul, maybe realizing belatedly what had just happened. And he looked alarmed.

'I am really very sorry about your mother.'

Shrug.

'Particularly as you were the one who had to discover such a horrible sight.'

This time the shrug was accompanied by a gulping swallow, visible in the boy's thin neck, and Claire could see his entire frame was vibrating with a tremor he could not suppress, his left knee jerking uncontrollably.

Saul reached out and touched the boy gently on the shoulder. 'It will stay with you, Tommy, that terrible memory, but it will fade, like a pattern in the sun. And it won't always hurt so bad.'

'Really?' The boy tightened his jaw and clenched his fists. Then he raised his eyes. 'When?'

Saul seemed to understand, or maybe he'd anticipated the question. 'It varies,' he said gently. 'Everyone handles grief differently. And your grandmother' – a swift glance at Lynne – 'will help.'

There was silence. Claire realized Saul was waiting for the next move to come from the boy.

'Will it help when they . . .?' He stopped.

Saul nodded. 'With an arrest will come some relief, yes.' And again, he was silent.

When the silence didn't break, Saul asked, 'When did you dislike your mother most?'

'When she . . .' Again, he was working his jaw. 'When she . . .' He couldn't finish the sentence, which left Claire to wonder and try to find an ending which fitted.

When she lied?
When she brought men home?
When she cheapened herself?

'When she made up lies so we believed her and then laughed at us for being gullible.' Angry tears formed in the boy's eyes while Claire marvelled, yet again, at her patient's cruelty.

How could you, Poppy? Having children is not a blood sport.

To her disconcertion, Tommy Kelloway was staring directly at her through the two-way mirror. She had to reassure herself that he couldn't possibly see her.

Saul hadn't quite finished. 'When you came home,' he said, 'what was the first thing you noticed?'

Lynne started forward as though to protect the boy from this line of questioning, but Tommy had regained his equilibrium. 'The lights were all on,' he said. 'I noticed that first. Mum made a real thing about not wasting electricity. Switching the lights off.'

He waited, maybe for a prompt that was not going to come. 'And then I walked into the lounge. Mum was lying on the floor. I saw blood. Lots of it. And there was a smell.' He wrinkled up his noise as though he could still smell it. 'Something chemical as though she'd been cleaning the oven. I . . . I knelt down. Her jeans were pulled down so I could see her—' He couldn't finish. 'I went to tidy her up and it burnt me. The jelly-like stuff that was over her – you know. It burnt me too.' He looked aggrieved.

Saul put out a hand to encourage the boy.

'I washed it off and then Neil and me, we went outside. It was raining but we didn't care. We couldn't be in there. I dialled nine-nine-nine and asked for the police.' His face was twisted now, in distress.

Simultaneously Lynne stood up. 'I think that's—' Saul stayed her with his hand. 'Yes,' he said. 'That's enough for now.'

Claire watched him usher Lynne and Tommy out and then he stood, motionless, his chin on his chest, deep in thought. Moments later he was knocking at the door of the viewing room.

'The boys,' he said without preamble, 'are holding back a secret.'

She was startled. She hadn't thought that at all. She looked at him questioningly. 'How do you know? I didn't pick up on anything in particular.'

'Their hands were twitching,' Saul said, touching their fingers to each other. 'It's a classic illustration of agitation.'

'But surely they'd feel that anyway? They've just lost their mother in appalling circumstances.'

'Indeed,' he said. But his blue eyes were troubled and he suddenly looked tired.

'You think they know something they're not telling us?'

'I don't think it,' he said steadily. 'I know it.'

'But what . . .?' She couldn't complete the sentence.

It was only when she'd returned to her office that Claire started to unravel Saul's claim. It hit her how the entire scenario hung on the boys' statements: times, the diversion from home, what they'd found when they'd returned. And she realized the police had a lot of work to do.

TWENTY-EIGHT

6 p.m.

Back at her office, Claire faced a stack of work, letters to dictate, others to be written, statements about imminent court cases and some study. Sometimes she felt, like Teresa, that she was drowning in a workload which never eased or even paused. A sea of damaged humanity, stretching out their arms to her. Every time she picked up a set of notes or logged on to the computer she felt bogged down. It was six o'clock by the time she finally lifted her head and gave herself time to analyse her feelings of something creeping towards her, as though all these patients were marching in her direction. So again, she sat and thought. Tre Marshall had sat on the railway bridge many, many times before and he had always been coaxed down, either by the psychiatric SWAT team headed by Ryan, or Teresa, whom he knew and trusted – most of the time – or by the long-suffering police. At some point it was almost inevitable that he would fall. So was his death a mere coincidence?

Tempting.

But.

The police had not released details of the exact extent of the assault on Poppy Kelloway. In particular, the corrosive substance on her knickers. They had kept that back in the hope that this detail might entrap the killer.

So how had Tre known about the state Poppy had been found in? Coincidence? Liar, liar . . .?

She was shaking her head even as she asked herself the question. No. She was convinced Tre Marshall did not have it in him to torture and murder someone, whatever his beliefs. He had not committed the assault on Poppy. He might have watched her at the clinic, but had he even known her? It was too tempting to lay it at his door, believe that in a fit of agitation he had gone round to her house with a bottle of oven cleaner and killed her. If there had been less planning, Claire might have believed that and made a connection. But Poppy had been in on the plan. She had not cleared the house of children for Tre Marshall. But then . . . Another train of thought was funnelling through her mind. The fact that the boys were diverted out from the house depended on the boys' statements. What if . . .?

She was chilled at the thought and the implication and returned to the question of Tre Marshall, the second death of one of her patients in less than a fortnight. Where did he fit in? Anything Tre did was on impulse. What if someone had set him up, neatly planting that phrase, the silly little ditty into his mind? Had someone been pulling the strings of this vulnerable, cursed man whose apparent suicide was such a perfectly timed gift? The thought made her angry. She knew it would be only too tempting for the police to lay this murder at another psychiatric patient's door.

Except it wasn't true.

Had anyone been on the bridge with Tre? Surely not. But the image remained firmly fixed in her mind. Someone had persuaded him to jump into the void this time.

She looked up.

NHS clinics are strange places out of hours. Long, dimly lit corridors with echoes of footsteps, doors that swing to and fro, shadows behind them. Her office window overlooked one such long corridor, empty of people but never quite empty of sound or movement. For one of the first times ever she was desperate to leave. But when she stood up, she realized an envelope had been pushed under her door. When, she couldn't even guess. She couldn't swear that it hadn't been there when she'd returned after the boys' interviews with Saul. And she had been so absorbed in her work it was possible, if someone had been stealthy enough, that it had been pushed under while she'd been working.

She wouldn't have heard it.

She picked it up.

It was handwritten, and unmistakably addressed to her.

Dr Claire Roget. MBChB FRCPsych

They'd got her qualifications right. She unfolded the letter inside.

You think you're nearing the truth?

Ha! Ha! Ha!

What is truth, Doctor?

She dropped it as though it was alight. Then she picked up the phone.

TWENTY-NINE

8 p.m.

At first, she'd had trouble convincing DS Zed Willard that this letter had any connection to his case. His scepticism annoyed her.

But finally, he listened. 'Don't touch it,' he said. 'We'll check it for fingerprints but . . .'

He didn't get it, she realized. She was going to have to spell it out to him. 'Zed,' she said, 'this was pushed under the door of my office. Someone was here.'

'Ah.' Finally, he understood.

He repeated his offer. 'We can have an officer stationed at Greatbach, if you like.' His voice was tentative, anticipating her response.

But this time she accepted, even though she doubted it would achieve anything or protect any of them. That image of patients marching towards her cleared in her mind as she realized. They weren't threatening. They were beseeching.

She had to help see justice for them, the cloud of suspicion removed and the killer brought to justice. Even Poppy. They were too easy to push to the sidelines under the judgement that they were *receiving psychiatric treatment*, which to some people equated to criminal behaviour.

Wednesday 27 April, 8 a.m.

It was up to her. She'd realized that through the night, recognizing the role she had to play as advocate for her patients. And she could start by speaking to someone whose role she had, so far, failed to explore.

Robbie Kelloway, the three children's father.

Lynne Shute had said she'd been in contact with Robbie and they'd agreed amicably for the two boys and Holly-Anne to stay with her for the time being, to minimize disruption both emotionally and in their schooling.

That explained why Robbie Kelloway wasn't taking over custody of his three children at the moment and it made sense. But Claire wondered where exactly he fitted into all this.

Poppy's version had been that, without any help from her husband, she had struggled – heroically – to bring up the children on her own. It was a neat narrative but Claire doubted it was the truth.

Apart from the time Poppy claimed he'd tortured her (which she'd probably forgotten about the moment she'd said it), she had never been negative about him. If Claire asked her anything about Robbie or mentioned his name, Poppy would simply shrug and smile and say he played no part in either her or the children's lives.

She had found a number for him in Poppy's notes. A mobile. She trusted he still had the same contact details and dialled it without any real hope that he would pick up. But he did.

'Hello?' He sounded grounded and unsuspicious.

She introduced herself and was rewarded with a stony silence that stretched for what felt like minutes before he spoke. 'Well, Dr Roget, what on earth do you want with me?'

'I take it you know what's happened.'

'My mother-in-law rang to tell me. And the police have been in touch too. What I can't understand is why you, of all people, should be involved in a murder investigation. Surely that's down to the police?'

She bridled at his choice of phrase: *of all people*.

She could feel the hostility in his voice and anticipated his next salvo.

'After all, your track record in "curing" my wife of her unfortunate habit of relating fantasies as truth isn't exactly anything to be proud of, Doctor, is it?'

She could hear anger there too. But she picked up on something else. 'You call her your wife?'

'Yes.' He gave what sounded like a cynical chuckle. 'Poppy and I – well – we never actually got around to finalizing a divorce.'

Claire was silent. Another fallacy and a particularly pointless one. It made no difference to things now but, as in pondering many of Poppy's lies, she wondered why. What was the point of it?

'So,' he said, 'why are you ringing me?'

'I was wondering about the children.'

'Ah, yes,' he said. 'The children.'

'Poppy said—'

He interrupted. 'Let me guess. That I've had little to do with them in the years since we separated.'

'More or less.'

'I tried,' Robbie said. 'I really tried, but . . . I wanted to be a good father to my boys and little girl but let's say she made things difficult. Oh, she did it with subtlety. Everything one hundred per cent credible. Every time I tried to make contact she would throw some obstacle in front of it. Had we been divorced, perhaps I could have formalized access, but . . .' And there he stopped. 'I suppose,' he said very slowly. 'I was hoping. I hoped,' he substituted, 'that we'd get back together again. Pathetic, isn't it? And all the time my three children were growing up without me.'

She could hear bitterness and self-hatred in his voice now and Claire started to wonder about this absent father.

'Financially?' she ventured.

'That was another thing. I gave her money – regularly. And, of course, she kept the house. I didn't dare challenge her financially or I'm pretty sure things would have got even stickier. I did what I could,' he added, 'made the best of a bad job. So, Doctor . . .' He was mocking her now. 'How do you think *I* can help you?'

'Poppy's lies,' she began.

'Hmm.'

'Was she lying throughout your marriage?'

'No.' His voice was quiet, factual, unemotional now. He'd simmered down.

'Why not?'

'Because, Doctor, I threatened her.'

She was taken aback at his openness. 'With violence?'

'No. I just said I'd leave if she kept on making up ridiculous stories.'

'And did she?'

He sighed. 'No. Not for a while.'

'Then she started making up things about you?'

His initial silence answered the question. Then he spoke up. 'I said we were finished if she did it again.'

She picked up on the word. 'Again?'

'She'd started off by telling a load of whoppers about her family, her mum, her dad.'

Even though she sensed he was leading her away from himself, Claire was curious. 'What sort of whoppers?'

'That her dad was really wealthy and that he was a tax exile in Guernsey. I knew that was a load of crap. Her dad was unemployed, on the sick for alcoholism and living in Macclesfield.'

There was an awkward pause which Robbie finally filled. 'I don't understand why you're speaking to me.' He sounded truculent, defensive. 'Why are you even involved?' He paused. 'What do you want, Doctor Roget?'

'I'm just trying to help the police find your wife's killer.'

'I wouldn't have thought it was part of *your* job, assisting the police.' She could hear mockery as well as amusement in his voice, as though he was thinking: *Dr Claire Roget, amateur sleuth.*

'Sometimes it is.'

He hadn't quite finished. 'Do your patients know that?'

'It's my job to protect them and the general public.'

'Oh, well . . . Was that all you wanted to know?'

'Not really.' He was disinterested now, detaching himself from the conversation.

But Claire hadn't finished. 'What was it she said about *you* that wasn't true, that finally ended your marriage?'

'Nonsense about domestic violence. That's the diet she fed the kids on too, taking little vignettes from her own childhood and implanting them in her narrative about me.'

'Did that have a knock-on effect?'

'Sorry?'

'Were the police involved?'

'In something that was a fabrication?'

She could sense his anger rising, all light-hearted amusement gone now.

'Not that time, no.'

She heard the sarcasm as well as his rising fury.

'But I could see the way things were going. It was the end as far as I was concerned. I could never have trusted her again. It was best I cut and run. But I didn't think for a minute that she'd make things so difficult with the children. Particularly Tommy.'

She made a mental note to suggest to Saul Magnusson that he might introduce the subject of domestic violence with Tommy and Neil. Holly-Anne would have been too young to remember anything before her parents had separated eleven years ago. But Tommy, in particular, who would have been around six, would remember life when his parents were together.

Maybe that was the boys' secret.

'So, is that it?' He was patently anxious to end the call and, as she couldn't think of another relevant question, she capitulated.

'Yes.'

He'd hung up before she could say anything else, leaving her still puzzling over his role in his wife and children's lives – and Poppy's death.

She realized now why she had felt the need to contact him. He knew the truth so must have held some answers.

She recalled the meagre details Poppy had fed her about Robbie who, apart from not actually being her ex, opened up another tranche of possibilities.

And even though there seemed to have been no acrimony between them, instead a form of amused tolerance, during the phone call not once had he expressed any grief or shock about his wife's murder. Maybe he had anticipated all along that at some point her lies would provoke someone to violence. And now she knew the question she should have asked him.

Not *why* was she killed, but *who* do you think killed your wife?

Unless . . . and this was a possibility that maybe even the police hadn't considered. Unless *liar, liar, pants on fire* had been a distraction or a diversion.

And the torn appointment card?

Claire shook her head.

It was late when she left Greatbach, still puzzling over Poppy's murder while acknowledging that she had heard nothing from Detective Sergeant Zed Willard.

THIRTY

S aul poked his head round the door. 'You have a minute?'
'Come in.'
He closed the door very gently behind him. 'I'm seeing Holly-Anne later this morning. I wondered if you'd like to watch?'

'I would.'

'Good. Ten thirty.'

'Thanks.'

'I'll keep the questions to a minimum, you understand, nothing too upsetting. She's just a little girl, unlikely to have much insight into their home circumstances.' He looked thoughtful. 'And the bottom has been knocked out of her world.'

Claire nodded slowly. 'I wonder how she's settling in with her grandmother.'

'Oh, that part of it is working well. Holly-Anne is familiar with her grandmother. She's spent a lot of time with her. In fact, speaking to Lynne, I get the feeling life is better for all three of the children with her rather than with their . . . unpredictable mother.'

'That's what Lynne said to me.' She followed that up with, 'I don't want to interfere with your interview, but it might be an idea if you ask her about her father.'

'Really?'

'Yes.' And she related the gist of the conversation she'd had with Robbie yesterday evening.

Saul met her eyes. 'Uncovering the truth is even more difficult than usual in the light of Poppy Kelloway's inventiveness. Perhaps the children's grandmother might shed some light on things.'

'I'm meeting up with Lynne tomorrow.' She eyed him curiously and couldn't resist probing further. 'Have you thought more about the boys' interviews?'

He hesitated for a while, deep in thought before responding. 'I've spent some time pondering my impressions and spoken to the boys again. Only briefly this time.'

'But you haven't changed your mind about some hidden knowledge?'

'No. My thoughts were more analytical about the boys' characters and what clues they gave as to what they might hide.'

'And?' she prompted.

'Tommy, as you probably picked up, tries hard to be the man of the family, take over his father's role. He wants to appear tough, in control, but then he feels inadequate because he realizes he is not. That is why he is . . . truculent. Defensive and open to being exploited.'

She gave that some thought before adding, 'And Neil?'

'Dependant on his brother, who, incidentally he neither fears nor likes. He has a more complex and insecure character than his brother and is, I suspect, the more intelligent of the two. I suspect his mother's lies have confused him so he doesn't quite trust any adult. That trust has translated to fear.'

'So what role does their father have?'

Saul shook his head sadly. 'None. No role at all. He doesn't appear to . . .' He gave one of his rare grins. 'To figure in their lives.'

'Did you explore the fallout from that?'

'That was where I became unsure. There were conflicting messages.'

'What do you mean?'

'They say they don't see him, but that is not the truth.'

'But where?'

'I think at their grandmother's.'

She was silent. 'You think Holly-Anne might give something away?'

'One can only hope. I'll see you later?'

Claire spent much of the morning arranging for Dana Cheung to be transferred to a mother and baby unit soon. There she would still be supervised, but less closely, and she would be free from the psychiatric institution. Dana herself looked apprehensive. As well she might. When she had been admitted, her condition had been acute anxiety as well as suffering from psychosis. That had been two months ago. Nothing in psychiatry is quick – or certain.

During Saul's interview with Holly-Anne, as before Claire watched from the other side of the two-way mirror while Lynne observed from the corner. This time she was watching with much more attention, apparently nervous of the outcome.

Holly-Anne was a sweet-looking child, petite, with her mother's blonde hair and big blue eyes. In a white top and dark blue leggings, with pink trainers, she looked a typical eleven-year-old and displayed none of her brothers' anxiety, instead studying Saul with a boldness that reminded Claire of Poppy. Of course, unlike her brothers, she hadn't seen the worst of it, she hadn't seen her mother dead and she would have been largely protected from the details by her grandmother, who was watching over her like a hawk. Holly-Anne sat demurely, knees pressed together, again in an attitude reminiscent of Poppy, her hands resting on her lap, giving Saul a timid little smile now that could have melted hearts. Except Claire had seen Poppy dish out the exact same smile, particularly dazzling and sweet when she'd been spinning one of her sticky little lies, causing trouble for someone: voicing complaints about a rude receptionist, someone cutting her up in the car park, an attempt to squeeze money out of her by loan sharks or confidence tricksters, or someone at the school where she worked 'hitting on her'. All said with that same, sweet, convincing smile.

Claire glanced across at Poppy's mother. The lines around Lynne's mouth deepened as she pressed her lips together. It looked as though she was struggling to keep her comments tightly reined in. And she was scared for the child. Even through the glass, Claire could sense her anxiety.

Claire shifted her attention back to Holly-Anne, inventive under Saul's delicate questions, and didn't believe a word of it. She was the reincarnation of her mother except less proficient. Maybe Poppy had honed her skills as a child. 'Yes, I did see one of Mummy's boyfriends,' she volunteered. 'I think his name was . . .' She rolled her eyes towards the heavens, searching.

'Matteus,' she finally came up with.

Saul wasn't taken in for one minute. He was just as aware as she was that this was all a fabrication, a fiction born in little Holly-Anne's mind.

'Holly-Anne,' he prompted. 'What did Matteus look like?'

'He was . . .' And this was when Holly-Anne's age and naivety showed. 'A bit like – you know – the prince in *Frozen*. Really, really good looking.'

'Can you tell me what colour his hair was?'

'Oh. It was blond. Really yellow.' Believing she'd pulled off the deception, she smiled.

Holly-Anne's stories weren't as subtle as her mother's. She hadn't perfected the fine art of lying – not yet. But she'd learn. Claire glanced curiously at Lynne, who was watching her granddaughter with a certain amount of tension – more so than with the boys.

Wisely, Saul ignored the girl's fabrication, writing nothing down this time. He moved on. 'Tell me about the friend you had the sleepover with.'

'Oh.' She hadn't expected that and sounded disappointed. 'She's someone I sit next to at school.'

'Her name?' Saul's voice was gently coaxing.

'Shelley.' Holly-Anne's response was cautious. She hadn't quite got the measure of the psychiatrist and was looking slightly worried. And that, Claire sensed, was exactly how Saul wanted it. Not . . . quite . . . comfortable.

Holly-Anne shifted forward in her seat as Lynne leaned back in hers. Less watchful now she believed she understood Saul's methods.

Saul smiled at the girl. 'You were fond of your mother?'

The girl's eyes flickered as she decided how to answer this. 'Of course I was. I loved her – with all my heart.' She even tapped the left side of her chest.

'And your father?' Saul had asked the question so softly Claire hardly heard. But Lynne and Poppy both had. For the first time since the interview started they looked at each other, Holly-Anne taking her cue from her grandmother, who intervened. 'Dr Magnusson,' she said, 'I think it best if we could avoid that subject?' Her voice trailed away towards the end of the sentence. She was trying to semaphore the warning, that to pursue this line of questioning would upset her young granddaughter.

Saul gave her a little nod and returned to the subject of 'Matteus'. 'So this very handsome boyfriend of your mother's. When did you last see him?'

'About a week ago.'

Claire was shaking her head. This was complete fantasy. Zed Willard had made no mention of any yellow-haired boyfriend hanging around Poppy's home. 'Matteus' had not been the person she had reported hanging around outside her house the night she had died.

But Saul played along. 'Did she have many boyfriends, your mother?'

Holly-Anne shrugged. 'Not so many.' She'd run out of ideas. Or more likely she'd grown bored of the subject.

This was exactly how Poppy's stories would peter out. She'd simply grow bored with the whole effort of making them up. Her daughter had an added feature. She even gave a theatrical yawn combined with a staged mute appeal to her grandmother. Big eyes and a pleading expression as well as her hands pressed together. Like a prayer or a *Namaste*.

After a few more probing questions, Saul started to wind the interview up. 'And are you happy living with your grandmother?'

Lynne sat up, rigid, wondering how the girl would respond. Holly-Anne's head whipped round and she gave her grandmother a beatific, reassuring smile. 'I *love* living with her,' she gushed in an affected, little girl's voice.

Interestingly, Lynne's tension didn't dissipate.

THIRTY-ONE

Midday

Strangely enough, Claire's suspicions grew during a further consultation with Tony Ranucci later that day when he swaggered in and dropped into the chair. 'Wasn't due back for a while,' he commented. 'So, is there a problem?'

She could hardly tell him that she was checking up on him – again – because he was top of her list of suspects. 'No. I just wanted to check a few things.'

'Ah.' He was someone who didn't always think before he spoke. He was apt to blurt out his thoughts. 'Looks like her lies caught up with her then?'

'Lies?' she queried.

He leaned in. 'Liked tellin' her stories, didn't she?'

She made no comment, so he asked, 'They got anyone yet?' He was chewing gum, which made his questions as well as his manner appear casual, though she sensed they were anything but. Those lazy, dark eyes were watching her from beneath lowered lids.

She kept her response non-committal, while at the same time she was checking his blood results on the computer. He was still clean. And eagle-eyeing her, anxious to learn what she knew.

'What was she seein' you for?' He'd kept up the jaunty manner.
'You know I can't . . .'

'I know you can't.' There was the hint of mimicry in his rejoinder
and she looked at him sharply. Ranucci was clean and that cleanliness, his responses no longer blunted by drugs, were perceptive and
. . . troubling. Why on earth should she be troubled by it? Because
she'd picked up on something. That torn appointment card, as well
as the letter which had appeared in her office on Tuesday evening,
directed the same brand of knowledge and mockery towards her.

Ranucci was watching her, his face hawk-like, the sharp, Roman
nose almost quivering as though it could smell her subtext. She ran
his history through her mind. What had he been like before the
tragedy? she wondered. A hard-working, lithe chef, working all
hours to support his wife and baby daughter. In one great throw of
the dice, fuelled by snorts of cocaine, he had lost the lot, everything
that had meant anything to him. On his first visit, shaking from the
effects of cocaine withdrawal and bereavement, he had pulled out
his phone and slid across photograph after photograph of a beautiful
Italian woman and a plump little baby with soft, dark, curling hair
and her father's appealing dark eyes. When he had lifted his face
back to her it had been wet with tears. Only Italian men seemed to
know how to cry while still retaining their masculinity. As gently
as she could, she had talked to him and listened to his words, his
explanation for the events, the exhaustion of working all hours at
the beck and call of the head chef. But at the same time it registered
that he was taking no responsibility for the actual accident himself.
'We was forced off the road. It was too narrow for a coupla vehicles.
That big thing comin' the other way. I can see it now, still comin'
towards me. We hit a tree. I turned to say to Chiara, "You OK?"'
And then his words had dissolved in a layer of grief that was as
deep and inhospitable as a grave. 'She couldn't say nothin', Doctor.
I lost them both that night. Both of them. My two beautiful
girls, I used to call them.'

The police report had stated that no other vehicle was involved
and Ranucci's estimated speed was around seventy mph. Far too
fast, in their opinion, for a narrow, winding country lane and a
driver, particularly one charged with cocaine, to be travelling at that
speed. In some ways Ranucci was as inventive as Poppy had been.

She hadn't corrected his story.

To even utter the word *sorry* would have seemed inadequate as well as inappropriate, so she'd nodded and listened some more. And that night when she had reached home and Grant had been there, she had wondered. Could she ever adore him as much as Ranucci had, apparently, adored his wife? She didn't think so. She couldn't imagine him weeping over her photograph, splodging tears over her picture. Or was Ranucci's adoration simply a symptom of his guilt?

When Grant had asked her how her day had been, she had escaped upstairs and stood under the shower until she felt she could face him again. But that evening their entire relationship, held up to an unforgiving light, had felt a lie, their relationship superficial, because it did not, never would, live up to that intensity. Even though Ranucci had, in effect, killed the wife and daughter he had professed to love so much.

So . . . she had emerged from the shower and wrapped a towel around her. Crocodile tears.

And yet it was part of the reason why she and Grant had split up. Had she been expecting too much? Italian men were, after all, famous for showing their emotions.

Ranucci was speaking. 'Tragedy,' he said, chewing his gum, 'Innit?'

'Yes.'

She was watching him for the signs of grief she'd seen when he'd described the tragedy of his wife and daughter's deaths. But she saw none.

There had been no hint of animosity there and she drew her own conclusion: Ranucci was not one of the people Poppy Kelloway could hurt. He couldn't hide his emotions ergo he'd felt no animosity against her.

She checked through all his other details and felt sad as Ranucci left. Whatever the reason behind his wife and baby daughter's death, he was permanently affected. When he left, much of his swagger had dissipated.

She knew his attendance had been a fact-finding mission. For them both.

2 p.m.

Depressed, she climbed the stairs to the ward and consoled herself by spending some time with Dana before she was transferred to the mother and baby unit. Her patient was quiet that afternoon. Quiet and reflective when Claire asked her how she felt about her daughter now. Dana gave the matter prolonged thought before nodding and returning a simple but honest answer. 'I can't say I love her,' she said. 'I'm not even sure I like her.'

It was tempting to say *that will come*, but instead Claire waited.

And Dana gave an unexpected smile. 'I think I will,' she said. 'One day I think I will.' And her hand stole across to touch Claire's.

As Neil Armstrong said, 'One small step . . .'

THIRTY-TWO

S imon was walking towards her along the corridor and they stopped for a chat. He jerked his head towards the room she had just emerged from and Claire nodded. 'Nearly there,' she said. 'But if we rush it we lose any advantage.'

She became aware that he was still watching her out of the corner of his eye. The corridor was empty and he looked a bit down, which was so out of character that she asked him softly, 'Do you miss your wife?'

She sensed he was finding it hard to answer honestly; she was surprised that he was willing to talk about it at all.

'Yes,' he said finally. 'And no. Marianne was so different after she had a miscarriage.' He was shaking his head. 'It was like all her focus was on that unborn child. Nothing else existed except that. I just didn't know her any more. We had nothing left. Anything between us had been sucked out. And,' he admitted now, 'I felt I'd failed her.' He stopped speaking for a moment, reflecting. Then, 'We tried, Claire. We really did try. It just didn't work. And so . . .' He heaved out a big, regretful sigh. 'I had to get away. I had to escape. England seemed about far enough. When she came over those couple of months ago, I thought . . .' He considered this. 'I *hoped* things would be different, but they weren't. So here I am. Still.'

He looked at her, his face rueful. 'It's the way it is.'

'Are you in touch now?'

He didn't respond straight away but sidestepped the question. 'She's having therapy,' he said. And smiled at her.

She said something she'd been thinking for a while. 'You should have talked this through. Not run away.'

His grin widened. 'Are you trying to export me back to Aus?'

'Absolutely not. I love having you as my registrar and on the top floor at home. But we have to live the best lives we can.'

He was watching her very carefully at this. 'Ri-ight. And are you?'

Which reminded her of her half-brother's approaching wedding and the trip to Chester – alone this time – to pick up her outfit.

She put a hand on his arm and focused on Simon's situation rather than her own. 'If she's having therapy . . .' she said.

'It's taking a while.'

'As you know, psychiatry's a long, slow business, Simon,' she said, 'often with unsatisfactory or uncertain outcomes.' Then she smiled and mocked him. 'If you prefer a quick fix, maybe you should have taken up surgery?'

He met her smile with one of his own before asking, 'Are the police making any advances in the Poppy Kelloway case?'

'I haven't heard. There's nothing on the news and the police haven't been in touch with me.'

'Can't see what good planting a PC outside the place will do.'

DS Zed Willard had kept to his word about having an officer stand guard at Greatbach. 'Me neither. I think it's supposed to make us feel safe.'

'Does it?'

She shook her head.

'I just hope they get someone soon.'

'Me too.' Maybe her response had been more heartfelt than usual. Certainly Simon had picked up on it. 'You think they're going to catch whoever it was?'

'I just don't know. I hope so.' She tried to make a dubious joke out of it. 'I don't want our patients to be popped off one by one.'

It had started as a lame joke but as she descended the stairs to return to her office it sounded increasingly hollow. While Poppy Kelloway's killer was at large and Tre Marshall dead, and who knew the story behind that, she couldn't shake off the possibility that Greatbach, and she in particular, was in the killer's sights.

3 p.m.

Saul Magnusson was hovering outside Claire's office and she realized he'd been waiting to speak to her about Poppy's three children. 'Let me just get a coffee,' she said. 'I'm practically dehydrated. You want one?'

'I'll stick to water. I still haven't got over the luxury of being able to drink it straight from the tap. How many countries would love to have that privilege.'

'Well, I need a caffeine fix. Why don't you wait in my office and we can talk?'

She unlocked the door and let him in. That was a new practice since the letter had been pushed under her door. She now locked it whether she was inside or not. Only she and Rita had a key. Up until now the thought of an intruder had never seemed threatening. But things had changed.

Saul was sitting in one of the chairs to the side of the desk. Best practice was not to put a desk between yourself and your patient, but Claire needed a work surface and the room was small. Three chairs, one behind the desk which held a computer, and the small space felt crowded. Even the window overlooking the corridor seemed designed to pin her in.

Saul waited until she settled down, his long legs almost touching the opposing wall.

She turned to face him. 'So?' That was when she realized she was dreading hearing what he had to say.

'I have had another session with the boys,' he said. 'Together this time. This gave me a chance to observe their interaction. They have very different personalities. You probably picked that up from watching the two interviews.'

She nodded while anticipating what he would say next.

'Tommy,' he began, 'is a very angry boy. Sullen and resentful. Quite powerful emotions. He's also a bully. He thought I couldn't see but I was looking out for it. He was gripping his brother's arm.'

'What are you saying?' She'd asked the question while not wanting to hear the answer.

'They are lying.'

She was appalled. 'Surely you can't think . . .?' She couldn't finish the sentence.

He touched her arm. 'No. No. I don't believe they killed their mother.' He paused. 'But I do believe they were complicit.'

It was what she'd feared when she'd heard the story of the two boys going out on the town together.

'But almost the whole case hinges on their testimony.'

He nodded.

'And Holly-Anne's,' she added, more thoughtfully.

'What I want to explore now is their motive. Someone's influence is behind this. I've already said how I think they're holding something back. Claire . . .'

She looked straight into his cold blue eyes.

'I wonder about their father. I would very much like to meet Mr Kelloway, the man who has, it seems, the perfect alibi.'

'I've spoken to him.'

'And?'

'He sounds balanced – measured. I didn't pick up on any resentment against his wife.'

'Wife? I thought they were divorced.'

'Apparently not. He claims he supported Poppy financially – which unsurprisingly contradicts Poppy's version – but it does explain how she managed financially. I always wondered.'

Saul was nodding. 'Is he bitter against his ex-wife? Sorry, wife?'

'I think he's angry about her limiting access to his three children.'

'Might he have encouraged the boys to take action?'

'I don't know,' she said. 'I don't think I know any of it anymore.'

Saul continued as though he hadn't heard her last remark. 'Their mother's fantasies had a marked effect on each of the three children, but differently. Tommy became a bully. Neil crawled into a shell, and Holly-Anne . . . You saw how she was? Emulating her mother. Making it up as she went along?'

'Yes.'

'They are all damaged. Claire . . .' He was eager now. 'I think we should speak to the police.'

'And say what, Saul? We have nothing concrete. This is all pure conjecture.'

'I think you should alert them. We should work alongside them now. This was not so much a crime as a conspiracy.'

'It's too soon.'

But he wasn't giving up. 'I can't point the finger in one direction or another. Certainly not to implicate children whose knowledge of the crime might be very sparse. But I know the police. They discount children as accessories. They believe them when they shouldn't.' He followed that up with, 'You need to speak to the police, Claire, before there is another tragedy.'

'I'll seriously consider it. But you need to find out what they're holding back, Saul. Explore their motive, as you say. Just telling the police that we think the children are lying won't get them very far, and it won't be enough to prevent another crime. We need more.'

'When Poppy . . .' He said the name as though it was a foreign sound, stumbling over the second syllable: Pop*pee*. 'I don't believe there was any new man. You see how much hangs on the boys' evidence? And the police found no forensic evidence of an intruder.'

'They did find some DNA evidence, but they've failed to identify it.'

'So it's nobody on their database.'

'No.'

'That doesn't surprise me.'

But she had threaded that fact into the narrative. 'It can't be her brother then. He has a criminal record.'

Saul's eyes penetrated her. 'For what?'

But she shook her head. 'I don't know.'

'It might be an idea to find out.' He paused. 'All three children were in thrall to their mother. She controlled them. And that can breed resentment. Particularly in a boy of seventeen years old. And then there is his brother and the little sister who follow in their mother's footsteps. I tried to find out what particular lies Poppy fed to her children, but the boys have grown a protective shield around them. Yet I can only think they knew what was true and what not. What I am less clear about is the real role their father played.' He gave a brief, impish smile. 'I am always suspicious of an alibi that is so indisputable.'

She shook her head, smiling too. 'It checks out – believe me.'

'Ah.' Saul continued, 'All three children have told me separately and together that their mother told them their father had a new life and had forgotten about them. It seems he played no part in their lives.'

'And is angry about that.'

'Understandably. And then there is a grandmother who appears to act as a surrogate and this uncle who suddenly seems to have popped up in her life.'

'He's probably been in prison.'

'Again, you should find out more.'

'I will.'

He stood up. 'She played a dangerous game, your patient. At some point her malice was going to result in violence. People get angry when they are lied to, Claire. These are the ingredients for a toxic soup. The question is which part did each of these people play? And who was the instigator?'

'You're convinced a member of her family murdered her?'

'I believe they had a hand in it. Are you willing to talk to the police?'

She nodded. 'Soon.'

'Before it is too late, Claire.'

THIRTY-THREE

3.15 p.m.

With the new insight Saul had given her, Claire felt nervous about meeting up with Lynne. But that was the arrangement. She'd thought at the time the outpatient clinic seemed a bit exposed, too many people, reasoning that since her daughter's murder, Lynne was a recognizable figure. Now she regretted that decision.

She turned up promptly, her eyes watchful and shrewd while, remembering Saul Magnusson's dark hints, Claire studied her. Today she looked younger than her years. Perhaps she was beginning to recover from the events of two weeks ago. Maybe she was pulling herself together in the interests of her grandchildren. Possibly, having the grandchildren live with her was enough of a distraction from her own grief. But perhaps the explanation was something darker. Perhaps her plan had played out.

Whatever the explanation, Lynne was dressed smartly in a navy jacket and well-fitting trousers over a striped blue and white fisherman's T-shirt. And there was something else about her that seemed to support Saul's theory, something confident, as though she'd won something.

She started politely. 'Thanks for seeing me, Doctor.'

'No problem,' Claire responded. 'Actually, I was hoping you might have some information that might help me understand your daughter a little better.'

The knives were quickly out. 'A bit late, don't you think?'

Now was not the time for recriminations.

Claire kept her cool. 'My focus was on my patient and her history, Lynne. You always knew that Poppy's tendencies could not be cured, simply managed and discouraged.'

Poppy's mother's features sharpened. She reached her hands out, palms upwards, in an expression of appeal. 'What's the point – now?'

'How did it all start?' Claire asked gently. 'What triggered it?'

'Didn't you ask her that?'

'Many times. And each time I got a different answer.'

'It was so long ago . . .'

She seemed to scan her memories. 'She was just a little girl. Looking back, I didn't realize it was the start of anything significant. I certainly didn't realize it would go on and on until even I couldn't separate fact from fiction.' She drew in a deep, regretful breath and lowered her voice. 'Neither did I realize it was infectious.'

Claire knew she was talking primarily about Holly-Anne – maybe the boys too.

Later she would pick this sentence apart, letter by letter, and reflect where it fitted into the narrative. But for now she asked, 'So how *did* it start?'

'She was so convincing. She was a little girl. About five, I think. She was due an injection at the surgery. My phone went off and I stepped outside to take the call. It was my solicitor and I couldn't ignore it. It was important.'

Claire waited.

'When I came back into the clinic room, Poppy was crying. I thought it was just the injection. I knew she'd been frightened but she tugged my arm. I apologized to the nurse and we left. On the way home Poppy said the nurse had pinched her and said she should have been strangled at birth.' Lynne's eyes appealed at Claire. 'What would *you* do?'

Claire had no answer.

'I made a complaint. The nurse denied it but Poppy insisted and the nurse lost her job. It didn't even occur to me that my daughter was lying. I didn't think a little girl of five years old could or would lie. She was so convincing. I knew she didn't like the nurse for some reason. But to do that, make up a lie. Why, Doctor? What was the point? She had nothing to gain.'

'It gave her a sense of superiority,' Claire said, abstracted, her mind dealing with the here and now. But Lynne Shute was waiting for a fuller answer.

'Power,' Claire continued. 'She felt a sense of cleverness. And sometimes a substitute narrative can help children deal with difficulties in their lives over which they would otherwise have no or limited control.'

'Could you *ever* have cured her?'

Claire felt Lynne was seeking reassurance. She shook her head.

'So why did you keep seeing her?'

'It was part of the court's directive. And I never stopped hoping we could modify her behaviour. I tried to warn her there could be consequences.'

Now they understood each other.

There was one more point Lynne seemed to want to explore. 'Could you have prevented . . .?' She didn't need to complete the sentence.

Claire shook her head.

And then the atmosphere in the small room changed.

'Have you been helping the police?' Her voice had sharpened, her eyes hostile.

'I don't have anything concrete to offer the police, Lynne. The only real input I've had is to suggest the children spend time with our child psychiatrist.'

Lynne moved forward, eager and yet apprehensive. 'And has he unearthed anything that might help?'

Claire played safe. 'I really don't know. You should ask him. You were present, surely, at all of his consultations?'

That resulted in another sharp look.

Lynne left soon after, leaving Claire alone in her empty office to think, testing some of Poppy's assertions.

Who had told her the brothers didn't get on? Poppy. Who had told her that Holly-Anne had 'no friends'? Poppy.

It was the same with the versions she had given of her husband's (not ex-husband's) failure to provide for her and the children, as well as the reason behind the lack of contact between father and children. Where was Lynne in all this? She must have known the truth.

And she realized now the significance of these latest enlightenments. Tommy dominated his younger brother. It seemed that, in this, Poppy had spoken the truth. Enough to persuade him to lie to the police about that night? Likewise, if Holly-Anne was far from being the innocent little angel, but her mother's spawn, how did these three details change the real version?

And how did this impact on their grandmother and uncle? What part did they play in the story?

THIRTY-FOUR

At around seven p.m. Claire stood up, realizing how late it was. She should be on her way home now. But first she thought she would pay Dana a last visit. She was due to be transferred to the mother and baby unit in the morning.

It was dark in the stairwell, a place she'd always found a little spooky with echoing voices which came from one of the other floors. You could never be absolutely certain which one. Sometimes the hum of the floor cleaner's polishing machine mingled with a shout or a scream. Who knew where it came from or from whom? Disturbed patients frequently shout and scream.

When she reached the top floor, it was the silence that she noted, an eerie silence in the fading light that was equally disturbing. She pushed open the door. At first all seemed normal, civilized, quiet and peaceful. Two nurses sat at the nurses' station. They were having a report and looked up as she approached. 'I'm just going to pop in and see Dana,' she said as she passed them.

She listened outside the door.

Dana was weeping, pleading with someone over her phone. She hadn't even noticed Claire enter. Claire stood for a moment as she took stock of the situation. The mobile was set to speaker phone so she recognized the voice on the other end. Fangsu giving a tirade of abuse about her daughter-in-law being an unfit mother, saying that Lily Rose should be with her, that she would make sure the child was safe from evil spirits . . . and so on.

Claire grabbed the phone off her patient. 'Mrs Cheung,' she said furiously, 'it's Dr Roget here and I heard what you said to my patient. I will *not* allow you to jeopardize her recovery. She is now much better and may be able to care for her daughter in the future. If you can't help her in her recovery then I suggest you leave her alone. Do you understand?'

There was a shocked silence on the other end and then the call was ended.

While her patient looked at her with round eyes, Claire was furious. She knew how delicate this situation was. And she saw now, only too clearly, where it could lead.

She sat on the bed and, in a move that might not have been approved by the Royal College, put her arm round her patient and let her weep, pour out all her misgivings, saying again and again how unsuitable she was, what a poor wife and mother she was, while Claire had to try to undo the damage Dana's mother-in-law had inflicted.

She made a mental note to speak to Edward Reakin in the morning. As a clinical psychologist, he could visit Dana in her new location and turn this case around, because it was complex. Try and undo the harm that had been done, or at least some of it, Claire now fully realized, by her mother-in-law.

As they sat in silence, Dana Cheung weeping on her shoulder, Claire was reminded of another day, early on, when Poppy Kelloway had first been referred. Like Dana today, Poppy had broken down, something unusual in her patient, almost unique. Holly-Anne had been six years old. Lively and constantly tugging at her mother's arm if she felt she wasn't getting enough attention. Poppy had had trouble coping with the energetic little girl and was full of complaints. 'I'm not getting much sleep. I'm a terrible mother. I'm too tired and I'm constantly short of money.' Yet Claire had noted that her patient was dressed expensively and, if her nose was not deceiving her, was wearing Chanel perfume and not some cheap fake.

She'd asked her then, 'Doesn't Holly's father help out?'

Poppy had sniffed out her response. 'Robbie?' She'd given Claire a sly look which had made Claire want to respond, *Who else?*

But she'd kept that question to herself.

'He doesn't help with any of them. He doesn't want to.'

The claim had stunned her at the time because, as part of her assessment, she'd interviewed Robbie soon after, and he had denied it. He had a good job, as a sports coach for a semi-professional rugby team. Why wouldn't he support his own children? he'd asked bluntly, and she had sensed his veracity. As well as outrage peppered with a certain amount of male pride.

'All three of them?'

Robbie was a handsome guy, with a square face and determined chin. Watching him, she'd realized. While Poppy had been a bare-faced liar, her husband was the opposite. Unable to vocalize anything but the truth – the whole truth. Nothing but.

She stayed with Dana until her night sedation was taking effect, and then she slipped away back to her office to pick up her bag.

And was relieved to hear a knock on the door.

THIRTY-FIVE

7.45 p.m.

'Saul and I are going for a curry. You wanna come?'

Sometimes Simon Bracknell's appeal was that he was so boyish, reminding her of *Just William*, right down to the ginger hair and freckles. Stick a different pair of glasses on him and he'd be just right for the part. Added to that was his openness and bluntness.

'Sure,' she said, feeling the smile spread across her face like jam over a sticky toddler's and just as sweet. 'I would.'

'That place in Burslem still open?'

'It is. Why don't we park at my place and then walk up? Then we can have two glasses of wine,' she added mischievously.

'Or a beer or two.' Simon's face grew even happier and she felt reassured by his buoyancy, hoping he was coming to terms with the decisions he had made that had led to his current single status and position as her lodger. And maybe, one day, he and Marianne would be reconciled. Or maybe not.

'I'd better book.'

'Your boyfriend want to come?'

And suddenly she felt a white heat of annoyance. 'He isn't my boyfriend. Not any more. Not really,' she added more honestly.

Simon was unabashed. 'So, if he isn't your boyfriend, what is he? Friend with benefits after your weekend away?'

She prevaricated. 'I hate that phrase. It's cheap.'

Simon simply grinned and pushed his glasses up his nose. 'As you wish,' he said. 'And if you are booking, can you make it eight thirty so we'll have a chance to shower the day away?'

She couldn't stop the smile warming her face, spreading, it felt, from ear to ear. 'Certainly, Your Highness.'

But the choices of the day were not over.

8 p.m.

She was just getting changed when Grant came on the line sounding both jaunty and confident. 'I've just finished cooking the most delicious meal, Claire,' he said. 'You'd better come over and help me eat it.'

That was when she began to feel awkward. 'I can't,' she said. 'Not tonight.'

'Work?' How could one syllable sound so suspicious, even hostile?

Though she could have justified an affirmative, her inconvenient honesty won the toss. 'Not exactly.'

'Oh?' An even shorter expression of suspicion.

'Having a curry with a couple of colleagues.'

'Right. Well . . .' She could hear him sucking in a long breath. 'There's something I need to talk to you about.' And she knew, instinctively, that it was connected with the woman who had answered the phone. Yes, at some point she and Grant would have to have 'the conversation' but, coward-like, she wanted it to be later rather than sooner.

Give me a few days' grace. 'Tomorrow,' she managed. 'Come round to Waterloo Road.'

'I'll see you there.' His voice was tight and neither had pinned down an exact time.

The night at the Kismet restaurant turned out to be more raucous than Claire had anticipated. Simon and Saul had, it seemed, formed a matey bond, blokey, but not offensively so. They joked and brought up various scenarios which seemed mainly to involve white-knuckle experiences of the sort that Claire would have hated. Bungee jumping, swimming with sharks, rock climbing without ropes. Anything without a safety net. But the banter was jolly, noisy and friendly. A distraction from the thoughts that haunted her mind, visions of children who hated their mother. Enough to kill her? A mother whose relationships were equally tainted. This evening, away from it all, was a balm to Claire's soul. *Let the police do their job*, she thought. *It's nothing to do with you.*

And as she met her colleagues' eyes across the table it was as though they had all nodded and come to a tacit agreement. *Say nothing.*

As they walked back to Waterloo Road together she realized neither Simon nor Saul had mentioned Poppy's murder. Maybe, she tinkered with the thought, as they stepped along the pavement, the curry evening had been a two-pronged ambush to take her mind away from it.

THIRTY-SIX

Friday 29 April, 9 a.m.

But however much she tried to convince herself that investigating her patient's murder was a job for the police, Claire knew she had a duty to speak to DS Zed Willard. But when she tried the number he had given her, it went straight through to answerphone. She left a non-committal message, that her call was a simple enquiry as to how the investigation was going. She felt that she and Saul had only part of the explanation. And they had no evidence, only opinions. Theirs was a theory which would need proof. She prevaricated with the line that until they could help with something more tangible, they should leave the police to work it out for themselves. And then prove it in a court of law. Trouble was that without understanding the deviousness of the lead characters they might struggle, because it was a vital part of the narrative.

Her discomfort was like an itch in her back, one she could never quite reach and which would not go away. But, like a Geiger counter bleeping furiously, the sensation increased in intensity when her thoughts focused on the boys.

It would help to speak to one person.

Saul, like most doctors, carried a bleep. She dialled the number and waited for him to call back.

He must have recognized her office number because moments later he was outside her window, attracting her attention with a soft knock.

She beckoned him in.

'I know what it is you're thinking. Unravelling the boys' statements about their night out.'

They looked at one another for a long moment, communicating silently, but neither anxious to say the words.

'Their night out,' she said. 'It wasn't their mother who suggested and paid for it.'

She recalled Poppy's words. The boys who hated each other. True.

The fact that Claire knew Poppy wouldn't have paid for that night out. True.

Or for a taxi home. True.

'But someone did.'

She watched his face, knowing she didn't need to spell it out for him. He had seen, met and spoken to the child soldiers of Sudan, known that if a boy – or girl for that matter – could lift a gun they could fire it. If their psyche was damaged or indoctrinated enough they could be persuaded to do anything.

But torture . . . their own mother? Hardly realizing it, she was shaking her head. Perhaps following her thoughts, Saul Magnusson was watching her. He too was shaking his head, but it was aimed at gently dissuading her, though as she looked into those icy-blue eyes she read some doubt in there too.

'I will continue to see all three of them,' he said. 'I am keeping all possibilities open. I know there is something they are not telling me. But I find it hard to believe,' he added gently, 'that the murder of their mother is that thing. It is something else, something equally relevant to the investigation.'

He seemed lost in thought for a moment, then looked at her directly. 'What about you, Claire? How is your exploration of your patients going?'

'Stalled at the moment,' she said. 'I've got to know some of them better but I can't say I've made any progress towards Poppy's murder.' She wanted to add that she believed the person behind the crime was someone close to home. It had to be someone who knew her children.

Maybe Saul felt he should lighten her mood. 'And now you have your brother's wedding to look forward to.'

'Thanks for reminding me. I have to pick up my outfit tomorrow.'

'And I am sure you will look very nice in it,' he finished formally.

He was smirking as he let himself out through the door.

She had meant to spend the morning dictating some letters but found it hard to concentrate. Just after lunch she gave up and told Rita she would be taking the rest of the day off. She had to shop for tonight's meal with Grant. Looking at her watch, she realized she just had time for a quick coffee with Julia before dinner. They met at a shop near her surgery in Hanley.

Gina turned up too.

'And can we keep off the subject of Poppy Kelloway?'

'Sure.' Gina answered for both of them. But maybe they'd picked up on the sour note in her voice.

Julia changed the subject slightly and asked about her wedding outfit, picking up quickly on the illicit weekend in Chester. Again, the two friends exchanged glances.

Gina put a finger on her chin. 'So there we have the reason behind this emergency meeting: Grant Steadman.'

'I'm meeting up with him tonight,' Claire said gloomily. 'And I just know he'll issue an ultimatum.'

Gina met her eyes. 'Your decision,' she said.

Julia added sensibly, 'You can't have it both ways, Claire. You can't keep him on a string forever. He's a bloke. He wants more than supporting your elbow at a family wedding and the odd illicit weekend away.'

Gina chipped in. 'To devote time and energy to your profession often means your partner feeling neglected unless she – or he – is *extremely* understanding.'

Exchanged glances again. 'And we don't think Grant is really that sort of man.'

Which caused Claire to heave out another heavy sigh.

Luckily, or perhaps kindly, Julia changed the subject. 'I had a letter back from one of your colleagues,' she said, 'about a child who'd been bedwetting since his father had walked out.'

'That'll be Saul Magnusson. He's a newly appointed paediatric psychiatrist.'

'About time we had one of those. I and, I guess, plenty of my colleagues in general practice have got lists of children with psychiatric problems – everything from eating disorders to ADHD. And it isn't just in the poorer areas, Claire.' She was warming to her subject. 'Plenty of the kids in the Westlands have their own set of problems – drugs, excessive and unrealistic parental ambition, social media bullying. You name it, it's skulking around. I feel sorry for kids today. In a way they've never been so lucky and in another they've never been so unlucky.'

'What's he like?' Gina asked in her soft voice.

'Who?'

'This Dr Magnusson. Does he have a partner?'

Claire couldn't help but smile. 'What is it with couples who want to pair up every singleton they know?'

They were waiting. 'He's an adventurer,' Claire said. 'Worked for MSF, the Red Cross, various charities going to far-flung places in the world, practising medicine at the rough end, sleeping under canvas and living on whatever rations the locals have to eat or the charities provide. And when he's not saving the souls of these poor kids, he's fond of white-knuckle sports. I spent yesterday evening listening to him and Simon trying to outdo each other with their scary and terrifying experiences.'

They were both laughing. 'Who won?'

'Simon, I think. Paddle boarding off the Gold Coast, he swam alongside a great white shark. Saul managed to look really impressed.'

'If that's what he's like, what brought him to Stoke?' Gina was nothing if not persistent. 'It's hardly Afghanistan or Syria, Kyiv, Eritrea or the Congo. Or even,' she finished with a smile, 'the Gold Coast.'

'I think . . .' Claire pondered this for a moment. 'I think something got a bit too much for him. Something happened that really upset him. He's come to Stoke to lick his wounds, but he won't be here for long. He'll soon be gone.' She didn't mention the fact that Saul had told her he'd admired her work.

Gina looked disappointed. Claire stood up. 'Which reminds me. I should be going too,' she said. 'I want to—'

Right on cue her phone rang and she recognized the number. It was Zed Willard. She answered briefly before cutting him off. 'Can I ring you back in, say, five minutes?'

'Sure.'

With that she paid her third of the bill, kissed her friends goodbye, and left.

THIRTY-SEVEN

5.40 p.m.

Claire waited until she was back in her car and parked along a side street before she rang Zed back.

'How is your case going?' She could hear the nip in her voice, partly caused, she knew, by what she was going to tell him, and how far she might be willing to go.

His answer was vague. 'Some blind endings, some false trails, nothing that's led anywhere – so far.'

He sounded down in the mouth.

'Poppy's mother said something this afternoon that sort of clarified things.'

'Really?' She felt his interest had quickened.

'Well, it maybe explains to some extent where all the lying began.'

He was waiting.

And she told him the story of the nurse and the injection, the power a little girl's lie had achieved.

'There was only Poppy's word.'

'So how could this be relevant to our investigation?' He sounded frustrated.

She had to give more. 'I don't know, except . . . it isn't only adults that can be convincing liars.' It was on the tip of her tongue to go further and mention the fact that Saul felt the three children had played a part in this, but she didn't dare. They needed to unearth solid facts. Zed Willard had already made it clear it was facts he wanted, not psychiatric mumbo-jumbo, rich with conjecture and poor on evidence.

She was met with silence this time, and asked whether they had any other leads.

'We're working on it, Claire,' he said gloomily, 'but the truth is we haven't much to go on.'

'I thought you had some DNA evidence?'

'Unidentified.'

'Do you have *anything*?' she asked incredulously.

'We have too much.' It burst out of him in a fit of frustration. 'We have a plethora of cars and people. It was a fine night and the world and its wife were out walking the dog, mostly, it seems, in hoodies and big coats as it wasn't very warm. Added to that there was a Bible class in the Christadelphian Hall, a Zumba class in the village hall, a kids' karate session in the CofE church hall, and any number of people playing football on the green. We can't check up on them all.' He paused and let his frustration boil over.

'We were hoping that your child psychiatrist might glean something from one of the three children, but so far . . . nothing.'

Maybe her comment had landed and he was giving her a lead in to say more. But she held back. 'It takes time, Zed. These children have been traumatized.' She kept back the fact that she had watched the boys being interviewed and that she and Saul had spent time discussing the case.

'We don't have time.' On the other end there was a long silence. 'We're worried that someone somewhere knows the full truth and that makes us concerned for their safety.' It was obvious now why he was ringing. 'If they know something,' he added.

She tried to divert him. 'Do you mean one of the children?'

Zed didn't answer at first, and then he said slowly, 'Someone out there knows the truth. Someone other than the person who committed that hideous act on your patient. Tell me, Claire.' His tone was distant now, cold and unfriendly. He sensed she was holding something back. 'What sort of person does that to another? What's in their psyche?'

She knew he wasn't asking for a psychiatric profile. This outburst had been triggered by something else. Maybe he too was inching towards an unpalatable conclusion.

She made an attempt at an appropriate response. 'Someone who gives vent to their anger. A cold, calculating anger. Someone who wanted her to acknowledge her lies. That's who – and why.' She was not only telling him, she was instructing herself.

DS Willard fired his responses like bullets from an automatic pistol. 'I don't believe this simply happened. Looking at the crime

I believe it was pre-planned. And this is the thing that's foxing me, Claire. Somehow this killer persuaded her to get rid of the kids that night.' She realized now he was far from uncovering the truth.

He continued, 'I've spoken to Patricia's mother. This was not a usual occurrence. So our killer is smart and persuasive. You get my drift?'

She was silent, giving Zed Willard a chance to ask her outright. 'I wondered if you'd found any patients who might fit the profile yet?' He tried to lighten the question. 'Anyone on your roster?'

Plenty, she thought, knowing that some of her patients had had good reason to hate Poppy. *Too many.*

Yet perhaps they were barking up the wrong tree by focussing on her patients. 'No one who stands out particularly. What about the brother who seems to have suddenly appeared in her life after an absence?'

'Prison,' he said.

'For violent crime?'

At which point DS Zed Willard unexpectedly exploded into laughter. 'Depends on your definition of violent crime. A complete wanker.' He quickly apologized. 'Sorry. Drake Shute held up a post office with a banana in a bag. The assistant believed it was a gun and handed over a thousand pounds in cash. She was terrified, then spoof jokes were popping up all over the place. To the assistant it was anything but a joke.'

'A pretty sick joke. But surely?'

'I'll stop you there. He has an alibi.'

'His mother?'

'Yep. Watching TV for the early part of the night. Curtains open, seen by neighbours.'

'And later?'

'He was at his local, chatting up the barmaid, which landed him in a bit of trouble as her husband was in the darts team.'

'He's clear then.'

'Yeah.' His frustration boiled over. 'So far we've had a spaghetti jar full of leads that's taken us nowhere. If you come up with any suggestions, let me know.'

'I will.'

'Thanks.'

His tone was dry and humourless.

THIRTY-EIGHT

7.45 p.m.

Friday night had come round all too quickly. Grant had texted to say he would be round by eight o'clock and she had some fish in the steamer and a bowl of salad with a bottle of wine chilling. But she was nervous. She sensed that tonight would be a watershed, a point of no return. Once she'd crossed the Rubicon there would be no turning back. Not this time. If she searched her heart, she knew she couldn't commit to the fable, the family relationship he wanted. But neither did she want to let him go.

It wasn't like her to duck an issue. But she couldn't have it both ways.

She was already drinking a glass of wine when she heard the doorbell echo into the hall.

She held the wine in her mouth, tasting the black grape flavour on her tongue before swallowing it. Then she went to answer the door.

He was standing on the doorstep, his grin half anxious, half as warm as the heart that went with it. He was dressed in clean jeans and an open-necked pale blue linen shirt with loafers on his feet and a jacket slung over his shoulders, a bottle of wine in his hand. 'Hi.' He went to kiss her cheek, moving towards her mouth. With difficulty she moved back and sensed his heartbeat but managed a smile.

'Hi,' she returned before adding, 'come in,' while wondering when this awkwardness had grown between them like a mushroom springing up overnight from damp dark soil.

He followed her into the kitchen, making only one comment. 'Aussie boyfriend not here tonight?'

'He's not my . . .' Then she realized he'd only said that to get a rise out of her. He didn't really believe it. 'No. He's out. And anyway, he tends to stay up on the top floor.' Honesty forced her to add, 'Most of the time.' She turned to toss the salad. 'I think he might be getting back with his wife.'

'That's nice.'

She knew he didn't care. He was here on a mission of his own.

'Hmm.' He sat down and plonked a bottle of wine on the table. 'You want to eat first or . . .?'

She had the feeling once they'd spoken she would lose her appetite.

'Let's eat.' Anything to postpone the moment when she knew he would leave.

They ate in silence, only making desultory comments about the food.

Claire could eat only half, though Grant seemed to have his usual healthy appetite.

When he put his knife and fork together she knew she couldn't put this moment off any longer.

Finally, the moment had come. 'Well?'

He knew she was perfectly aware what he wanted just as surely as she knew she could never give it. She shook her head slowly. 'I'm sorry,' she said.

Grant's face sagged. She had dealt him a blow. And the fact that he'd anticipated it made it worse. He grabbed his jacket from the back of the chair. 'That's that then,' he said, looking her straight in the eye. 'I can't say I'm surprised but I hoped, considering everything, that you might have changed your mind.' He paused, maybe to give her a last chance, but she shook her head.

'I'm sorry,' she said again. She'd meant to say so much more, something about loving him always, but she knew it would sound insincere. And it would be. In a relationship she would go so far. And no further. Which wasn't how it should be.

He came towards her and gripped her shoulder. 'You're sure?'

She forced herself to nod.

'OK,' he said in a voice heavy with weariness. 'Well, that's that, I guess. And I should probably tell you now, before you hear it from someone else.

'The voice you heard when you rang. I'm considering expanding my interiors business by going into partnership with someone I know. Her name is Olivia. She sort of deals in antiques and curios, fabrics and such like. We're working on perfecting "a look".' He scratched the words into the air and she knew by the tears that were forming behind her eyelids that this really was the end. 'I had to make sure, you see, Claire. If there was any chance we could be together – on my terms – I would have grabbed at it. Olivia isn't like you. She doesn't have a career that absorbs her life. I'm sorry, Claire,' he said. 'I'm really sorry it's finally ending this way. I'm sorry for what couldn't be. I'm sorry I let you down that time. I had to give it one last chance but you've made your decision.' He grinned at her. 'Your way or the highway.'

Then in sudden frustration, he said, 'Oh, what's the point?' and walked out.

She heard the click of the front door as it closed behind him, the sound of his van backing out of the drive, the sudden acceleration out on to the main road. And then there was silence, leaving her with thoughts slowly forming, misshapen but final. No more on/off boyfriend. No more live in/live out lover. No more push me/pull you.

He was gone.

She was alone and she burst into tears. The end of any love affair is so sad and empty compared to the white-hot passion of its beginning.

She went back into the kitchen and smelled his aftershave – Terre d'Hermès, a smell she breathed in, evoking his presence. But he was gone to this . . . Olivia. She poured herself another glass of wine and stared around the four walls of the kitchen. And the worst thing? She'd known this was coming. She'd anticipated it like the vibrations that travel along a railway track when the train is still miles and miles away. Invisible while making its presence felt.

'You're on your own now, Claire Roget,' she muttered.

'*Made your bed.*' Her mother's voice barked in her ear.

Her next coherent thought was The Wedding. It was three weeks away. And she was going to have to face it alone, wrapped in the cold mantle of loneliness to run the gauntlet of her mother's hostile judgement, that her daughter hadn't even managed to hold on to her boyfriend.

'Shit,' she said and went to bed.

But it was no escape. All around her she sensed space. It felt as empty as a vacuum.

THIRTY-NINE

Saturday 30 April, 7 a.m.

Claire's first thought on waking was regret for having drunk so much wine last night. It hadn't helped.

Her second thought was that this was the last day of April. Tomorrow would be the first of May which would bring her to three short weeks before the wedding.

She almost picked up the phone to ask for a temporary truce, just on that one day. But Grant would have greeted the request with scorn. Once he had made a decision, he did not retract.

The trip to Chester reminded her of that last weekend, the walks along the river, finding the boutique, the laughing, the picnic lunches, the dinners and the nights.

The woman in the shop greeted her as though she was an old friend. 'Boyfriend not with you?'

It would have felt too long and complicated to go into any sort of explanation, so Claire simply said, 'No,' then tried on the outfit to check the alterations were correct, watched her pack it up and headed home.

Sunday found her following her least favourite pursuit – house cleaning. There was no sign of Simon, and the top floor – his bedroom and bathroom – was his responsibility, so she left that, and used up her energy scrubbing out the kitchen cupboards, radio on full blast to boost her efforts.

Monday 1 May, 8.30 a.m.

The week began with a shock and a threat as a new candidate entered the equation.

She was in her office when her phone rang and Rita told her a Lisa Graham wanted to speak to her.

Distracted, the name only rang a bell at first. 'Find out what she wants, what it's concerning.'

Moments later Rita was back. 'She's most insistent she speak to you.' She paused, adding almost in a whisper, 'She mentioned Poppy Kelloway.'

And then Claire remembered. Lisa Graham was the sister of Harry Bloxham, the gas fitter victim of Poppy's lies.

She was on high alert. 'Put her through.'

Moments later her phone clicked. 'Hello, this is Dr Roget. You wanted to speak with me?'

'I do. My name is Lisa Graham. You remember me?'

She recalled the barrage of letters and allegations. Her response was cautious. 'I remember you, Lisa.' She thought it unwise to make reference to her brother. It would probably unleash a further torrent of abuse.

'I heard about your patient. The bitch who caused my brother's death.'

Claire made no comment.

'She got her just deserts in the end.'

'Some might—'

Lisa cut in. 'Someone felt she didn't deserve to live. Someone felt she should be punished. And from what I hear, the punishment fit the crime. There must be a load of people who would have set fire to that wicked liar's pants.'

That shook Claire. How did Lisa know this detail? As far as she knew it had been deliberately held back from the press reports because it could be used to trip up any false confessors.

Claire couldn't work out what the point of this call was. Was it to fish out any details or was it purely to gloat?

Harry Bloxham's sister had been furious at the false allegation which had led to her brother's death. How furious? Had her anger festered into violence?

All along she had assumed Poppy's killer was a man. What if it had been a woman? Could it have been a woman?

'Why are you ringing me, Lisa?'

That upfront question caused the woman to hesitate before she found an answer. 'I just wanted you to acknowledge that justice has been done.'

'This wasn't justice, Lisa. This was murder. Your brother died because of her lies. I acknowledge that. But he killed himself. Someone *murdered* Poppy.'

'Justifiably.' She wasn't backing down.

'How did you make the connection?'

'Oh, you mean the "liar, liar, pants on fire" thing?'

Claire waited.

'It was all over the Internet.'

They'd thought they'd kept it out of the media. Someone must have leaked it, Claire thought, her anger boiling over.

'Goodbye,' she said, and ended the call.

She sat for a while, worrying about this development. Maybe they should look into the vindictive sister's movements on the night that Poppy had died. In the end she rang DS Zed Willard and left a message for him to call her back.

What she didn't say in her message was that he needed to plug the leak. But Lisa's phone call had answered one question which had been bugging her. She now knew how Tre Marshall had learned the words.

FORTY

Tuesday 3 May, 6.15 a.m.

Something had changed deep inside Claire. She knew that as she sat up in bed, drank coffee and faced the day. She felt different. If she'd been forced to find a word for how she felt, that word would have been *freedom*.

He had cut her free. Life was no longer a compromise. It might have stunned her at the time, but now she didn't need to feel guilty or sad. Now she only wanted him to be happy with this Olivia, to have all that life could offer. She wanted him to use his talent combined with her gifts. *You be good to him,* she warned. *Give him all I wouldn't. Or else.*

One day Grant Steadman would have all the love, the partner, the children, everything he'd ever wanted and he would forget about her. But, cliché that it was, she also knew she would always love him. And while she hoped they would remain friends, she knew, realistically, that they wouldn't. He would have too much in his own life.

Be happy, she whispered, and began to plan her day.

She was going to go for an early-bird swim in the pool. At least twenty lengths splashing in an American crawl and as fast as she could go. Then she would head in to Greatbach, sit down and review the list of patients Rita had left whose appointments had coincided with Poppy's again. Just in case there was a link she'd missed. Neither Lynne nor Drake Shute or Robbie could have committed the murder. It must have been someone else. But someone had persuaded all three children to leave their mother alone in the house. Who?

Was it possible the person was one of her patients? She recalled the three children, sitting in a line, obedient and passive. She had cross-checked Poppy's attendances with her other patients, but had not even considered the children.

She fingered the notes still sitting on her desk. And while she didn't approve of offender profiling, there could be clues in a person's deepest psyche that could act as a signpost.

While Detective Sergeant Zed Willard and his team would do the heavy work – check CCTV records, take statements, interview suspects, analyse data, send things in bags to the forensic lab – she would burrow down into the minds of her patients and unearth their innermost secrets, discover if anyone might have hated Poppy Kelloway so much they had planned, even revelled in, watching her 'pay' for her lies.

It still troubled her that the details of Poppy's murder had been leaked, but that was a police matter. For her part she could not ignore Lisa Graham's triumphant phone call. She would have been delighted enough to want to drag Greatbach and its staff in.

Swimming up and down a lane in the pool is a perfect way to focus the mind.

For the first few lengths, once she'd acclimatized to the pool temperature and settled into a steady rhythm, another image haunted her. More personal. Walking up the aisle – alone – running the gauntlet of her mother's gaze as critical as Fangsu Cheung's when she'd watched Dana's attempt to mother Lily Rose.

The first part of her plan worked well. She swam fast enough to make herself breathless and her arms and legs ache while her waist felt taut, strong, ready for action. But when she'd towelled herself and her newly streaked hair was almost dry she couldn't resist checking her phone. Nothing.

What did you expect? she said to herself angrily. It was final. That weekend in Chester had been their last tango.

He'd made that clear. She realized he'd been working up to it. Grant came to decisions slowly, pedalling towards them using logic and anticipating consequences. It had probably taken him months to arrive at this decision, all the while this unknown woman had been sidling in close and intimate. Filling the gap she had left. She gave herself another lecture, borrowing a well-known phrase from her mother: '*So get used to it.*'

As she drove to the clinic she continued the conversation with herself, agreeing with her friends' comments. *You can't keep him in the wings to be trotted out when you have an evening spare or need a significant other for a formal occasion. Be honest with yourself, Claire, that was what you did. Used him as a puppet to be taken out of his box when you wanted to play with him.*

It really wasn't a nice thought. She didn't like this image of herself.

And as she parked up, her thoughts turned to deeper analysis. Why did she shy away from commitment? Why did she not want a steady partner, a family? It wasn't to do with Grant. There was some inner explanation. She'd thought she'd supplied enough answers: his mother's dependence, his silent abandonment of her when his sister had been dying, her career, but all of a sudden she wasn't so sure.

FORTY-ONE

Tuesday 3 May, 9.15 a.m.

The pile of notes Rita had left on Claire's desk was still high enough to almost topple to the floor. But then Poppy had been attending clinic for a little over five years. There were bound to have been many encounters between her and other patients and she had no record or precise memory of the times her children had attended with her. Claire had no pressing engagements this morning. Dana had now been safely transferred to the mother and baby unit, and Simon and Salena could deal with the wards and any emergencies that cropped up. If they had anything they couldn't handle they'd soon ring her. In the meantime, she set her mind to sifting through the other patients.

Her hand hovered with regret over Tre Marshall's notes, the word DECEASED now written with a thick permanent marker. No doubt she would be asked to write a report for the coroner on his death. She'd have to attend the coroner's court in person to make a statement. She started composing a description of his diagnosis and previously stable condition. Maybe the information leaked about Poppy's death had triggered his deterioration. Tre could perceive all sorts of links between him and random events. And it was perfectly possible he'd not meant to kill himself but simply to calm himself by watching the trains. He'd been there before. For him it was a place of tranquillity. The fall *could* have been an accident. Then she sat up, questions burrowing through her mind, that one phrase that she found so disturbing. *What is truth?* The same phrase which had been in the anonymous note under her door. One which seemed to question the judgement on Poppy Kelloway's lies.

Nipping at the heels of these two thoughts was another one. If Tre Marshall had climbed on to the railway bridge without meaning to commit suicide, was it possible that someone had pushed him?

She was opening the first set of notes when her mobile phone tinkled out a tune. This time she did recognize the name and number.

'Zed?'

'Yeah.'

'You know someone has leaked the details of Poppy's death on to the Internet?'

'How do you know?'

'Come on,' she said. 'If it's on the Internet, *everyone* knows.'

'We're dealing with it.'

'Good. I want to ask you something else.'

'Tre Marshall?' he guessed.

'Yeah.'

'Why? It was a suicide, surely?'

'Is there CCTV at the station?'

'Some. Why?'

'Was he alone?'

'Yeah.'

'It's not possible someone pushed him?'

'No. He was on his own. Not sure how this reflects on Greatbach, but it was a suicide. Possibly a slip.' He was responding as carefully as if he was giving evidence in a court of law. But it heartened her.

'There's something else.' And she told him about Lisa Graham's phone call. His response was a stunned silence. Then she heard him draw in a deep breath. 'What are you suggesting?' There was a note of caution in his voice.

'Maybe you should look into her.'

'We already considered her,' he said slowly. 'But . . .' And there he stopped.

'Any luck on the DNA?'

'Not so far. We've involved Interpol.'

'You think it was someone . . .?'

'Brought in for the purpose.'

'So not one of my patients.'

'It's still possible. If it was a contract killing, someone here was involved. And we're chasing up your child psychiatrist. Something in all three of the children's statements isn't adding up.'

She took a deep breath. 'As in . . .?'

'If it was their mother who persuaded them to go out that night, then Poppy was the instigator.'

He was getting there but trailing behind her and Saul's conclusions.

'You had Poppy's mobile phone and computer. Did you find her dating sites, her emails? Other contacts? People at work?'

'Most of the stuff had been wiped.'

'When?'

'A day or two before her death. There was nothing older than two days.'

He gave a sharp little bark of a laugh. 'I'd have a hand on a collar by now if your patient had left a vapour trail, but she didn't, Claire. Her computer was wiped. Her bank statements prove the fact that she was on dating sites but there's no details. Her finances were healthy. She lived well within her means.'

Claire had a cold feeling as she stepped outside her comfort zone. 'Zed,' she said slowly, 'have you considered the boys' statements might not be the truth?'

By his silence she realized he had. 'But the little girl was away for the night too.'

Now they were both silent, each reluctant to take the next step.

'You really think . . .?'

She forced herself to say it, to keep her voice steady. 'We think it's something that should be considered.'

'Wow.' She could almost hear his brain cranking. 'You've discussed this with the psychiatrist?'

'Yes, I have.'

'He hasn't said any of this to us.'

'I thought it was too soon. He needs more time with Poppy's children. He can't just leak out theories.'

'I suppose not. But you think we should consider them suspects?' He was digging blind. 'Working together?' Disbelief made his voice almost shrill.

'Keep it at the back of your mind for now, Zed.' She hesitated. 'Along with these so-called boyfriends.'

'If the boys – and their sister,' the words were almost choking out of him, 'were colluding, then it's possible there was no boyfriend.' He too was flapping about in the breeze.

He was defensive now, as confused and frustrated by Poppy's pointless lies as she had been for the past five years.

'Her murder was real enough,' she reminded him.

'OK.' He sounded weary now. 'So what are you up to today?'

'Going back to the notes, seeing if I have a patient who could have bumped into Poppy and her family here and whose psychiatric profile fits with that of a killer.'

'Thanks, Claire.'

'Poppy obviously really pissed someone off, someone who feels very bitter and angry with her. The pants thing would make me believe the reason behind the assault was a lie that damaged someone. But it might not be. It could be a deliberate diversion sending us on the wrong track. There are plenty of reasons why she might have provoked someone. Not just by lying. Lisa's brother's suicide is one of the more extreme examples. Poppy could be sharply cruel in other ways. She damaged her children by lies primarily about their father and his so-called refusal to see them. I'm calling in patients who might have resented her. But it's not a complete list. And it doesn't necessarily have to be one of my patients. It might not have anything to do with Greatbach.'

'But the torn appointment card,' he reminded her.

She'd thought of something else. They needed to find any flaw in the boys' statements. 'Zed,' she responded with sudden urgency, 'just run through the timeline with me.'

'I thought you knew it off by heart.'

She waited. 'Boys home around one a.m. Five minutes later they make the call. The forensic medical examiner saw her at a little after one and put the time of death at somewhere between ten and eleven. And the Four Crosses have CCTV?'

'We've been there. It's pretty hopeless. I couldn't identify my own brother on it. It's fuzzy and dark and most of the kids have their head down. We can take another look but it isn't conclusive.'

Hating herself, she added, 'Maybe check on the friend Holly-Anne was with too.'

'You really think this is a kids' thing?' He sounded disbelieving and Claire could only hope he was right.

FORTY-TWO

The call had ended but it had left Claire feeling uneasy. Images haunted her as though the fallout from Poppy's murder was creeping nearer. The images were graphic: Poppy's body burning, her hands desperately grabbing at her pants, trying to tear away the substance that was burning into her flesh. Tre hovering over the bridge, his thoughts like black demons drawing him down, a hand on his back pressing him forward. Ranucci with his cocky dismissal of Poppy's advances. The two teenage boys, giving their versions of events. Drake Shute, the children's uncle, waving a banana in a bag in the face of a terrified assistant who was convinced it was a loaded gun. Robbie Kelloway with his confident and clear but uncompromising judgement over his wife. Holly-Anne, bare-faced and unashamed as she spoke her childishly naive lies, already hinting that one day it would mature into a talent as damaging and dangerous as her mother's. Finally, Lynne's firm judgement that her grand-children would be better off living with her.

So much illusion that threatened to stick. But at least the images obliterated all thoughts of Grant and the ordeal that soon faced her – attending her half-brother's wedding with an empty space at her side.

8.30 p.m.

It was getting late by the time Claire left work and the sky threatened thunder, with black clouds racing towards her. In a minute the heavens would open and she would be soaked in her thin sweater and trousers. She had not thought to bring a mac that morning. And it was a ten-minute run to her car which was parked at the far end of the car park. She stood, rooted, preparing to run. And then, simultaneously, two things happened. There was a crack of thunder and she felt a hand on her shoulder. 'What are you thinking of? You'll get soaked.'

She stood, motionless. The crack of thunder had seemed as biblical a judgement as Pilate's phrase, which still haunted her. She had looked up the phrase online: *Truth is what you think is true*.

But that wasn't right. Illusion is not truth.

'Do you *want* to get wet?' Saul wasn't giving up but was watching her with concern which he tried to turn into a joke. 'Are you trying to find out if your clothes are properly waterproof? Or is it in your mind to catch pneumonia?'

He was part laughing and part serious.

And she couldn't explain except for a rather pathetic, 'I don't know. Caught in the moment maybe. Lost in thought.'

Then the storm really did break, rain gushing down the drainpipes together with lightning illuminating the entire vision in black and white. It made Greatbach look like a Victorian mental hospital haunted by ghosts and ghouls, nightmarish enough for a horror movie. They dashed for the archway.

'You must think I'm an idiot.'

Saul Magnusson shook his head. 'No. Sometimes it is good to observe the weather even though I wouldn't mind if it went a whole day without raining.'

She laughed. 'In Stoke?'

He laughed too then she turned, meaning to head to her car in a break in the rain.

But she stopped and turned to look at him, simultaneously sensing his awkwardness and realizing how very little she knew about him. Nothing about his personal life. And then she felt guilty. She'd never asked. He'd been appointed on the strength of his excellent work with traumatized children all over the world. But once he'd been appointed, apart from the curry they'd shared with Simon, she'd made no real effort to make him feel at home. She simply didn't know him, didn't even know where he lived, whether he had a partner, children of his own, anything.

She would make amends. 'Saul,' she said, 'are you busy right now?'

'Now?' He looked surprised. 'You mean now? This moment?'

'Yeah.' She was already beginning to regret her forwardness and wished she could retrieve her words. Particularly as he was frowning at her, confused and a little embarrassed.

'No. I am not busy.'

He seemed to be waiting for her next move, his head on one side, his expression questioning.

'We could perhaps go for a drink or something?' She felt she had to justify the invitation. 'I wouldn't mind hearing a bit more about your impression of Poppy's children.'

'Ah.' His face cleared and she realized he'd worried why she was being so friendly. The thought quickly followed that this was a man who'd deliberately built walls around himself, fending off any intrusion. He valued and protected his privacy. Now he had an explanation for her invitation, he was visibly relaxing, his face creasing into a lopsided grin. 'Lead on,' he said. 'But I don't know any wine bars around here.'

'I do. You can follow me.'

He climbed into his battered Fiat, folding his long limbs behind the steering wheel into a car which looked far too small for him, and followed her.

When they arrived at the wine bar he waited, politely, for her to enter first, holding the door open with one long arm. When they'd sat down and each had a drink – she a wine spritzer, he a beer – he looked at her and began with a compliment. 'I really do like your new hair.'

She touched it self-consciously. 'It was a friend who suggested it.'

'Your boyfriend?'

'No. A female friend. Anyway, he's not my boyfriend anymore.'

He studied her face. 'And is that sad?'

'A mixture.' She puffed out a long sigh. 'He wanted something . . . different.'

'As in?'

'The whole thing: marriage, kids, everything.'

'And you don't?'

'I think it would prove restrictive. It would descend into endless carping and quibbling.'

'Don't all marriages?'

She looked at him sharply. She hadn't expected such cynicism from him. It showed another side to his character. She went on to explain a little bit about Grant's business and the fact that he'd recently teamed up with an antiques dealer. 'And it seems like . . .' She found she couldn't go on, the words turning unexpectedly sour in her mouth.

'So is he still going with you to your brother's wedding?'

'I didn't realize you knew about that.'

'I've heard you mention it to Simon.'

That drew another sigh. 'I guess not. I can hardly rent him for the day.'

'No.' He waited for a minute before giving a rueful smile. 'On your own then.'

'I guess so. Nothing sadder, is there, than going to a wedding on your own.' She drew her shoulders up. 'Anyway,' she said brightly, anxious to divert the subject, 'that isn't what we're doing here, is it?'

'No. You want to know a bit more about Poppy Kelloway's three children.'

'Is it really possible they were involved . . .?' She couldn't complete the sentence.

For a moment Saul Magnusson looked far away and sad. 'I'm afraid when it comes to children, almost anything is possible. I have seen . . .' He sighed. 'Too much to trust that a child's body does not always translate to a child's mind. Not as we in the West understand them.'

She took a long sip of her drink then set the glass firmly down on the table. 'So what about them?'

'You should probably remember that all three of them have been brought up in an . . . unusual way. To believe it is clever to tell a lie.'

She nodded.

'Also,' he continued, 'contact with their father has been deceitful. Your patient discouraged it. Worse, she tried to tell them that their father did not want to see them.' He drew in a breath. 'That is quite cruel. If they found out the truth, they would have been very, very angry.'

'How might they have found out their father did really care about them?'

He looked at her. 'You say their father has been in touch with Poppy's mother.'

It was enough.

His eyes were serious. 'I have not seen her. At least not without her children present. I certainly have not been in a position to question her. When the children are with me she stays carefully silent. Maybe through manners. Perhaps because she does not want to influence them. But she sits there, listening to their stories.'

She picked up on the word. 'Stories as in lies?'

'Who knows?'

Again, she picked up on a word. 'What do they know, Saul?'

'Much more than they're telling.' He was curious now. 'But you met them before.'

'Only a few times . . .' She was thoughtful. 'And that was when Poppy had an appointment with me. They just sat outside, quiet and obedient. Compliant,' she added after a moment's thought. 'I think they were in fear of their mother.'

'Tommy is the ringleader. Where he led his brother and sister followed. He's old enough to understand his mother and see through her lies. All those fantasies, stories about being kidnapped, rich boyfriends, expensive jewellery she'd been given. But there was one lie he could not forgive.'

'His dad.'

'So, I would suggest that the police look again at Mr Kelloway. Maybe not him personally, but look into any contacts he might have with the criminal world.'

Then Claire held up a hand. 'I've thought of something else.'

Saul looked questioningly at her.

'She was always saying she was hard up. But I remember seeing her wearing an expensive watch one day,' she said slowly.

'There are some very good fakes out there.' His voice was gentle and held a hint of mockery.

'I know. And I'm no expert. But I can ask Zed.'

'Zed?'

'Detective Sergeant Zed Willard. He's in charge of the investigation into Poppy's murder. He'll know whether any expensive stuff has been found at the house.'

Saul shrugged. 'Even if he does, it doesn't prove anything.'

'But maybe it does, in an indirect way. She always claimed she was short of money. She wouldn't have had enough to buy herself designer stuff. Not unless she had another source of income.'

'Like . . .?'

'Well, Robbie or a boyfriend, someone or something else.'

'Something else? You mean blackmail?'

'I don't know,' she said, suddenly tired.

He was watching her. 'I fear young Tommy has carried the burden of his mother's deceit. Resentment which has built up into adulthood.'

She didn't want to ask the question but it came out anyway. 'Did he kill his mother?'

'Had the torture not happened I might have thought it was possible in a fit of anger. But I had a copy of Mrs Kelloway's post-mortem. That boy did not slit his mother's throat.'

'How can you be so sure?'

'He has not had the necessary conditioning. Claire,' he said gently. 'I'm thinking about boy – and girl – soldiers who have watched brutal killings – often of their own family members – almost from birth. They've watched their peer group, their friends, commit murder. That is the mindset that produces a child able to torture and murder their own mother.'

He continued, 'And besides, he would have had to convince his brother. If Tommy colluded then so did Neil. And Holly-Anne.'

The thought of all three children being involved in their mother's hideous murder was still too abhorrent for Claire to imagine. But looking into Saul's face she realized he had already jumped over this particular chasm.

She picked up on something, an evasive twitch at the corner of his mouth. Something had triggered a memory and he was wondering whether to share it with her. She waited, giving him an opportunity, and when he didn't respond she prompted him. 'Saul?'

Surprisingly, he reached across the table to touch her hand.

'Don't spare me,' she said.

He leaned across, his beer glass in his hand. 'When I was in the DRC,' he began, while she processed DRC into Democratic Republic of Congo, 'I was sent to a village where they had an outbreak of cholera. When I got there, I found there had been some crimes committed and many people had abandoned their homes.' His eyes flickered, their clarity replaced by something else for a moment. 'There was a boy there. He was young. About ten but he looked older. I questioned him about where everyone was. He told me they had left because of the cholera. But I didn't believe him.'

'Why not? It seems a logical step if their water was polluted.'

'That wasn't it. I couldn't understand why he, alone, had stayed. The boy had a tic . . .' Saul reached out and touched the corner of her eye. 'Just there. There was nothing he could do about it, but he was frightened I would find something out that he didn't want me to know. And that translated into this tiny tic whenever he crossed over from the truth to lies.'

'Like Tommy's twitching.'

'Exactly. And Neil digs his fingers into his palm. Only Holly-Anne has no "tell".' He shrugged. 'Maybe it's because she is too young, or maybe she shares her mother's talents. Anyway, returning to the Congolese boy, I gradually pieced together his story.'

She wanted to know and yet she didn't. And Saul spared her. 'I won't go into the events that this boy had caused but believe me, he was a killer. Not only that but he was a liar too. And those lies had consequences.'

'Like Poppy's,' she murmured.

'Yes. This boy's lies had led to suspicion between the villagers and ultimately that had led to bloodshed. We found a cache of weapons, stolen goods, but worst of all was his pollution of the river which was their only source of water. He had left the carcass of a goat he'd slaughtered upriver as well as leaving some other animal faeces. The people left believing there was bad *juju* in the village. And he ended up with all the possessions the villagers could not carry. He alone had spread all that fear.'

'What did you do?'

Saul leaned back in his chair, surveying her with some amusement and some curiosity. 'What did I do? Tell me, Claire, what would you have done?'

'Taken him to the authorities.'

'Where he would have been beaten to death.'

She was silent. She didn't understand the law and rules of this country.

'I spoke to him and then I left.'

'Before . . .?'

He shrugged. 'I cannot be judge, jury and executioner.'

She was silent with no words left to say.

'I told you that story to illustrate what children can be capable of, particularly when their upbringing has been damaged.'

And now she wondered what life experience had sent Saul to the troubled areas of the world. His blue eyes locked into hers but she found no answer there. Instead, he nodded and moved on. 'Neil is a nice boy with, I imagine, his mother's easy charm?'

'Yes.' And it was true. Poppy had had an 'easy charm' about her.
'And Holly-Anne?'

He didn't answer her comment directly but mused, 'It is a burden,
isn't it? Two older brothers. A mother who dances around the truth.
This little girl was always walking across the shifting sands between
fact and fiction. So she made up her own rules to deal with life.'

Claire was silent for a moment. And then she asked a question
she'd never really considered. 'Did they love their mother?'

Again, that penetrating gaze of those icy-blue eyes that seemed
to bore into her soul. 'Did you?' He asked the question so quietly
she could almost have thought it had come from inside her
head. She tried to shake it away as Saul Magnusson watched her.

'I am sorry,' he said. 'I am stepping on your toes. Yes?'

'Sort of. Saul . . .' She changed the subject quickly. 'What really
happened that evening?'

'This is the boys' story,' he reminded her. 'She is not around to
either confirm or refute it.'

'Are you seeing them again?'

'Oh yes. I still have work to do.'

They were both silent until she insisted. 'But whether she was
expecting them or not, she must have allowed the boys to go out
as well as Holly-Anne going to stay with a friend. Someone *was*
there and they tortured and killed her.'

He put a large hand on her arm. 'It is for the police to work on.
Not you, Claire. And not really me. All we can do is pass on our
insight.'

'I can't help but wonder.'

'I understand that. And I also understand you feel some . . .
responsibility. That is right, isn't it?'

She shrugged. 'Understandably.'

'No. I disagree. Your job is not to anticipate when a patient's
actions resulted in their death.'

'But if her killer was another of my patients . . .'

'I can see why you might think that. Damaged souls sitting side
by side in a waiting room. It is, possibly, a point worth considering.
When Poppy was in with you, I presume her children would have
stayed outside – on their own.'

She nodded. 'That thought crossed my mind too.'

FORTY-THREE

I t was a warm day and only a couple of weeks before the dreaded
wedding. She had heard nothing from Grant. Not a phone call,
a text or an email. Nothing, which had left an unexpectedly large
void in her life.

So, what did you expect? She lectured herself. *That he would
come crawling back? Not going to happen. Not ever.*

But, like many couples/friends they had had almost a running
commentary on each other's days – except for that great big six-
month hole when his sister had been dying. Now she felt the silence
acutely and checked her phone many times a day feeling empty
disappointment at the blank screen. She had to face it. He had gone.

And it hurt. She was surprised at how much it did hurt. It was
as though some of the joy had been sucked out of her life. No one
to share good or bad things with.

It did not matter how many times she told herself to get used to
it, the fact was she was struggling. Clinics, ward rounds, consultations all seemed to hold a mundane sameness, grey and colourless.
And the impending wedding made it worse. So a phone call from
Detective Sergeant Zed Willard was a welcome punch away of the
clouds which covered the sun. And she could hear the warmth and
welcome in her voice as she spoke to him, the tone an octave higher.

'Zed. Nice to hear from you.'

He was taken aback. 'Didn't quite expect *that* much enthusiasm.'

'How is the case coming along?'

'Slowly.' His voice was guarded and she knew he was holding
something back. To fill the silence, she asked her question. 'One time
when Poppy attended clinic I think she was wearing an expensive
watch – unless it was a fake,' she finished.

'It wasn't,' he said grudgingly. 'It was the real McCoy. A Rolex
lady's watch, according to our research. Worth around two grand.'

She'd known there was more to this. 'Zed, she was a school
secretary, bringing up three children alone,' she pointed out. 'Where

would she have found two thousand pounds for a watch? She barely had the money to afford school dinners. So she said,' she finished miserably. This habit of Poppy's throwing obstacles even in the investigation of her murder was discombobulating.

'We're working on it,' he said testily.

She felt chastened.

And then he got to the reason behind his call. 'Do you know a man called Cornelius Rotherham?'

'Yes.' She couldn't hide her surprise. Professor Rotherham was the last person she'd expected him to mention. 'Why?'

'Tell me about him.'

'He's a slightly eccentric academic.'

'He's a strange one, then?'

She felt like saying: *All my patients are strange in one way or another, but doesn't that include almost the entire population? Isn't that what makes us unique, each in our own, very individual way?*

What she actually said was, 'Some of my patients are. It's the ones who appear normal who are the worry. So what's your point, Zed? Why are you asking about Professor Rotherham specifically?' At the same time, she was aware that the situation between them was deteriorating into confrontation, a battle between her profession and his duty.

'Well, this man, this Professor Rotherham, appears to have had some . . .' She was aware he was choosing his words with huge care, dancing on tiptoes between words. 'He appears to have had some . . . dealings with your patient.'

'Poppy? That seems very unlikely to me. What sort of dealings?' She felt outrage and sympathy as well as an instinct to protect this highly intelligent, eccentric PhD from Cambridge, retired because of his OCD affliction when he had started to refuse to stand in the class-room with his students in case they spread disease. The impact of the Covid-19 pandemic on Professor Rotherham had been profound.

'She was seen going to his flat.'

'Wha-at?' She couldn't have been more astonished. She knew about the flat, the ground floor of a Victorian house in the Westlands, constantly scrubbed and disinfected. Teresa Coren had attempted to visit, just to check on his home circumstances, and had been stopped at the threshold, given a mask and gloves, a paper forensic overall and overshoes. The place had stunk of disinfectant and it had been obvious he'd been uncomfortable right through her ten-minute visit. The thought of Poppy visiting his apartment didn't make any sense.

He had told her on more than one occasion that he liked to keep himself to himself. He was one of life's loners.

She needed to pick the obvious hole in this story. 'Who saw her?'

'A neighbour.'

'Which neighbour?' The question was pretty pointless as, fairly obviously, she didn't actually know *any* of Professor Rotherham's neighbours.

'The phone call was anonymous.'

'I see.'

And she did. This version failed to convince her.

'Male or female?'

'Sorry?'

'Was it a man or a woman?' She knew she was sounding waspish but she needed to follow this particular story right down to the bottom of the rabbit hole.

'*I* didn't take the call,' he said, sounding equally waspish – if not more so.

'So have your officers tracked down the "neighbour" who dished out this story?'

'Not – so – far.'

She felt angry then on behalf of this tortured academic picked out because he was 'different', and unable to defend himself.

'We'll be searching his flat.'

Policemen tramping through his precious, protected space? It would be torture.

'Do you want someone from the Community Mental Health Team to be there?' she asked.

'Thank you, but no.'

'Be careful,' she advised. 'Be respectful. He will find any intrusion into his private domain very stressful and difficult.' She knew she had to tell him then. 'He has OCD, Zed.'

'Aaah.' The long *aaah* told her he understood. 'I'll tell the officers. They'll be wearing white suits, masks, overshoes. The lot,' he promised.

And that was all she could expect. If the police had a lead that pointed towards the professor, they had no option but to follow it. But thinking about the effect this invasion would have on her patient, she heaved out a long sigh. He would feel . . . persecuted.

Her voice was chilly at the next sentence. 'Do you have anyone else in your sights?'

'Someone called Ryder – John Ryder.'

Another all too familiar name.

She thought about Ryder. He was bitter and angry – and like many people whose fortunes have had a sharp downturn, he failed to see his own role in this. None of it was his fault. His ex-wife was a 'bitch', his child's mind being poisoned against him. His bitterness shone out of him as a red, warning light.

And then there had been that knife assault against his ex-wife.

But she then remembered Poppy's words. *He's a right weird one.*

'She did know him, Zed, but she recognized the dangers of him.'

'He has a history of a knife threat.'

'Against his ex-wife whom he blamed for all his problems – rather than himself.'

But while she couldn't see Ryder and Poppy forming any sort of relationship, she *could* imagine him being angry enough to have poured caustic soda over her knickers, watch her desperately try to peel them off, which only spread it on to her hands, increasing the torture. Only then would he have killed her. John Ryder's fury would easily have reached boiling point. It was never far off that anyway. The question was why? And if this was the true version, it reverted to the original theory that Poppy had been the one to organize all three children to be out that night. Unless the three children – or maybe just Tommy – had colluded with him.

Zed Willard was waiting for her to comment. When she didn't, he gave her one more name. And it was the one name she had been hoping she wouldn't hear.

'Italian guy,' he said. 'Tony Ranucci.'

'What do you want to know?'

His voice was gentler now, friendlier, almost conciliatory. 'We don't need your professional insight right now. But if we can build a case and bring it to court, we might need a psychiatric assessment. Otherwise you could well be off the hook.'

She sensed he was smiling as they ended the call.

But off the hook wasn't really where she wanted to be or where she belonged. She was at the centre of this. He had tossed the names of three of her patients into the ring – two of whom were already on her own list – and left her to ponder them some more. Surely Poppy had not visited the professor at his home? If she had, her price might well have been a Rolex watch. Had she missed some vital ingredient in his mental make-up? She felt frustrated, this time with herself, for her inability to find Poppy's killer through psychi-atric analysis. She had the facts; she had her own professional experience. She knew these people as well as the victim. It was quite possible that she knew the killer – even intimately. But she was failing to slot them together.

DS Willard could do the scientific stuff, tie up forensic evidence, the so-far unidentified DNA and the court case, but her interest was exploring the trigger factors and mindset behind her patient's death. There was mockery as well as cruelty. And to understand that she would need to drill back down into Poppy's lies. It would be a learning curve, but one she could use in the future as an alert to future homicidal tendencies. And she had the feeling that DS Willard had missed the most significant names off the list.

She considered reminding him of it, but perhaps Zed would think the worst – that she was deliberately diverting suspicion away from her patients. She knew what they needed – the truth from the boys. In other words, a confession. Zed wouldn't take Saul's theory seriously otherwise.

But she did have a plan – and a list. As well as an idea. And she had also decided to ask Simon if he would accompany her to Adam and Adele's wedding.

Coward that she was, she couldn't face going alone.

FORTY-FOUR

9 p.m.

Claire was sitting alone in an empty house when her mobile tinkled out a Michael Bublé tune, her latest download.

Something about not having met someone yet. Very appropriate, she thought wryly, and, recognizing the number, she answered the call.

'God, Sis, I'm getting really nervous now.'

'Bit late for that.' She was smiling and she knew he'd hear it in her voice.

'Every time the subject comes up there seems to be some new

detail, something else they haven't thought of. Claire, what the fuck are fascinators?'

'A couple of feathers or something. Women wear them these days instead of hats.'

'Oh – is that all?'

'That's all.' She chuckled. 'You sound disappointed.'

'I was getting worried. I thought . . . Never mind what I thought.'

She was laughing so hard she almost didn't pick up on his follow-up.

'And favours?' She could picture his brow, wrinkled up, worrying over yet another detail.

'Just a little gift to put at the side of guests' place settings.'

'Oh.'

'Adam . . .' She tried to reassure him. 'You're just having typical pre-wedding nerves. That's all. It'll be all right on the day. Everything will work out fine. You and Adele really love each other. That's all that matters.' She felt a twinge of envy. She and Grant hadn't loved each other – enough. 'Enjoy the wedding. And you do have the honeymoon to look forward to. Just the two of you.'

'Mmm.' His mood wasn't lightening. 'Anyway. You and Grant will be there.'

'Umm.'

While she felt guilty for adding to his concerns, she knew he was going to have to know the truth at some point. Preferably before the wedding day.

And, typical Adam, his concerns shifted immediately. 'Oh, Sis, I'm so sorry. What an awful time for you to break up.'

'Yeah. Timing's not great.' She heard the hardness in her voice, something gritty and brittle, at the same time tough and repellent. Maybe he heard it too.

'So, what you going to do?' He paused. 'Come on your own?'

'I thought I'd ask one of my colleagues to come with me.'

'Gre-eat.' She heard false enthusiasm combined with uphill encouragement. Like pushing a wheelchair up a steep incline.

Yeah, she thought. *Great except I haven't actually asked him yet.*

He echoed his earlier words. 'Shitty time to break up.'

And for the first time in years she felt indignant. She wanted to say: *Everyone's lives don't simply revolve round your and Adele's wedding.* She swallowed the mean thought and picked up on him.

'Sorted your suit out yet?' She knew the answer – he'd got it weeks ago – but at least it moved the conversation on. They talked for a few more minutes and she sensed that her half-brother was relaxing, moving away from his petty concerns and sounding happier. After a while, as the conversation became desultory with brief silences, they said their goodbyes and ended the call.

Which was when she heard Simon sneak in, quietly, softly surreptitious, moving like a pantomime cat burglar on tiptoes across the hallway which, like many homes in the Potteries and elsewhere, was paved with encaustic Minton tiles so the sound of even stockinged feet was audible. Then he barged into the umbrella stand and cursed. At which point she stood up and opened the door. A bit surprised to read a look of guilt on his face. 'Where have you been?'

'Ah.' He started to say, 'Nowhere,' but something stopped him. Maybe, unlike Poppy Kelloway, he was not a habitual or a natural liar. 'I sort of met up with . . .' Another pause, during which his face turned beetroot red. 'Teresa,' he confessed and all was revealed, but it introduced a problem for her. Teresa Coren was quite attractive, with a nicely rounded figure and – as far as Claire knew – she was single.

Simon's colour deepened. 'We've been seeing each other for a couple of months now. Just as friends. You know – confidants.' He was waiting for her to make some comment, she realized.

The one she managed was limp, to say the least. 'That's nice.'

Simon looked relieved. 'Yeah.'

But at the back of her mind, sweeping aside her own naturally selfish response, she did want to point out that he and his wife, Marianne, had been separated for less than a year since he had left her to work in England. Also that he'd said she was having therapy. Surely that held out some hope for a future together? Or was she doing her usual – failing to see when relationships had ended? They didn't hang on forever.

But her mind was focused on something else, returning to the vision of herself attending the wedding on her own. The field had narrowed – or rather emptied, since she hadn't had a back-up plan. Her next thought was *thank goodness she hadn't named a plus one to her brother*. Did she dare ask Saul Magnusson when she had no idea whether he was married or single, or in a relationship, or even whether he was straight or gay, never mind anything else about him? Embarrassment and humiliation loomed. Now if she did ask Simon to accompany her to the wedding, Teresa would, quite definitely, interpret it as her making a play for him. She felt her own colour rise as she said again, 'That's nice,' before returning to her sitting room and closing the door behind her.

Nothing rubs in one's single state more than seeing everyone around you paired up. She was even tempted, again, to ring Grant and ask him if he would do this one thing for her. One – last – thing. But now pride stepped in, barring her way. She couldn't do it.

And Zed had dumped those names at her door, leaving her to winkle out the truth.

FORTY-FIVE

Thursday 5 May, 10 a.m.

Claire spent the following morning wondering how best she could find some information which would help find Poppy's killer, recognizing at the same time that 'help' wouldn't be enough. Neither would 'pointing the police in the right direction'. They needed proof. Hard evidence. And that was something she probably wouldn't be able to give. Unless one of her patients confessed and then repeated that confession to the police. Had she moved on from her suspicions of the boys? No. She still believed they were lying, but she did not credit them with matricide, particularly when it included torture.

Tackle your problems one by one, her grandmother used to say. And so she would.

There was one image she could erase: that of her mother's lips pursed with disapproval when she noted her daughter, who was a constant thorn in her side, entering the church alone, sitting in a pew with an empty space next to her, taking her seat at the reception, the *Claire's partner* or, worse, *Grant Steadman* card in front of an empty chair. She would meet her mother's eyes and read their verdict. Stripes in her hair, fancy silk outfit. All to no avail. *I knew you weren't worth anything and now he thinks so too.*

The look of shared sympathy from her two aunts whose marriages had both catastrophically broken down. No one there from her father's side, of course. Her father. She allowed herself a brief thought. What had he been like, this Monsieur Roget, who had cared nothing for his daughter? If he had bolted because his wife was, as he might have seen it, mad, why had his abandonment been so complete? Or was there a different story? Had her mother acted in the same way as Poppy had and denied him access as a form of punishment to both?

I will find out, she vowed.

But by Thursday afternoon she had stopped feeling sorry for herself. She'd tried on her outfit and given herself a confident little grin; she could brave this one out. In the end, she thought, it was she who had dumped Grant. Not the other way round. So she turned her mind around, as slowly but surely as a juggernaut.

She still believed she had the key to Poppy's killer. She had the facts; she had the insight. It was up to her to use the talents she had. Face-to-face she would be able to trip up the killer, make her own mind up on the damaged psyche they might be trying their best to conceal, gauge their response to questions. If she asked the 'right' questions. In that way the police would always lag behind her.

She listed their attributes.

The person had ego. They harboured hatred. If she had been forced to bet which of her patients was most likely to carry out a savage, vindictive murder, she would have formed a list, and put Ranucci right at the top.

But it didn't quite fit. Ranucci had some of the ingredients, but not all. He could have committed the knife attack. But the corrosive gel? That wasn't his style.

And then there was Professor Rotherham. She didn't believe in this anonymous phone call about a blonde female visitor. Someone had been trying to focus the police's investigation on him. But there was something DS Willard didn't know that she did: his obsession with the classics, in particular the specific punishments inflicted by the Gods.

But she could see no connection except the coincidence of shared appointment days. She shook her head. Poppy would have given him a wide berth.

There were some concerns about the professor. However, his career had not been destroyed by one of Poppy's selected lies but by his sickness. She remembered him telling her once, his face stricken pale, that he could actually *see* bacteria crawling, proliferating in milliseconds until they covered an entire surface. And viruses. The Covid-19 epidemic had not only been torture for him, it had also worsened his condition. She had doubled his dose of anxiolytics but it had hardly kept him out of long-term supervision. He had teetered on the edge ever since. It wouldn't have taken more than a puff of a breeze to blow him right over.

Her thoughts were interrupted by her phone. And the number was Detective Sergeant Zed Willard.

Again?

'Hi.' He sounded jaunty.

She greeted him with caution. 'Hello.'

'We've got a suspect – or at least we're . . .' He corrected that to the truth: 'We're questioning someone.'

'Who?' Her eyes drifted across the piece of paper where she been drafting her list of patients, one question in her mind. Which one?

She felt she quickly had to add in a reassurance: 'I'll obviously keep it to myself.'

'His name is Peter.' He was still sounding jaunty. 'He was a maths teacher who worked at the school Poppy worked at before she started at Highfields.'

Her first thought was relief. *Not one of my patients.* But it was quickly followed by a sense of guilt. She'd let her attention be focused on them initially before considering anyone else. The term *under a psychiatrist* blanketed any unusual, concerning or potentially criminal behaviour.

'Tell me more about him,' she said cautiously.

'He's a good-looking man with jet-black hair, over six foot tall and with a certain, arrogant bearing. He fits the bill beautifully. And he's been on her Tinder profile.'

'What was his subject?'

'English. He has a Polish wife who lives in Krakow.'

'So what was Poppy's contribution?'

'She said she'd seen him with a Year Ten pupil.'

She was still cautious, almost fearing to believe that this was, at last, the truth. 'How did you find this out?'

'Looked into her past employers.'

'And . . .?'

'He left the school soon after. Never returned to teaching. His wife, with whom he was very much in love, by all accounts, never did leave her native Poland.'

'And was the allegation true?' Her mind drifted, cloud-like. *Was anything Poppy Kelloway said true? If only her stories could have been tossed in the air with a winnowing fan then the lies would blow away, like chaff, in the wind, and the truth descend to the ground to be picked over.*

'So, what's brought him to your attention? Poppy told so many lies, Zed. Loads of them must have resulted in harm.'

'He's confessed they dated.'

'And she didn't recognize him?'

'Apparently not.'

'Zed, I don't want to burst your balloon, but Poppy remembered things and faces in particular. She would have known who he was. If she dated him . . .' She let him draw his own conclusion.

'She did.' He sounded hurt and for the first time he also sounded dubious. 'He's a prime suspect and he doesn't have an alibi.'

'Do you have any evidence?'

'Not yet,' he said tightly. 'But we're waiting for a result on that sample of DNA found at the scene. We'll see if it's a match.' Now he was sounding pleased with himself again. While he didn't like her questions, she realized DS Zed Willard was convinced he had the right man and she had to concede, it fitted.

Profile? Check.

Opportunity? Check.

But the question boring into her mind was *where did the boys fit into all this?*

'And the neighbour who saw Poppy go into the professor's home?' She felt indignant on behalf of her patient.

There was an awkward pause. 'Doesn't seem to have come to anything. We've appealed for her to come forward but . . . nothing. We're treating it as a hoax call.'

So it was a she.

And then he added something that chilled her, because he spoke with a casualness she recognized as affected. 'Anything more come out of your bloke's interviews with the children?'

She knew why he was asking. He was searching for some corroborative witness testimony.

She forced herself to stick to the facts. 'Apart from both of us having the distinct feeling that each of the three children is hiding something – still nothing concrete.' She didn't mention both their convictions that the boys were lying about the circumstances surrounding their night out.

'Is he seeing them again?'

'Yes.'

'Good.'

So they were questioning a person of interest, but she had voiced her concern about their 'prime suspect' being Professor Rotherham. Still, she was worried. Among the allegations against him when he had lost his job were consequences, not of his OCD, but of surreptitious touching. And that bothered her.

She didn't believe that DS Willard was right that this Peter was the guilty one. Her worry was that *she* knew who was.

FORTY-SIX

7.45 p.m.

Simon Bracknell was coming down the stairs as she let herself in to the house. 'I was just going to cook,' he said. 'You going out or do you fancy a bit?'

'Not going out,' she said, perhaps more shortly than she'd meant because he gave her a hard look. 'You OK? You seem a bit down.'

'I'm fine. Think I'll have a shower.'

But as she passed him on the step he scrutinized her. 'Not going out with the boyfriend?'

That was when she turned to face him. 'There is no boyfriend, Simon. Not anymore.'

'Oh, jeez, I'm sorry.' He touched his glasses, adjusting them on his nose, a habit she'd noted when he was uncomfortable.

She tried to shrug, as though it was nothing, but she didn't quite pull it off and he picked up on her mood. 'You want to talk about it? What happened?'

'Nothing. That's the point. We weren't going anywhere.'

He met her eyes for a moment then put a hand on her shoulder. 'Wine in the kitchen,' he offered. 'Maybe you could do with it?'

She nodded, suddenly finding she couldn't speak. She felt

overwhelmed with emotion, sadness at facing the truth with Grant, on top of her concern about Poppy's murder. Not so much that she hadn't really helped the investigation as a rampant fear that was taking hold of her. If Poppy's torture for lying had been *pants on fire*, what was in store for her, the psychiatrist who couldn't cure her patients?

She followed Simon into the kitchen where he pulled the cork from a bottle of wine, set two glasses down on the table and pulled out a chair.

He sat opposite her, waiting for her to speak. And finally she did, repeating herself. 'It wasn't going to go anywhere, Simon.'

'Why not, Claire?'

He used her name rarely but it set the tone between them. Pals.

'Because . . .' She fumbled for the right phrase. 'He wanted more. He wanted more than I could give.'

Simon rested his chin on his fist. 'Yeah,' he said, waiting for her to enlarge.

'My work. He always resented it. I'd feel I had to run home at the end of the day. He was always sort of disapproving, not . . .'

This time it was Simon who shrugged. 'I know it's a cliché,' he said, 'but life isn't all work, you know. There's more to it than that.'

'Children,' she managed.

He had an answer to this too. 'People – women – mothers – fathers. People manage it.'

She shook her head. 'It went deeper than that,' she said.

He waited and then guessed. 'Possessive mother?'

He smiled. 'Then try mine for size. She's just the opposite. I don't think she knows – or cares – whether I'm dead or alive.'

This was an unexpected shared intimacy. 'Mine too.'

'So there you are.' He raised his glass. 'Here's to the single life.'

'But Teresa?'

'Ah. More of a friend than a girlfriend. That's it.'

Once she would have asked: *And does she know this . . . limitation on the relationship?* But right now she felt too raw to explore the depths of others' amity.

But she did ask him something she'd avoided before. 'What really went wrong with you and Marianne?'

'A bit like you and Grant,' he said. 'Needy. Too needy.' He sucked in a breath. 'Pathologically needy.'

'And you . . .?' She couldn't finish.

'Couldn't satisfy it. I know, I know,' he said, his face going pink, before she'd had the chance to comment. 'It was the only way I could have made her happy. Worked at first. But it didn't take long before I felt suffocated.'

'But she'd just had a . . .'

He looked guilty now. 'There was never going to be a right time, Claire. If not then, it would have been something else sooner or later.'

'But—?'

She didn't finish the sentence because he asked her a question.

'So, what about the wedding? It's only a couple of weeks, isn't it? You going to go it alone?'

She drained her glass and didn't answer. And he didn't offer.

FORTY-SEVEN

Friday 6 May, 8.15 a.m.

Claire was driving into work when, quite unexpectedly, a rogue thought made her smile. Weren't there agencies who supplied hot blokes to attend functions? She pictured herself in the outfit, high heels, spectacular jewelled headband, beautiful lace skirt billowing out over the closely fitted silk suit, on the arm of a suited and booted male model type, complete with slicked-back hair and oily manner. Her smile broadened. But then she realized that everyone there – including her mother, stepfather, Adam and Adele – would sniff out the fake, and the smile was quickly superseded with a feeling of blind panic. She had less than three weeks to go.

She parked the car and walked slowly through the arch into the quadrangle, as always sensing the peace that came from being in the pretty area, with its small mounds of grass, few trees and paved walkways. It ameliorated the threat of the tall grey walls that overlooked it. The juxtaposition of the pastoral central area to the forbidding presence that overlooked it was a deliberate contrast. She had offered an opinion on the design, recognizing it would be a place for patients to recover some of the sense of peace that they'd been lacking.

Simon was behind her and caught her up. He must have left the house not long after she had. She felt slightly awkward having opened up the night before on her misgivings surrounding the impending wedding. She sensed he wanted to say something but was holding back. She tilted her head to one side and waited. And finally he came out with it.

'If you're desperate . . .' he began.

She lifted her eyebrows at the word. She didn't do *desperate*.

'I mean . . .' Simon had gingery hair and freckles. Normally his face was pale. Obviously he had kept well protected from the Sydney sun. Now his complexion was raspberry as he tried to backtrack. 'I don't mean desperate . . .' He blundered on. 'But – well – if you need an arm.' And then he got it out, speaking quickly, the words tumbling out of his mouth. 'I'm not doing anything that weekend. I can – that is – if you want . . .'

She took pity on him. 'Are you offering me your arm for my half-brother's wedding?'

He nodded, obviously relieved she had removed the burden.

'Thank you, Simon. I'd really like that. It's good of you to offer.' She had to broach the subject. 'Teresa won't . . .?' Her voice tailed off.

He was shaking his head. 'God, no. It's not that sort of relationship. Not really . . . intense, you know?'

'Oh.' And all of a sudden she felt awkward and changed the subject. 'Do you have a suit?'

That put a grin on his face. 'Believe it or not, Claire, I do. I can look respectable sometimes.'

They both, simultaneously, let out a long breath and laughed.

He, because his offer had been accepted in the spirit in which it had been offered and she because, well, quite clearly it had got her out of a hole. The hired hot male model had never really been an option.

They parted at the door and she headed for Rita's room, which was a little along the corridor from her own office.

She found the secretary bent forward, peering into the computer screen, only looking up when Claire reached her.

'Morning,' Rita said. She looked confused. 'Professor Rotherham has asked to see you.'

They looked at each other, each reading the other's thoughts. Rita knew why Claire had been asking for certain patients' notes. So her voice was small as she added, 'He was only in a few days ago, wasn't he?'

Claire nodded and felt chilled as a sudden thought hit her. Who better to clean up a crime scene than someone with an addiction to cleanliness? And then there was Professor Rotherham's intelligence, his strong sense of justice, his obsession with classical torture. And the lead the police had failed to follow up but dropped in the light of their new suspect.

She felt a prickling sensation covering her skin from top to toe. The professor had been a patient of hers for about as long as Poppy had, but she felt a sudden reluctance to meet up with him.

Rita was watching her over the rim of her glasses. 'You think he's connected with the . . . What happened to . . .?' She didn't have to enlarge.

Rita was the queen of euphemisms. Not for a moment would she use such a blunt word as *murder*. Had the circumstances been different, Claire might have smiled. Instead, she felt a sudden snatch at her heart before lecturing herself. She couldn't do this – be apprehensive with every patient she saw. She didn't believe DS Zed Willard was fingering the right collar. Her next thought was to chide herself. What on earth was she playing at? Did she think she was a detective? Playing at judge and jury? Did she think she had some sixth sense, some magical instinct?

Common sense was telling her: This – isn't – safe. If the professor was the perpetrator, she had read him wrong, seeing him through the spectrum of pity, as a mild-mannered intellectual with a terrible affliction.

She steadied herself, trying to bring logic into her reasoning. She had training and experience with all sorts of felons – stupid ones, clever ones, people who used a diagnosis to hang every single deceitful, cruel or evil action on and excuse them from the justice system. And those who genuinely lacked all logic and reason. Those who were, in fact, insane and could not be held accountable for their actions. Then she lectured herself. Poppy's murder might not be the work of a mentally healthy person, but there was a certain cunningness about it. There had been planning; the children had been persuaded. That was the point at which she stumbled. *Had* they been persuaded?

Perhaps Poppy had even contributed to the planning and plotting herself without realizing what the consequences would be.

Deep in thought, Claire headed back towards her office.

She needed to spend some time settling herself as well as refreshing her previous notes and preparing for the correct and probing questions. But halfway along the corridor she met Saul Magnusson. He stopped her. 'Claire, I'm seeing the Kelloway boys this afternoon and wondered—'

She interrupted him. People were milling along the corridor and she worried they might be overheard. 'Shall we go into my office, Saul? More private.'

'Of course.'

She waited until she had shut the door and they were both sitting down before she prompted him. 'So?'

'I am seeing the boys again later on today,' he repeated before enlarging. 'I think I'm close to finding out what they're hiding. I'm worried about them.'

'And Holly-Anne?'

'I am less concerned. She has the character of her mother, I suspect. But the boys are different. Angry and at the same time they are frightened.'

She tried to find an innocent explanation. 'Possibly about their future with Lynne?'

He was still frowning. 'No. And that is another thing. She sits there when I speak to them, not intervening at all, but when I suggested we have another appropriate adult present, she was not happy.'

'What do you think's going on there?'

'She is worried I will unearth something.'

'Saul, how about we bring Robbie into the picture?'

'Why? They have had little to do with their father. He has a cast-iron alibi.' He was frowning. 'I don't understand how you think he can help.'

'Call it instinct, Saul. I think we're going to need him.'

'Very well. I will speak to Mrs Shute.'

'And, if I could sit in?'

His face was warm. 'Of course, Claire. Of course.'

He stood up. 'I hear you've found someone to escort you to your brother's wedding?'

She didn't correct him as to the exact relationship between her and Adam. It wasn't important.

His eyes twinkled. 'A clinic is not only a hotbed for *staphylococcus aureus,*' he said. 'Gossip grows and proliferates as though it was sitting on a blood agar plate.'

She heard his chuckles echoing as his long legs paced along the corridor.

Claire's next task was slightly more worrying. She made the appointment with Professor Rotherham for Monday, knowing, by the fact that he picked up the phone before the first ring had completed, that he'd been waiting for her call.

FORTY-EIGHT

3.15 p.m.

Jarrod Stonier's appointment had been for three o'clock, but, as usual, Claire was running late, playing the game of catch-up which, like a roundabout with children eternally pushing it, never seemed to stop. One could neither get on or off. You could only keep going – round and round.

He sauntered in, one hand in his pocket, the other pushing open the door, and she studied him. Was he Poppy's killer? It was a tempting thought. He was not a likeable character and, recognizing that, he played on it, maximizing his effect on others for his own gratification.

He looked smug.

'Sit down,' she invited.

Jarrod was a thin guy with a permanent shuffle. He'd been referred five years ago after a spate of problems at work, around the same time as Poppy. He'd been a refuse collector, working for the local council. But he'd flared up and lashed out at a colleague. Then he'd dropped the contents of a bin all over the road when the householder had objected to being blocked in by the bin lorry. He had also been in an 'altercation' with an impatient driver who couldn't get past him, a problem he'd expressed by keeping his hand on the horn. That had resulted in the car driver's windscreen being in conflict with a wheelie bin hurled by Stonier. He'd very nearly killed the man.

And so he had been sacked, which had persuaded him to smother the local council offices with graffiti, using the F-word liberally.

Somehow, these crimes had resulted in a short spell of community service followed by a referral for anger management with Edward Reakin, their psychologist. Edward had quickly passed the baton on to Claire, suggesting that a more appropriate diagnosis would be narcissistic personality disorder.

Today Jarrod slouched in wearing what almost constituted his uniform: jeans and a dark red baggy hoodie with a pair of grubby trainers on his large feet. He dropped into the chair, lifted his eyes to hers and gave her a grudging smile. 'Didn't think I'd be seeing you for a few months yet, Doctor.' The 'doctor' epithet had been added in a tone of deep irony. 'In fact, I thought you'd discharged me.'

'I thought I'd better check up on you.' She kept the reason to herself.

He shrugged and gave her a long, searching look.

She began along well-trodden pathways. 'I think last time we met you were going for a job?'

Another shrug. He knew they'd been along this road many, many times before; the results were always fruitless.

Though she knew the detail, she pretended to scan his notes. 'Stacking the shelves at night at the supermarket. You still doing that?'

He shrugged again but she was watching him, silently waiting for his answer which he gave – eventually, reluctantly. 'Yeah. Zero hours. Pay's crap.'

'I expect it is,' she agreed.

He waited for her next question, eyes warily flicking around the room.

'You're still living in the rented flat in . . . Bucknall?'

'Yeah.'

'So tell me. How is that working out?'

Quite suddenly Stonier's face grew suspicious. He studied her, eyes narrowing. 'Why am I really here, Dr Roget?' This time there was a touch of anxiety in his voice.

'I needed to—'

He was watching her while shaking his head. 'No. It isn't that.'

They both waited, the tension in the room palpable.

And then he drew himself in, his shoulders hunched, chin jutting out, mouth stroppy. 'It's to do with that patient of yours. Isn't it? The one that was murdered in her own house.' He was speaking quickly, anxious to get the words out, his mouth twisted into a distorted smile. 'You think I had something to do with it?' She could hear the incredulity in his tone. And could see the reason behind his anxiety.

It was based on history. Whenever anything went wrong in his vicinity he always got blamed. He was used to it, shouldering the accusations like a donkey carrying a load. Claire had always suspected he had more insight than he led others to believe. His 'eruptions' had been sudden and volcanic, but his insight after the events had been almost profound. And as he'd led her towards this train of thought she followed his lead. 'Well, you were friends – for a time.'

'Yeah. Until . . .' He stopped. Right there. She was tempted to prompt him. *Until . . .?* But she resisted the temptation and waited, silently. Jarrod didn't respond well to being prompted. He would speak when he was ready and tell her only what he *wanted* her to know.

He was chewing over these decisions before deciding to speak. 'We saw each other for a bit,' he said. 'But she was trouble.'

'In what way?' She was trying to sound disinterested, but her mind was super-charged.

He leaned back in his chair, lowered his eyelids. 'Put all sorts of stuff about me online,' he said, his voice low. 'Fake stuff. Lies.'

'Was it?'

At which point Stonier leaned back in his chair, puffing out a frustrated breath. '*You* choose, Doctor,' he challenged. '*You* decide. You're supposed to know me, know my history. Inside out.'

She was tempted to smile.

He carried on. 'You're supposed to understand me. To know what I'm capable of. You think I'm into rape? Slapping a girl around? Stealing?' He edged forward in his chair. 'I'm the first to admit I get a bit . . .' He searched around for an appropriate phrase. 'Out of hand. I lose my rag. I get it. I kind of fizz up when I get riled. But go for a woman? Never. You know my history, Doctor. Women I don't touch.'

She realized then that Stonier knew no details about Poppy's murder.

He grinned, displaying white but crooked teeth. 'I don't do that stuff.' He stood up, shoulders straight now, taller than she'd realized. 'I don't *need* to do that stuff.'

'OK,' she said steadily, changing tack as completely and suddenly as if the wind had changed direction. North to south, east to west. 'Then help us. Tell me what she said about you.'

'She tweeted stuff, saying I'd raped her. Then she tried to get some money out of me. Said three hundred quid should fix it. Where the heck am I going to get three hundred quid? Tell me that.'

'Why didn't you take this to the police?'

'Hah.' His response was laden with sarcasm, mockery and disdain. 'You think they'd believe anything good about me? Little Miss Sunshine would have had it all her own way. I've got a bad past. I'm the first to admit that, but I don't do women.'

He'd reached the door where he turned round. 'If I were you, seeing stuff online, I'd be looking for someone who's been inside. Someone who's into that sort of thing.'

'Torture?'

He nodded. 'And for your information, the police have already interviewed me so you don't need to see me for at least six months. If ever.'

And with that he walked out.

FORTY-NINE

5 p.m.

C laire was heading for the top floor where she had patients to review, some to discharge, when she peered out of the window, towards the quadrangle. She could see Simon Bracknell talking to Teresa Coren. There seemed to be some awkwardness between them and she could guess what the issue was. Simon was speaking but looking around him, distracted or else wishing he was anywhere but there, while Teresa's focus was purely on him, intense as a laser beam. She was leaning forward, pulling on his arm. Claire drew back from the window, anxious not to be seen. She had the distinct feeling Simon was justifying his promise to accompany her to the wedding. And Teresa was not happy with it.

Sometimes life was just too complicated.

At six o'clock Claire found herself back in her office with little more than a pile of letters to check and sign. The corridor was empty, the hospital abandoned by the end of the day. The exit was sudden, as instant as if a siren had sounded – one moment bustling corridors, telephones ringing, people knocking on her door. The next – silence. Emptiness, the feeling of sudden abandonment as complete as the desertion of a war zone. It was especially noticeable on a Friday afternoon.

Almost seven o'clock. She had time to try Zed Willard's number.

He answered, sounding hassled. There was a lot of background noise. The hospital might have emptied out but the police worked twenty-four seven, their shifts probably busier by night than by day. Even over the phone she sensed the full, forceful energy of a major police investigation, the bustle behind him. And noted that it didn't sound triumphant or exuberant, no hand slapping because they had someone in custody. She wondered what had happened to Peter, the man they had been questioning.

'Claire,' he said shortly, his voice as abrupt as a bullet, irritation at the interruption leaking through. 'How are you?' But he spoke quickly, fulfilling a polite request – nothing more.

'I'm good,' she began. 'I just wondered . . .?'

'No.' His voice was still short, clipped, angry and frustrated. 'No arrests yet.'

Had they been face-to-face, she might have asked – gently, of course – how the investigation was going, really. It might, at least, have opened up a conversation. But she sensed things were going badly and she could hear a hum in the background. 'I'm sorry,' she said, resorting to a useful phrase: 'Now isn't a good time.'

'I'll ring you. Later.' And the line went dead.

So she sat, chin in her hands, worrying. His latest suspect, it seemed, was slipping away. Which left the field open.

On Monday morning Professor Cornelius Rotherham arrived at her clinic.

FIFTY

Monday 9 May, 11 a.m.

The professor was a hugely intelligent man, with a domed forehead, piercing blue eyes, sparse white hair and a stoop. He always smelled clean, of bleach and disinfectant, a spicy pine scent which he carried around him like an aura. 'Thank you for seeing me.' His voice was gruff and he looked ashamed, something she'd never picked up on before – not in this intensity. He was still wearing his gloves, she noted. And she recalled the memory Zed Willard had shared with her, that the crime scene had been cleaned with the thoroughness of NCIS. But at the back of her mind was this tale of a mystery blonde, someone who superficially, at least, resembled Poppy, reported by an anonymous caller. All this flashed through Claire's mind. As did the red button on her side of the desk which connected with the hospital security team.

He dropped heavily into the chair, breathing hard as though this had been an exertion.

'You asked to see me, Professor. So . . .' She kept her voice friendly. 'What's the problem?'

'The police have been talking to my neighbours.' There was a note of panic in his voice.

'Do you know why?'

'No. And that's what troubles me.' Then he added, more honestly, 'But I think I can guess.'

'So . . .?'

'For some . . .' he hesitated, '. . . ridiculous reason they seem to link this savage murder with me.'

She cursed that the details of the murder had leaked into public knowledge. But at the same time she was surprised the professor was showing such interest in the case. Current affairs, particularly details of crimes, were not his usual diet.

'And the police have been to my flat. They arrived with a team of four . . .' He gulped in air. 'Suited and booted.'

She skirted around the specifics. 'I understand they're looking at a number of my patients.'

'Why?'

'Because Mrs Kelloway was also a patient here.'

'Yes, but why me?'

'You knew her, didn't you, Professor?'

Interestingly, he was looking shame-faced. 'Not to my knowledge.' As always with him, there was this strange mix of dignity and – she had to admit it – imbalance.

She reminded herself that the mystery caller had not been identified. While Zed Willard had credited the story, it had not been verified. 'I think you met her here.'

'I did?' His voice was squeaky. Frightened.

'Yes.' She kept her tone casual. 'I believe you both attended here on a few of the same days.'

'Really?' He was increasingly uncomfortable. 'You've checked that?'

She nodded.

'I hadn't realized.' His voice was thin and he was starting to breathe heavily, pursing his lips, blowing out and sucking in, gasping like a goldfish. Claire watched the metamorphosis with analytical interest. This had all the hallmarks of a guilty man. But, she reminded herself, the professor could not be expected to react to stress in a predictable way. It didn't necessarily indicate guilt. 'The police . . .' He was looking like a cornered rat. 'They wanted to know how well I knew her.' He looked shamefaced now. 'How well? I *didn't* know her. I didn't. She was a complete stranger to me.'

'So,' she improvised, trying to calm him, 'what could you tell them?'

'Nothing. I couldn't help them. Poor girl. Children, I understand.'

'Three.'

'Oh dear.' His eyes were watering. 'Oh dear. I don't even know what to say.'

She watched him for a while, trying to understand his mindset, wishing she could dig out the truth – somehow. After all, Rotherham's neighbours . . . And that was where she stopped dead. Who was this anonymous 'neighbour'?

'I think someone rang the police with the story that they'd seen someone who looked like Mrs Kelloway leave your flat.' She offered him an alternative explanation. 'Could it have been someone else, do you think, someone who looked like her, who your neighbours saw visiting you?'

Professor Cornelius Rotherham let out a breath in a rasping hoarse exhalation. 'What did she look like?' His voice was both fearful and quiet.

'Surely you've seen the pictures in the paper?'

He shook his head. 'I tend to get my news from local radio.'

'She was small, petite, in her forties.' This sketchy description transported her right back, Poppy breezing into her room, her personality bright and as full of life as she was full of lies. Even if it had been a deceitful existence, there had been an unarguable charm about her. And that had been her weapon. But she drew you in only to spit you out, still laughing.

Professor Rotherham blinked. 'I can't think of anyone like that. I might,' he resumed, shaking his head slowly and frowning, 'have seen her *here*. I really don't know. I can't remember. I'm sorry.'

She waited.

'No one comes to my flat,' he stated. 'It is a very private place. It was an unwarranted intrusion.'

'So where do you think this rumour came from?'

'From – from – fantasy land.' His eyes appealed to her to believe him. 'Someone made it up.'

Possibly, she thought.

'Well, Professor. If the police have any real evidence – not just hearsay, or a possible misidentification – that you actually did have some . . .'

He broke in. 'They searched my flat.' She knew what agony this would be for him. Strangers, police, tramping through his sterile environment.

And then he reached the heart of his request. 'Stop them,' he begged. 'Stop them. Tell them to leave me alone. I can't stand it. They won't listen to me, but they might take some note of you.' He was actually wringing his gloved hands then putting them together, beseeching her in prayer. 'Please, Doctor, put out some sort of defence of me. Explain to them. I can't have people just coming into my environment. Polluting it. I would never. I would . . .' He stopped and lowered his eyes and she realized something else, something deeper. The professor had a dirty little secret.

Not all of the case constructed around his dismissal had been due to OCD. There had been less tangible reports of inappropriate behaviour. He wouldn't be the first man to hire a prostitute while afterwards being stricken with guilt. And so he tried and tried again to scrub the encounter away.

'I'll do what I can,' she promised.

And, polite as ever, he thanked her, stood up and left.

Bang on cue, her mobile buzzed in her pocket.

Zed Willard dived straight in, his voice brisk and short. 'We've found evidence at your professor's place,' he said, 'in spite of his scrubbing the place practically sterile.'

'It's part of his condition,' she said wearily, realizing he didn't sound triumphant but crestfallen.

'I thought we should tell you. The long blonde hair we found at Professor Rotherham's flat does not match Poppy Kelloway. It seems . . .' She knew he was smiling now. She was familiar with that smile. It could be indulgent, friendly, kind. Warm. Since Poppy's death it had been missing in action.

'Your professor occasionally has – shall we call it – urges?'

She completed the sentiment. 'And pays for it.'

'Yeah.' Now he allowed himself a little chuckle.

FIFTY-ONE

C laire had no more than two minutes to reflect on this new-found insight before she saw Simon peering round the door. And he looked worried. Instinctively she knew why. His next words confirmed it.

'Dress code?' he said. 'I'm guessing it's not shorts and T?' He was trying to make a joke of it but she knew he was genuinely anxious.

'I thought you said you had a suit. Oh . . .' She realized now. 'You have a *lounge* suit.' And at a guess it had been Teresa who would have pointed out that the usual dress code for a wedding was a *morning* suit. She cursed herself for her thoughtlessness and tried to make up for it.

'We can hire it. I'll pay as I'm the one who's put you in this position.'

'No need for that,' he said, 'but I am heartily relieved. My wardrobe's a bit sparse and . . .' He stopped there, giving her a chance to observe his everyday uniform of open-necked shirt, chinos and loafers. No socks. She smiled. Everyone at Adam and Adele's wedding would be *properly* attired. Dressed like this, Simon would be worse dressed than the waiters.

Aloud, she said, 'We'd better make an appointment at the hire shop.'

'Yeah.' He gave a hesitant grin and she realized just what a favour he was doing for her, getting dressed up, attending an English country wedding. This was well outside his comfort zone. 'Thanks,' she said warmly – and meant it.

'No bother. Happy to help.'

'Umm.' She felt awkward even bringing this up – it was partly the result of her witnessing the scene from the window. 'Teresa's OK with this, is she?'

He looked bemused. 'Yeah, why wouldn't she be?'

'I thought you two were . . .' Feeling even more awkward, she broke off. 'Never mind.'

He turned to go but hovered on the threshold. 'Do they do shoes?'

'I'm not sure. We'll find out.'

'Thanks,' he said again and left while she wondered. He wasn't paying much rent to her – barely covering his expenses, electricity and gas. So what was he spending his money on? His wife? The divorce?

Who knew? And there was another difficulty she should probably face. She was wondering how much of her family dynamics she should fill him in on.

Maybe just a very sketchy outline?

The next hour was spent in a joint consultation with Edward Reakin and Dana Cheung, who had been brought from the residential home where she had been placed for a, hopefully, final assessment. Maybe it was time to let her go to her own home, with Lily Rose, providing the toxic mother-in-law wasn't there to goad her and erode her rapidly increasing confidence as a mother. Having arranged three weeks' holiday, Graham was over from Qatar. He sat, tight-lipped, slightly bemused and very quiet at the back of the room, playing no part in the interview. His baby daughter was asleep in his arms. Periodically he looked down at her, his face full of emotions: puzzlement, affection, pride and a certain gritty loyalty which extended to both wife and daughter. They would both be safe with him. He planned to take them back to Qatar with him which would, of course, put the family out of reach of the Greatbach team. So it was doubly important they get this right.

Playing no active part, Claire watched as Edward Reakin asked his questions, gently teasing out Dana's new-found mental health. 'So how do you feel today, Dana?' There was never any hint of a threat in his voice.

And Dana sensed it. Her eyes flickered over Edward's face and Claire sensed she felt safe. Reassured. Cocooned.

Even so far as to smile. 'I feel OK,' she said slowly and carefully. She aimed a swift glance at her husband and daughter. Then looked back at Edward. 'Still not absolutely confident about Lily. I still worry I could hurt her.'

'All new mothers feel like this, Dana. You aren't alone in lacking confidence.'

'No, but few women have had such terrible feelings towards their baby.' Again, she looked across the room at her husband as though he might have an answer. 'At the hungry ghost who sucks things into its small mouth.' Her eyes widened and filled with tears. 'Where did all those terrible thoughts come from?'

Claire could have answered quite easily, but this was Edward's interview. She was here as a bystander, a witness. Not as a clinician. Edward pondered the question, taking it in with full seriousness. Then said, 'When two cultures meet, Dana, there often is a certain amount of suspicion and misunderstanding. What seems normal in one country can feel threatening in another.' He gave one of his rare smiles. 'But there is a benefit too. Your daughter will have the joy of straddling two wonderful cultures.'

Claire could have applauded his diplomacy.

'With your husband's support, all will be well.'

Claire switched her focus to Graham Cheung. He was a bulky, stocky man, the diametric opposite of his delicately built wife, with her tiny feet and hands. His world was huge steel super structures, not this quiet, plain room with a fragile wife and newborn baby. He was an engineer and liked certainty – not guess work. But he was trying his best. He bent towards his wife and Dana stretched out one of those small hands.

'So, when do you think we'll be OK, that I won't need to worry all the time?'

Claire spoke up. 'Maybe three months with some careful monitoring. Your wife's already made huge progress. With the medication and Mr Reakin's input we can work towards that.'

He stood up. Not quite as tall as she. And pumped her hand. 'Thank you, Doctor. You're giving me some hope.' His voice was hoarse, his face tired. 'My mum. She's been a real help.'

'She needs to be gentle and encouraging towards your wife.'

Graham Cheung managed a tight smile.

FIFTY-TWO

'*My mum. She's been a real help.*' Claire pondered the phrase Graham Cheung had used. Poppy had used those exact same words.

It was time to share her theory with the police, but first she needed to check a few details. She could hear the stress in DS Willard's voice even as he responded. She sensed the police investigation was going round and round in circles.

'Zed,' she said. 'The friend that Holly-Anne was staying with. Did *you* talk to her?'

He sounded irritated at her intrusion. 'No. One of our officers simply confirmed that Holly-Anne was where she said she was.' He burst out then. 'We're talking about a little girl who's eleven years old, Claire. I hardly think it's relevant.'

How could she tell him? It was *all* relevant, each tiny, seemingly unimportant detail.

She couldn't tell him what was in her mind.

Zed Willard went on, 'Why on earth are you interested in a little girl who was having a sleepover with a friend? I think lots of little girls do this, don't they?' He still sounded angry – and aggrieved. She'd picked up on that note in his voice and now wondered at its significance before shelving it. Something she would think about later. For now, she needed to focus.

'Was the sleepover the friend's idea, or Holly-Anne's?'

'Does that matter?'

'I wouldn't have asked unless I thought it did.'

'Well . . .' He was rifling through some papers. 'Apparently it was Holly-Anne who asked the friend if she could stay that night.'

As she'd thought.

'And,' he continued, making her wince at the sarcasm in his voice, 'Holly-Anne was exactly where she said she was until she was picked up by another of our officers and taken to her grandmother's.'

Claire heard and felt her revulsion. The grandmother who was convinced her three grandchildren would be better off living with her than with their lying, deceitful mother.

Well. Grandma Lynne had got what she wanted.

She thanked Zed Willard for the information and heard complete bemusement in his voice. And he did apologize. 'I'm sorry,' he said. 'Things are very difficult at the moment.' He hesitated. 'We do have one thing,' he said, tacking on, 'Apparently.'

She waited.

'A match for the DNA. A Darius Bogdan. He's a thirty-four-year psychopath with a long criminal record of extreme violence. He's from just outside Bucharest. It's pretty certain he was working under contract but . . .'

His voice trailed away. She could anticipate the questions. A contract killer had to have an employer. However appropriate, the caustic soda gel was hardly a torture weapon of choice unless someone had suggested it. Someone who had known Poppy.

'Basically,' he confessed, 'we're missing large parts of this case. Until we have all the pieces, we're going to struggle to bring it to court.'

'May I make a suggestion?'

He listened without comment and she told him not to worry but when she'd put the phone down she wished she could have reassured him with some concrete details. It was almost six o'clock. Without much hope, she tried Saul Magnusson's bleep only to be told it had been switched off. Wherever he lived, he would be on his way home now.

First thing tomorrow, she vowed, she and Saul would work together and tease out the truth. But right now, she remembered, she and Simon had an appointment with a gentleman's outfitter.

FIFTY-THREE

An Aussie transformed.

Claire hardly recognized Simon Bracknell when he emerged from the changing room after a lot of huffing and puffing from behind the curtain.

In a morning suit, collar and tie, he might look thoroughly uncomfortable, but with his hair slicked down, and wearing highly polished black, patent shoes, he looked the part. Tall, slim, a bashful grin.

'Hope I'll do.'

She realized she was gaping, her mouth dropped open. 'Sorry. Yes. It's absolutely perfect. You'll do fine.'

Mentally she was rubbing her hands. *This would do in front of her mother.*

She arranged pick-up with the outfitter and, still laughing at the transformation, they headed for the pub. Simon was in good humour. 'I wondered who the posh guy in the mirror was. And then I realized. Maybe,' he added, as though a thought had just struck him like a bolt of lightning, 'Maybe I'll even enjoy this wedding.'

'I doubt it,' she said darkly and proceeded to sketch out the family dynamics. That sobered him up until he grinned again. 'Give me a good chance to study human nature.'

'At its worst,' she said, raising her glass for a toast. 'But thanks.'

'My pleasure.'

'Hmm. I think I'd moderate your joy.'

Tuesday 10 May, 8.30 a.m.

Claire arrived at work early specifically to catch Saul Magnusson before he started his day's work. She found him outside his office.

She told him about the Romanian and he listened, knowing what she was asking him.

10 a.m.

They arrived on time, a huddled group, each one appearing dependent on the other.

Lynne Shute appeared shrunken. She knew her fate. Holly-Anne clutched her hand and the two boys walked like automatons, stiff little soldiers. Even when they sat, they still appeared wooden.

Lynne should have taken charge, answered for them all, but it was as though events had finally hit home.

Saul opened the discussion. 'I will ask some questions,' he said, speaking slowly and frowning, the words dragging out of him. Not one of them really wanted these questions answered.

Saul spoke to the youngest of the group. 'Holly-Anne,' he said. The girl's response was to clutch her grandmother's arm so tightly that Lynne Shute winced, tried to release the girl's fingers.

'Who suggested you ask your friend if you could stay over that night?'

The girl didn't need to answer. Her frightened look at her grandmother told all.

Saul nodded, as though she had given her answer.

He turned his attention to Tommy and Neil. 'And you?' he asked.

The boys looked at each other. Tommy answered for them both. 'It was our grandmother.'

'She gave you the money for the club and for the taxi home?'

Both boys nodded.

Lynne was collapsed in her chair.

Claire spoke then. 'Why?' she said. And that resulted in Lynne sitting up, her eyes blazing. 'They have a father,' she said, shaking her head now. 'They should have been with him, not learning her rotten ways. What would happen to them, do you think, learning a trade of lies and deceit, making up things? I didn't kill her, but my daughter deserved all she got.'

'Really?' Claire could not believe it.

Lynne smiled. 'Drake gave me the idea.' Her smile broadened. 'And I liked it.'

Claire was horrified.

'Drake had the idea of the little . . . embellishments. He thought it would put the police off the scent.'

'And Holly-Anne, the boys?'

That was when Claire understood the depths of Lynne's evil.

Lynne turned to smile at them. 'They've learnt to trust that their grandma will always do what's best for them.'

Later, when Claire spoke to DS Willard, he filled in the gaps. 'Bogdan had a friend who was in prison with Drake Shute,' he said. 'That is one link in the chain.'

'Whose idea was the caustic soda?'

'Drake's. He had the idea that if the emphasis was put on her lies and the psychiatric unit, it would draw attention away from the family and towards . . .' He paused. 'Likewise the mocking note sent to your office and the couple of glasses.' Now he looked embarrassed, but Claire could fill in the missing words. All too easy to pin the tail on the donkey.

'So that explains the torn-up appointment card, and the man that Edward saw with Poppy. Will the children be charged?'

'We'll discuss that with the CPS, but it's possible they didn't know all the details. We also have access to Lynne Shute's bank account. Life is cheap,' he said.

Life is cheap, she thought, wondering if that was so, why the medical profession tried so hard to save it. And then her thoughts turned to something else. She had always thought of children as being innocent. She never would again.

Sitting, alone in her office, she felt the earth shift.

FIFTY-FOUR

Thursday 12 May, 10 a.m.

There are winners and there are losers. Robbie Kelloway had taken over responsibility for his children who had been released into his care. He had asked to meet up with Claire and she had acceded. It would probably be the last contact she would have with Poppy Kelloway's family. They entered her clinic room, Robbie Kelloway with his arms resting on the shoulders of his sons. Holly-Anne trailed behind them.

Robbie was a good-looking man, tall, with an open face, thick dark hair and an appealing grin. He shook hands with both Claire and Saul Magnusson. 'It's a relief to finally meet you,' he said, before addressing Claire. 'Thank you for all you tried to do for her. I'm sure you did your best under the circumstances.'

Claire nodded.

'I want you to know,' he said, 'I tried everything to make things normal but she could always outmanoeuvre me. She lied to the courts and she was so credible. And every time I tried to see them they were always somewhere else. And the worst thing?' He looked at each child in turn. 'She fed them stories about how I didn't care, that I didn't give her any money, that I was trying to starve her out, that I'd cheated on her. She even told them I wasn't their father anyway.' He was shaking his head as he spoke. 'There was no end to the crap she made up about me. And when the kids were little they believed it. But children grow up.' He was looking at Tommy now who returned the look with a watery smile.

'Everything she said was a lie. Stuff about the children, rumours she'd spread. I don't know what it was.' Now he looked bemused. 'I could never work it out. It wasn't as though she hated me. It was more a sort of game.'

'What about Lynne?'

'Lynne.' Now he smiled faintly. 'She did what she could – under the circumstances. The best thing was to spend as much time with the three of them. Poppy couldn't afford to fall out with the one person she needed. But when the kids started asking questions, and more importantly when they showed signs of picking up their mother's bad habit . . .' He drew a breath. 'I think she was talked into it. Drake worked on her. At least that's what she's told me. And she was stupid enough to believe it wouldn't be tracked back to her.' His face changed. 'I still can't believe they committed such a horrible crime.' He fell silent for a few seconds before continuing. 'The boys wanted to come and live with me.' He turned around then. 'Not so sure about you,' he said to his daughter, who looked back at him with something both defiant and devious in her face.

Maybe lying is hereditary, hidden in one of the genes.

FIFTY-FIVE

Grant, it seemed, hadn't quite finished things with her. She found his number when she switched her phone back on, exhausted by the revelations of the past hour.

She called him back.

'Thanks for getting back to me.' His tone was sarcastic. 'I just wondered if you'd got fixed up for the wedding.'

Which, inexplicably, made her feel guilty because he was looking after her. She was quick with her reply. 'Yes. Thanks. Don't worry.'

'That Aussie registrar came up trumps then?' His voice was sour.

'That Aussie registrar has a girlfriend and, as a favour, has agreed

to dress up in a hired penguin suit and accompany me.' Her voice
lowered as she added, 'I couldn't quite face going to the wedding
alone. Not with – well, things as they are.'

'OK. That's good.' His voice was staccato. 'Good,' he repeated,
and she sensed he was reluctant to hang up. 'You're all right then?'

'I'm fine, Grant.' *Now who was the liar?*

She deliberately didn't ask how he was. His voice was false with
a forced jollity she'd heard before. *Maybe they both were.*

He gave a little huff of laughter. 'Still trying to do the work of
the entire police force?'

'We've worked together,' she said, 'to unearth the truth.'

And unconsciously Grant echoed the phrase that had been ringing
around her mind. 'What is truth?'

She didn't even try to answer and his next wish was sincere.
'Look after yourself, Claire.'

'I will. You too.' And they ended the call.

DS Willard was the next to call. And she instantly understood
that the question he asked had been preying on his mind.

'The boys,' he said. 'How much did they know?'

She'd given this much thought herself. 'I don't believe they really
understood the full details of what was going to happen. When they
got home it was too late.'

That was the only version she could accept.

FIFTY-SIX

6 p.m.

I t had been a harrowing day. But as surely as sun follows rain,
spring follows winter, and relief comes after pain, her evening
provided light entertainment.

Simon was having a try-on of his suit, not forgetting the pair of
shiny black patent shoes that the hire company had provided.

He stood in front of her as uncomfortable as a dressing-up artist.
He fingered the starched white collar and looked at her beseechingly.
'Really?'

She saw his point and tried her hardest not to laugh, instead making an effort to console him. 'Everyone will be wearing the same.'

Again, he said, 'Really? Everyone?'

'Except the ladies.'

'Right. Well, I'm telling you now, Claire, you really owe me one.'

'I do. An extra week's holiday?'

FIFTY-SEVEN

Friday 13 May, 11 a.m.

Claire closed Poppy Kelloway's notes, marking them DECEASED. They could be sent to the records department where they would sit alongside all the other patients who'd died, including Tre Marshall.

And the rest of the pile? The patients whose notes she had been combing for any sign that they had been involved? She was as guilty as the others searching through their histories to see whether they were the culprit. She put them on the table where they would be picked up by the porters and returned to the library until their next appointment.

Saturday 21 May, 11.45 a.m.

Claire watched her mother file into the church, lulled by the background of soft organ music. Adam stood at the top of the aisle, his nervousness palpable to all who sat and waited for the bride. Her mother's attention was focused entirely on her son, sparing only a flicker of shame for her daughter and a brief look of surprise at Claire's escort. Simon had simply folded his arms and grinned at her. Her mother had marched past while Claire had watched her with a combination of anger and acceptance while wondering. Had the problems all begun with an illness as painful as Dana Cheung's?

She fielded Simon's look of surprise as her mother had passed, stopping only when she reached the top of the aisle to give her son a kiss. He'd leant across and, in a hoarse, shocked whisper, said, 'That's your mum?'

She hardly made the effort to nod, even setting aside her theory that her mother had been ill around the time of her birth. She guessed she might never know. Unless she found her father.

Simon found her hand and gave it a tight squeeze, which she returned.

'Thank you for coming.'

'No problem.'

And that was it. No problem.

And so they sat through the service. And later?

Adam insisted she be beside him for at least some of the photographs. He put his arm around her for one, drawing her closer. This would be the picture she would hold in her mind. Not the other.

On her way home from the wedding, Claire called in at the mother and baby unit and found Dana breastfeeding her baby, watched over by Graham. She looked up at Claire, maternal pride beaming out of her as bright as a laser. 'Thank you,' she said before bending and kissing the baby's downy head.

Dana would not be a damaging mother as Poppy Kelloway had been or as Claire's mother still was. This was a positive, tangible result from her work and, like Poppy's bad influence, would reverberate down the generations.